Parrot Prose

A CORAL SHORES
VETERINARY MYSTERY

DL Mitchell

©2025 by DL Mitchell
All rights reserved. No part of this book may be reproduced, stored in a retrieval system or transmitted in any form or by any means without the prior written permission of the publishers, except by a reviewer who may quote brief passages in a review to be printed in a newspaper, magazine or journal.

The author grants the final approval for this literary material.

First printing

This is a work of fiction. Names, characters, businesses, places, events, and incidents are either the products of the author's imagination or used in a fictitious manner. Any resemblance to actual persons, living or dead, or actual events is purely coincidental.

ISBN: 978-1-68513-560-7
PUBLISHED BY BLACK ROSE WRITING
www.blackrosewriting.com

Printed in the United States of America
Suggested Retail Price (SRP) $20.95

Parrot Prose is printed in Baskerville

*As a planet-friendly publisher, Black Rose Writing does its best to eliminate unnecessary waste to reduce paper usage and energy costs, while never compromising the reading experience. As a result, the final word count vs. page count may not meet common expectations.

Always, for Blair and Maddy.

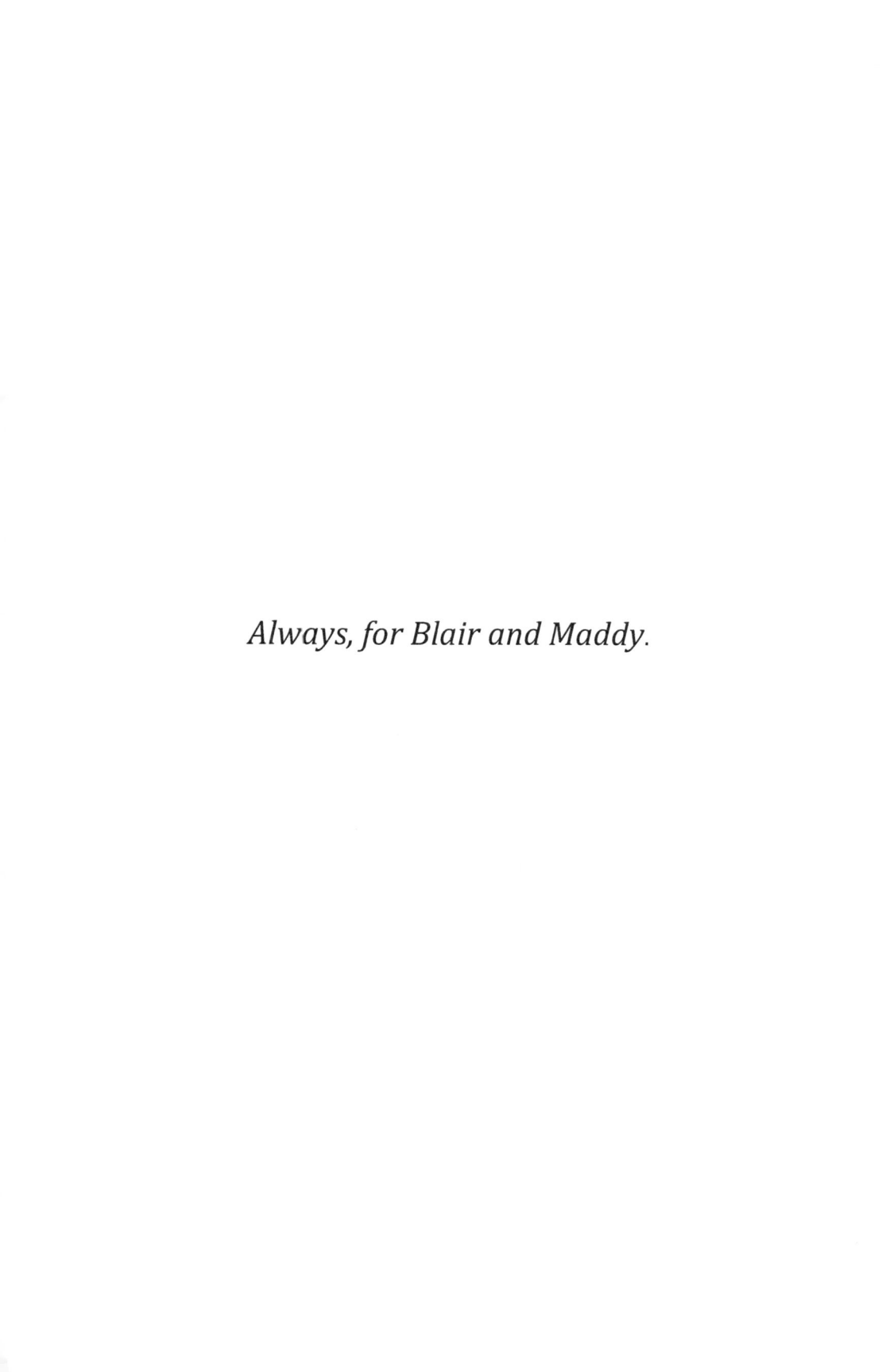

SPECIAL THANKS

My family and friends are my biggest cheerleaders. They celebrate all my successes and are there when I need words of encouragement. Without them, none of this is possible. I always want to make them proud.

To my friend, Denise, who helped me come up with much of the plot for *Parrot Prose* while drinking margaritas poolside in Key West. Gosh, we laughed. She's also an amazing beta reader and amateur editor. I think she missed her calling, but of course, it's never too late.

Pam, AKA my "CFE"—*client, friend, editor*. You are a talented writer, and I've learned so much from you. I cherish your support and enthusiasm for the Coral Shores series.

Lauryn, my dearest friend, is that person who's always there when I need a host for my book launch, a beta reader, social media guru, or words of advice. You're a beautiful, smart, and creative person with the most perfect, twisted sense of humor.

Thank you to my fellow members of the Atlanta Chapter of Sisters in Crime and the Atlanta Writers Club for introducing me to the publishing world. Whenever my creative energy is low, I'm instantly boosted after spending time with this creative community.

Kudos to the entire team at Black Rose Writing. You're small but mighty, and I'm grateful every day to be one of your authors.

My clients and their furry family members are constant sources of inspiration. I'm honored to be your veterinarian.

I saved the best for last—mystery readers! Your enthusiasm for *Trust the Terrier* made this sequel possible. Taking the time to share kind words of support and encouragement fuels me to keep writing.

Parrot Prose

CHAPTER ONE

"Hello. Whatcha doing? Hello. Whatcha doing?" The high-pitched cacophony emanated from the hospital lobby.

Anthony leaned against the doorway to Emily's office. "Sounds like our appointment is here. Tiki Lulu, our very own local celebrity." Anthony's smile stretched from ear to ear—his enthusiasm on full display.

"I haven't forgotten." As the sole owner of the Coral Shores Veterinary Hospital, Emily had to be flexible, although exotic pets really weren't her thing. She didn't mind seeing the occasional guinea pig or hamster, but avian medicine was daunting. And she avoided treating reptiles altogether. Dr. Dinsmore had been Tiki's veterinarian, but since his retirement, that privilege fell to Emily.

"Don't worry," Anthony said, to bolster her confidence. "I'm comfortable holding Tiki. We had two African Grey parrots at my previous hospital, and they were great patients. Have you checked out Tiki's posts on Flix yet? I think he's got close to a million followers."

Emily was aware of Flix, the latest social media sensation where people posted short home videos. Her staff made such a fuss when Tiki's appointment had been scheduled, so she downloaded the app to check it out for herself. His entertaining videos were addictive. This sassy parrot had star quality, and his owner, Marilyn, was a hoot.

Thankfully, Emily didn't have to put on a brave face for Anthony. Best friends since high school, they could precisely communicate their thoughts and feelings with only a glance or a nod. The remaining staff would never know she dreaded the appointment. Parrots were tricky. Her knowledge of avian medicine was only part of the equation. Handling them safely to minimize their stress was the real challenge. She wanted to do a good job.

"I'll get them settled and will be right back." When Anthony returned minutes later, he said, "This is going to be fun, Em. Put your game face on."

"I guess it's time," Emily muttered under her breath. Preoccupied as she tried to remember the pearls of wisdom she learned during her avian and exotic rotation at vet school, Emily failed to notice her staff lingering nearby. Everyone hoped to catch a sneak peek of the iconic bird.

With her hand wrapped around the doorknob, she paused, then exhaled, pushed her shoulders back and smiled as she entered the exam room. "Hello, Mrs. Peña. Hello, Tiki Lulu. I'm Dr. Emily Benton. It's great to meet you."

"Hello. Come on in. Hello. Come on in," Tiki said from the perch of his very fancy travel cage. His head bobbed up and down as he shuffled side to side, adding some gusto to his greeting. His plumage was gorgeous. Shades of darker gray on his head and wings blended to a light gray on his body. White trimming on the feathers around his head contrasted with his black beak and yellow-gold eyes. His ruby red tail feathers were spectacular, even more stunning than in his videos.

"Tiki Lulu is beautiful," Emily complimented Mrs. Peña, as she approached. Parrot and vet evaluated each other, turning their heads from left to right in unison. Emily leaned closer to his cage. "You're very handsome, Tiki."

Tiki puffed his feathers and wagged his tail before saying, "Pretty bird. Pretty bird," forcing Emily to stifle a giggle.

"Don't mind Tiki. He talks a lot when he's nervous," Mrs. Peña said.

Tiki, who stood about twelve inches tall, stepped out of his cage when Mrs. Peña presented her forearm for him to perch. He gave a little shiver, preened a few feathers, settled in close to her body, then nestled into the crook of her neck. "Momo," he chirped as she kissed him on the head.

"It's nice to meet you, Dr. Benton. I can already tell Anthony is a parrot-person, and Tiki seems to like you both. Oh, and call me Marilyn."

Emily was glad she had watched the Flix videos before the appointment. Being prepared for Marilyn's physical appearance allowed her to maintain her professional composure. Marilyn was late middle-age, short, but stout in stature. Her wild, curly gray hair had a solitary red streak dyed to match the color of Tiki's tail feathers. She had even found an identical shade of red lipstick. Jeweled little parrots adorned her bright red reading glasses and matched her dangling parrot earrings. An oversized red t-shirt topped her linen flare-legged pants—embroidered around the hem was a perfect likeness of Tiki.

"So, we're doing a nail trim on Tiki today?" Emily asked.

"Yes, but can I ask a favor?"

"Sure." Emily hoped it didn't involve some advanced avian medical technique.

"I have something going on at home, and it might be stressful for Tiki to be around. Would it be possible for him to board with you at the hospital for the day? He's happy in his cage, and I've brought some of his food, filtered water, and snacks. I'll be back before closing time—if that's okay?" She clasped her hands together in a tight grip as she waited for their answer.

The request surprised Emily, which delayed her response. Anthony stepped in to help. "I think we can accommodate Tiki," he said, then glanced at Emily for approval to proceed. When she nodded, he continued. "I have a large office with lots of natural light. Tiki can hang out with me."

"Wonderful!" Marilyn said as a look of relief lightened her face. "Well, let's get Tiki's pedicure taken care of, and then I'll leave him with you. Tiki, does that sound good to you?"

Tiki's head bobbed up and down in agreement. "Momo."

In response to the amused look on Anthony and Emily's face, Marilyn explained. "Hugo, my late husband, called me Momo. I won't bore you with the origin story behind the name, but it was a term of endearment. After he got sick, he taught Tiki to say my nickname. My heart smiles every time I hear it. I miss Hugo so much." Marilyn turned toward Tiki and gently stroked the side of his neck.

Emily and Anthony smiled, then focused on the task at hand. Tiki's nail trim was a breeze. Marilyn's calm presence and Anthony's expertise with holding parrots allowed for a quick and stress-free procedure. Emily chided herself for dreading the appointment. During their conversation, Marilyn confirmed Tiki Lulu's avian doctor at the University of Florida vet school would handle his medical care, so she only planned to bring Tiki in for routine trims. Emily breathed a sigh of relief.

Marilyn helped transition Tiki into Anthony's office. The custom-made travel cage sat atop a detachable rolling base for easy transport. Once he seemed settled, she left the hospital.

Emily moved on to her afternoon appointments, which included puppy visits, skin and ear infections, and one fire ant allergic reaction. It all seemed anticlimactic after meeting Tiki. The staff took turns visiting the parrot, and as Emily passed by the office, she stopped in her tracks when she overheard Abigail, her head receptionist, and Anthony discussing Tiki's latest videos.

"What's this about a treasure?" Emily asked as she turned to enter his office.

Tiki interrupted her with a, "Hello. Whatcha doing?"

"He says that every time someone comes in here," Anthony said. "His vocabulary is super impressive—from what I've heard so far."

Abigail waved her hands in the air, clearly struggling to contain her excitement. "Tiki is the clue to a buried treasure."

"What are you talking about?" Emily hadn't watched all of his posts and missed the part about a treasure.

"Well, Marilyn is an eccentric, almost-billionaire. Her husband passed away a couple of years ago. I think he made his fortune in sugar cane and rum in the Caribbean Islands. Anyway, Marilyn created this scavenger hunt that leads to a two hundred-thousand-dollar treasure. Every week, she posts a video of Tiki sharing a clue to the next treasure hunt location. Sometimes he even dresses up in a pirate costume. That's why he's gone viral. The local TV channel featured the story on last night's news."

"Wow. Marilyn didn't mention it today," Emily said.

"Maybe she assumed you knew," Anthony replied. "Plus, it had nothing to do with her appointment so no reason to bring it up."

Emily wasn't up to date on the latest social media trends. Her hands were full with running the hospital. After graduating from vet school and finishing her internship, she returned to Coral Shores to care for her mom. Her learning curve was steep, and she was still getting her bearings as she navigated the ins and outs of running a veterinary hospital. She tried to approach each new challenge with confidence, hard work, humor, and a willingness to learn from the people around her. Convincing Anthony to leave his head veterinary technician position in Tampa for the role of hospital manager had been an essential factor in her final decision to purchase the hospital from Dr. Dinsmore. They had always made a great team.

"How many clues have there been so far?" Emily asked.

"Three, I think. Tiki's followers are running all over south Florida looking for the treasure. What did you make of Marilyn's outfit?" Anthony smirked.

"She's colorful. I'll give her that," Emily said. Marilyn clearly loved parrots and Tiki in particular.

Anthony handed Emily a printout. "This is a list of Tiki's diet Marilyn included in the bag with his food and treats. It's no wonder he's so healthy. She knows her stuff, and it's obvious how bonded they are. She's had Tiki for over twenty years."

Emily looked at the list and then at Tiki Lulu, who returned her gaze. "Too bad we can't ask him where the treasure is buried."

"Treasure. Treasure. Ooh-la-la."

Emily, Abigail, and Anthony stared at one another, then at the parrot, eyes wide, before they erupted into laughter at Tiki's latest verbiage. Having him at the hospital was going to be an adventure.

Multiple times throughout her workday, Emily giggled to herself as she walked by Anthony's office. He tested the depth of Tiki's vocabulary by conversing with the precocious parrot. She overheard Tiki say, "Bye-bye, peek-a-boo, come here, love you, good boy, outside," and he could mimic the sound of a water fountain. Keeping Tiki entertained until Marilyn returned to pick him up would be fun for everyone.

Excited by the prospect of getting home on time for a change, Emily rushed to finish the day's medical notes. It was almost six o'clock, closing time, when Anthony walked into her office and sat in the chair beside her desk.

"Have you heard from Marilyn?" he asked.

"No, why?"

"Well, I thought she would've been here by now to take Tiki home. We're about to lock the doors, and I just checked with Abigail. She hasn't heard from her either."

"She might be stuck in traffic. Why don't you call her? I'll finish up here and join you in a couple of minutes," Emily said.

When she walked into Anthony's office, Tiki showed off his multilingual skills. "Hola. Hola."

"He's adorable." She smiled.

"He's more than that. I've never been around a bird with such a big personality and a vocabulary to match."

"Any updates from Marilyn?"

Anthony shook his head. "No. I called her home and her cellphone and had to leave a message. What should we do if she doesn't show up?"

"I don't want to leave Tiki alone overnight. I can pick up some takeout for dinner, and we can wait for Marilyn," Emily said.

"Okay. I agree about not leaving him here, if we can avoid it. I gave her my personal contact information in the message so she can reach us.

Well past closing, Emily and Anthony had finished their cheeseburgers and were debating what to do with Tiki. He ate the dinner Marilyn packed for him and seemed to settle in for a nap as the sun set. From his videos, Anthony knew Tiki lived in an outdoor aviary, so there was no need to cover his cage. Plus, the office would be quiet and dark until morning.

It was common for clients to delay picking up their pets from boarding when their plans changed at the last minute, but circumstances were different this time because of Tiki's celebrity status. Plus, he required special care and feeding. Marilyn didn't seem like the irresponsible type who would forget to contact them if she was going to be late. After one last attempt to reach her, Emily made the executive decision: Tiki would stay in Anthony's office overnight. He appeared calm and settled when they packed up to leave. They agreed to come early in the morning to check on him before the staff arrived. A feeling of apprehension overcame Emily as she locked the doors for the night.

CHAPTER TWO

Emily awoke from her nightmare, feeling suffocated and gasping to breathe. It all made perfect sense when she opened her eyes and found her almost twenty-pound, gray tabby Maine Coon cat sitting on her chest, staring at her, willing her to get up.

"Bella, I can't breathe," Emily said to her feline roommate. Bella responded with a flick of the tail, taking her time to walk across most of Emily's ribs before moving to the end of the bed where she sat with her back turned. "Okay, I'm getting up." Going back to sleep was not an option when Bella demanded to be fed.

Emily stumbled to the kitchen and hit the power button on her coffee maker before presenting Bella with her favorite tuna medley. With a mug full of super strong Italian roast in hand, Emily moved outside to her beachfront patio deck. Her cottage faced the Gulf of Mexico, and even though it didn't have direct sunrise views, the tropical sky was breathtaking with its streaks of red and gold. Coconut palms swayed in the light breeze, and the sweet smell of her climbing gardenias permeated the air. This was her happy place.

"Meow, meow." Bella announced her arrival, reminding Emily it was her happy place, too.

"Come on up." Emily tapped the cushion on her chaise lounge before scooting over to make room for her oversized cat. Emily's mother took respite in this same chair throughout her cancer treatments, with Bella by her side. After promising her mom she would always take care of Bella, Emily had recently started to enjoy this special space again without being overwhelmed with grief.

Two years had passed since she returned to her hometown and moved into her mother's cottage to care for her through those early days of doctor's appointments, chemotherapy treatments, and finally, at-home hospice care. She was grateful for that time with her mom, but being surrounded by those memories every day could be crushing. Her brother, Duncan, lived nearby with his young family, but his demanding career as a deputy sheriff made it difficult to be a caregiver, even though he had spent as much time with their mom as possible. Duncan wasn't interested in moving to their mom's place at the beach, so it had been easy for them to sort everything out after the funeral. That's when Emily made Coral Shores, and this cottage, her permanent home.

After one refill of her coffee, it was time to get ready for work. She needed to leave early to meet Anthony before the staff arrived. Last night, Emily watched all of Tiki's Flix posts about the treasure hunt. It was a big deal. Not only had Marilyn offered a two hundred-thousand-dollar prize to the winner, she also planned to donate the same amount to an animal-related charity the winner would choose from a short list of nonprofit animal or bird sanctuaries. The locations were to be revealed at the end of the contest. Local TV stations had taken an interest and were reporting daily updates on their newscasts.

Tiki Lulu was the lynchpin in the whole treasure scavenger hunt endeavor. Hints made during his latest video post would lead to a clue hidden within a wildlife center. Marilyn provided some context to the clues, but they were quite cryptic. So far, the locations spanned across south Florida at off-the-beaten-path attractions. Places the interstate highways had bypassed. Iconic old-Florida parks struggling to stay afloat. A by-product of the search for clues included an uptick in the number of people visiting these forgotten treasures, and the free publicity provided by the media. Marilyn had a well-established history of philanthropy centered on her support for diverse wildlife charities. This treasure hunt helped spotlight their important work.

Anthony called as Emily backed out of her driveway.

"Morning, Em. I couldn't sleep, and I wanted to make sure Tiki was okay."

"Are you already at the hospital?"

"Yup, for a while now. He's doing great and is super chatty. Take your time coming in. There were a few messages in the system, but none from Marilyn."

"I'm on my way. We can try all of her contact numbers again when I get there. See you soon."

Not hearing from Marilyn caused an uneasy feeling in the pit of her stomach that lingered throughout the short drive from her home on Gulf Beach Road to the veterinary hospital. Coral Shores was a sleepy oceanfront hamlet that prided itself on its Old Florida, small-town charm. Tourists flocked to the white sand beaches in search of keepsake seashells. As the sun cleared the horizon, marinas became busy hubs for boaters stocking up on fuel and bait before heading to the open water of the Gulf of Mexico. Locals greeted each other as they strolled along the causeway connecting the barrier island where Emily lived to the center of town. Under normal circumstances, the tropical water views along her drive had a calming influence, but not this morning.

There were so many issues to address if they didn't hear from Marilyn soon. Tiki had a special diet, and he couldn't stay in his travel cage forever. If they were lucky, Marilyn would arrive the moment the doors opened at eight o'clock, offering some innocent explanation for her delay. Until then, there was no point in stressing about the unknown.

• • •

"Want some tea, Momo? Want some tea?" Emily heard Tiki Lulu talking to Anthony as soon as she walked in the back door of the veterinary hospital. After watching Tiki's Flix videos, she learned his vocabulary approached one thousand words, and he could string together sentences on his own. He was quite remarkable.

"Morning." Emily rounded the corner to Anthony's office. "I'd love some tea. Thank you, Tiki."

Tiki bobbed his head up and down. "Good bird. Pretty bird."

"That's new." Emily turned her back and whispered to Anthony. "Do you think he's missing Marilyn?"

"Maybe, but I'm trying hard not to think about it too much. It was obvious how bonded they are, so I can only assume he misses her," Anthony said. "Marilyn must be a morning tea drinker."

"Can you imagine if Bella talked? It's best that I don't know what she's thinking. You should see the side-eye she gives me when I'm minutes late with her meals."

Anthony laughed. "I was about to call Marilyn. Fingers crossed."

Emily left to drop her stuff in her office and when she returned, Anthony hung up the phone.

"Any luck?"

"No. I tried her home and her cell. I left a message telling her Tiki is doing well, and we're here if she wants to come before the hospital opens. There's enough of his food for one to two more days." Anthony stared at Tiki, a deep crease forming in his brow.

To assuage his worries, Emily said, "I'm sure she'll call." Tiki enjoyed his time in Anthony's office even though they were both fully aware he needed a much larger and enriched habitat. His current setup wasn't ideal.

• • •

The veterinary hospital was a hub of activity. The cottage-style building exterior, complete with coral-colored shutters and flower boxes, welcomed clients inside to a friendly and comfortable lobby. Upholstered chairs and hardwood floors added to its charm.

The highlight of the morning included a follow-up appointment with Sara Lee, the fifteen-year-old Chiweenie, who suffered from food allergies and inflammatory bowel disease. She was half Chihuahua and half Dachshund, but her defining physical traits were her enormous ears that stood straight up on her head. Their size would be more appropriate on a German Shepherd. Sara Lee's owner, Susan, a well-known local artist and amateur mystic, had been one of Emily's mom's best friends. Susan now preferred to be called by her nickname, Otter, inspired by her spirit animal, the sea otter. Emily was still adjusting to the name.

Otter had only good news to share. After consulting with Emily, Sara Lee's stomach issues resolved by feeding an organic, hypoallergenic, homemade diet. They scheduled this appointment to recheck Sara Lee's blood work, but Otter declined. Since Mercury was in retrograde, now would not be a good time to run the test. She would return with Sara Lee next week when the moons were in alignment. It made perfect sense to Otter, and since Sara Lee seemed to be on the path to recovery, Emily agreed to wait.

"Emily, I mean, Dr. Benton. I think you look more like your mom every time I see you," Otter said, smiling as her eyes welled up. She shook her head to compose herself. "I miss your mom."

"Me too, Sus—" Emily corrected herself, "Otter," then changed the subject back to Sara Lee as she escorted them to the reception area. It was still too hard to talk about her mom. Otter was correct, though. Emily and her mom both had deep red hair, freckles across their noses, and pale blue eyes. Emily wore her long hair straight compared to her mom's wavy curls and was a few inches taller, but that was the only difference. Emily possessed the same natural beauty her mother had.

Anthony spent most of the day in his office entertaining Tiki. Emily tried all of Marilyn's contacts again after lunch, but still nothing. As closing time approached, Emily and Anthony sat down to discuss their plan of action.

"With Tiki settled here for the night, I think we should drive over to Marilyn's house. If she's home and needs us to keep Tiki for a few more days, we can at least get more of his special diet to have on hand. We wouldn't normally show up at a client's house, but I think the circumstances are unique."

Emily shrugged. "Worst-case scenario, we can leave a note at the house for someone to contact us. Where does she live?"

"I checked her client registration, and it's a twenty-minute drive. I'm not sure, but I think it's in a fancy neighborhood bordering the Burt Blenheim Wildlife Estuary. Not quite the Everglades, but close."

"Okay. I have some calls to return and medical files to update. Once the staff are gone, we'll head over." Anthony agreed, and they both got busy wrapping up their day.

• • •

The drive to Marilyn's house took them east, away from the ocean and the back bay. Once they passed the golf course communities of the suburbs, the landscape changed. Houses were sparse, and the marshland snaked with converging rivers that drained into the Florida Everglades National Park to the south. Without their GPS, they would never have found it. The home's ornate iron gate sat open, so they continued through the entrance onto a long, winding driveway, flanked with rows of towering royal palm trees. The shaded lane led to a massive, white stucco Spanish-style mansion complete with a landscaped circular drive centered on a blue mosaic water fountain.

"Wow. She's wealthy, but this is something else," Anthony said.

Emily drove to the front door and parked. Before the last turn in the driveway, they glimpsed a large, airy enclosure at the back of the house. They could only see a corner of the structure, but it looked similar to an aviary at a zoo or bird sanctuary. The entire setting was awe-inspiring.

"Do you see anyone?"

Anthony shook his head. It seemed strange for an estate of this size to be deserted—no signs of other vehicles or staff. They stepped out of the car and approached the custom, hand-carved front door, then used the heavy brass knocker shaped as a perched parrot to announce their arrival. Nobody answered after multiple knocks.

"Now, what should we do?" Anthony asked.

Emily's eyes narrowed as she spotted a path leading around the side of the house. "Maybe she's outside and can't hear us. Let's walk around the back to see if we can find someone."

"Okay, you're the boss." Anthony grinned. Even though Emily was the owner of the vet hospital, they were partners, tackling new challenges together as a team. "I want to get a look at that outdoor enclosure. Do you think they built it for Tiki?"

"Probably. It wouldn't surprise me if he had his own chef."

The unlocked side gate revealed a winding path bordered with tropical foliage, guiding them into the backyard. Tiki's outdoor aviary was twice as big as Emily's cottage and soared to the full height of the two-story mansion.

"This is amazing. No wonder Tiki is such a happy bird," Anthony said.

They stopped to take in all the details of his outdoor habitat. He had enough room for short flights, too many perches to count, and there were toys and feeding stations everywhere. A veritable oasis. The aviary could be accessed from the house through two sets of massive antique French doors. A large, comfortable seating area and dining table for twelve completed Marilyn and Tiki's sanctuary.

"I don't see anyone, do you?" Emily asked.

Anthony scanned the yard. "No. Why don't you go check out the other side of the house. I see a trail leading to the estuary behind us. Maybe she's out walking near the marsh."

"I sure hope there aren't any motion detector alarms on the property." Emily moved along the pathway bordering the back of the house. After rounding the corner, she saw an exterior door that hadn't been visible. It directly accessed the house without going through the aviary. She approached, then knocked. After no reply, she knocked again while peeking through the doorway window. "Oh," Emily gasped at the scene inside. At the same moment, Anthony started yelling from the tree line at the edge of the property.

"Em, help! Em!"

She had never heard such alarm and urgency in his voice, so she started sprinting. "I'm coming. I'm coming."

Anthony walked out from behind a fan palm. His face frozen with fear. As Emily approached, she noticed his hands were shaking.

"Are you okay?" Emily reached for him, then circled around to check for injuries.

"I'm fine," he said, even though his voice sounded anything but fine. Anthony pointed at a nearby row of palm trees. "I can't say the same for him."

Emily only had to walk a short distance off the path before she saw the body. She ran to the lifeless figure, prepared to render first aid.

"I already checked for a pulse," Anthony said. "Pretty sure he's dead."

Emily would have started CPR, except it would not change the outcome. They both stood there, staring at the body of someone they did not recognize. The man looked to be around thirty years old, had longish brown hair, and was wearing dirty jeans and cowboy boots. It was hard to draw their eyes away from his most defining feature—a gigantic wound on the side of his head. Half his skull had been bashed in.

Emily looked over her shoulder toward the dense estuary. "This jungle is freaking me out. Did you see anyone else?"

Anthony's eyes darted back and forth, scanning the property before answering, "No. Let's move toward the back of the house and call the police."

Unfortunately, this wasn't Emily's first time stumbling into a crime scene. Her hands trembled as she pulled the phone out of her pocket. She knew who to call.

CHAPTER THREE

"C'mon, Duncan. Pick up." Emily paced around Marilyn's backyard.

Her brother answered on the second ring. "Hey, Em. What's up?"

"We need your help. I'm with Anthony, and we didn't know if we should call 911 or if you can handle it."

"Are you okay?" Duncan asked, his tone shifting from jovial brother to serious law enforcement officer.

"We're fine. I'm at a client's house, and we just found a dead body. Pretty sure he was murdered."

"What! Again?" Duncan said.

Not that long ago, Emily and Anthony's lives became entangled in the murder investigation of their childhood piano teacher, Mrs. Eliza Klein. Emily received pushback from her brother, Deputy Sheriff Duncan Benton, and his partner, Detective Mike Lane, as she investigated the case on her own, even though her contribution had been essential in solving the crime.

"Yes—again. He isn't our client though. I have no idea who he is."

"Where are you?" he asked. Emily provided the address, and Duncan confirmed it fell within his jurisdiction. "I'll dispatch a patrol car and an EMT, and I'll be there as soon as possible. Don't touch anything."

Emily and Anthony had seen enough TV detective shows to know better than to disrupt the crime scene. Considered a necessity under the circumstances, they had touched the body to check for a pulse, but that was all.

"Em, let's sit down." Anthony pointed to a seating area closer to the aviary. "I don't feel so good."

Even though Anthony had been involved with Mrs. Klein's murder investigation, he had never seen a dead body before, not a human one, anyway. Emily's firsthand experience in that department helped her understand the resulting shock and trauma. Anthony had helped her process the flood of emotions after finding Mrs. Klein's body, and she needed to be there for him this time. She took his hand and led him to the bench.

Anthony stood six foot three inches tall, and if he was going to faint, it would be impossible for Emily to catch his sturdy frame. She rushed to get him seated, just in time. His friendly, handsome baby face had become ashen and drawn. Within a few minutes, the color returned to his cheeks and his breathing slowed.

After what seemed like an eternity, Emily heard sirens approaching the house. "Anthony, you stay here. I'll go around and meet them."

He didn't object. "Thanks, Em. My legs are still feeling wobbly." She patted his shoulder before running into the front yard.

The police and ambulance arrived together. Emily motioned for them to follow her, guiding them to the marsh and to the body. The police officer politely asked her to step back from the area, so she returned to the bench where she and Anthony waited for Duncan.

When Deputy Sheriff Duncan Benton walked into the backyard, anyone at the scene would guess he and Emily were related. His hair was more auburn than red, but the difference was academic. He motioned to Emily he would be right over, then talked with the first responders on scene. He disappeared into the marsh for a few minutes before instructing the officer to cordon off the area with police tape. Turning toward Emily and Anthony, he dropped his shoulders, let out a heavy sigh, and walked over to their seating area, taking a chair opposite the bench.

"You sure you're both okay?" he asked. Anthony nodded, but wasn't very convincing. He still looked nauseous, and his hands shook ever so slightly. "Take a couple of deep breaths, then tell me everything."

Emily took the lead to give Anthony more time to collect his thoughts. She told her brother all about Marilyn, Tiki, the treasure, and the reason they'd come to her house.

"You need to see this," Emily said, motioning for Duncan and Anthony to follow her to the back door.

Anthony teetered as he stood up, prompting both Duncan and Emily to reach for his arms to support him before he waved them off. He took a deep breath, clapped his hands together, and wriggled his shoulders.

"I'm okay now," Anthony said, before leading the way across the yard to the back door. Emily and Duncan looked at each other, then hustled to catch up to him.

"I was looking inside for Marilyn, or anyone else who might be at home. That's when Anthony found the body." Emily pointed through the window in the door. "It doesn't look good."

The living room appeared to be the scene of an altercation—an overturned end table, couch pushed askew, cushions tossed about, and pieces from a broken lamp spread across the floor. A large floral vase containing wilted flowers lay on its side, leaving behind a wet spot on the carpet. Duncan tried the doorknob, but it was locked. He knocked with authority, but nobody answered.

"I'm going to do a quick search around the house. Can you both wait for me on the bench?" he asked. Emily and Anthony agreed and moved back to their safe zone.

When Duncan returned, he was finishing up a call. "Okay, Mike. We'll see you soon." He hung up the phone.

"Was that Detective Lane?" Anthony asked before glancing at Emily.

"Yes, he's getting a search warrant to go into the house and will be here shortly."

Anthony leaned in to whisper, "I hope it won't be too awkward, Em?"

Emily had been dating Detective Mike Lane for a few months, but right now they were in a strange place, and she wasn't sure if their relationship was on or off. They both had demanding careers that made coordinating their schedules a challenge. Emily had fallen head over heels for Mike, but she wasn't certain those feelings were reciprocated.

"Not at all. I'm glad he's coming," she said, trying to sound brave. Anthony held her hand in solidarity.

"I don't understand why you need a search warrant," Anthony said. "There's a dead body, and obviously something bad happened inside the house. Can't you just break down the door?"

"Well, if I saw someone injured in the house, I would, but since we entered the backyard without authorization, it's a gray area. The search needs to be lawful—by the book. Mike will be here soon."

"I'm worried about Marilyn," Emily said. "She didn't keep her scheduled pickup time, and we can't reach her."

They were so consumed with the sight of the dead body; they'd forgotten about the original reason for their house call. Anthony and Emily faced challenges in providing Tiki's care, and now they had to make a longer-term plan.

Anthony's stomach growled loud enough for Emily to hear. He looked at her and shrugged his shoulders. "Actually, I've lost my appetite," he said. "But we need to figure out Tiki's diet. Duncan, do you think we can look to see if there's any special parrot food we can take back to the hospital?"

"I can't answer that right now. Not until we search the house and the property," he said.

"Are you okay if we wait?" Emily asked. Before Duncan answered, her own stomach started doing flip-flops. She suffered from an extreme case of butterflies. Detective Mike Lane walked into the backyard, leaving no doubt about his ability to take her breath away. He was tall and lean, with an athletic build developed from a lifetime of playing sports. His brown, wavy hair and hazel eyes weren't even his most attractive feature; that was his smile.

It had been almost two weeks since their last date, and despite it being a wonderful, romantic night, they hadn't been able to reconnect. Emily thought he might be trying to cool things off. She turned back to Anthony and caught him staring at her with a goofy grin on his face.

"I told you everything would be okay. Just talk to him, Em," he said.

She replied in a hushed tone. "I will, but this is a crime scene. Not exactly the best place for a relationship discussion."

Anthony shrugged. "I guess."

"Hi, Em." Mike greeted her first with a sheepish grin. "Hi, Anthony. Are you all right?"

Anthony replied, "It freaked me out at first, but I'm better now." He turned to Emily, nudging her with a subtle elbow to the ribs so she would answer him.

"Hi, Mike. We're good, but we're concerned about our client, Marilyn Peña. Can you check inside now?"

Mike waved the warrant in his hand. "Let's go," he said to Duncan. As he walked to the front of the house to join the crime scene technicians, he turned to look over his shoulder at Emily and their eyes locked. She sucked in a deep breath and smiled.

Anthony, who missed nothing, said, "You two will be fine. You need to figure out that whole work-life balance thing though."

She thought about it and agreed she had to prioritize her dating life before he slipped away.

"Our big project has us both running on empty," she said, motioning between Anthony and herself.

"But we have a little break coming soon. Make it happen, Em."

Anthony was in a more established relationship with his partner, Marc, when their workload exploded. His recent move into Marc's townhouse solidified their commitment, making it easier for Anthony to navigate work-related pressures with the help of a supportive partner. Emily and Mike were still in the early dating phase, and she thought he might have misunderstood the reason behind her absence. She wanted to take things to the next level, but they took a step backwards instead. Anthony was right. She and Mike needed to clear the air.

The police activity at Marilyn's house reached a crescendo as the sun set. The medical examiner had come and gone, taking the dead body with him. Duncan informed them the house was empty. They were relieved to find out Marilyn hadn't met the same demise, but they still didn't have any additional information concerning her whereabouts. Another hour passed as they waited for permission to search for Tiki's food.

The chorus of sounds emanating from the tropical canopy took on a musical quality when the frogs joined the constant sing-song provided by the cicadas. Emily and Anthony added their own drumbeat to the mix as they swatted away at the barrage of mosquitoes and no-see-ums that swarmed around them.

"Em, the bugs are getting bad. Do you want to wait in the car?" Anthony asked.

"Sure," she replied as they started walking toward the driveway. "I'm thinking our chances of getting into Marilyn's house are dwindling. If Duncan or Mike can't let us in now, I think we should go home."

"We have enough food for another day, and I can source Tiki's diet tomorrow. I'm thankful Marilyn left us the details when she dropped him off." Anthony paused. "What if she thought she was in danger? That might be why she left Tiki with us—to protect him."

"I don't know. Maybe." Before Emily speculated on what might have happened to Marilyn, Duncan came out of the house.

"I'm sorry you've been waiting so long. It'll be a few more hours before we finish processing her house."

"We get it," Emily replied. "Are you okay if we head home? We're getting eaten alive out here."

"Sure. I can get your statements tomorrow."

"What's going on in the house?" Anthony asked. "Was it worse than what we saw through the window?"

"Sorry. I can't answer that. It's an active crime scene."

Emily heard Anthony inhale and when she turned to gauge his response, he looked like he was holding his breath. Duncan's refusal to share any relevant info would not be well received. The last time Emily and Anthony found themselves intertwined in a murder investigation, the tension between the Benton siblings resulted in family friction. Nobody wanted to see that happen again, especially Anthony. They hoped Marilyn would reappear, safe and sound.

"Let's go, Em," Anthony said, prompting them to move toward the car. "I'll ask Marc if he can pick me up at your place."

"Okay. I can give you a ride to work in the morning," she said.

He pressed his hand against his forehead and shook his head. "I can't believe this happened again."

Emily agreed. It was déjà vu. For a second time, they'd found themselves responsible for a client's beloved pet after stumbling into a crime scene. Emily had brought Mrs. Klein's little terrier, Elvis, an innocent bystander, into her home, which caused Emily and Anthony's lives to become entangled in a murder investigation. The one positive outcome from such a tragic event occurred when Duncan and his wife, Jane, adopted Elvis into their family.

They were quiet on the drive back to Emily's beach cottage, except for the rumbling coming from their stomachs. It was way past dinnertime.

Finding a dead body could only be described as a traumatic life event, but it had been less personal this time. They'd known Mrs. Klein since they were kids. She had been their piano teacher, community leader, and mentor at the animal shelter and turtle rescue group. It became easier to distance themselves from the crime when the victim was a stranger, but that didn't change the fact someone out there would be missing their loved one.

Marc texted Anthony to let him know he'd be there soon and had brought them dinner.

"He's the best." Emily turned to Anthony and smiled. She loved seeing him so happy and settled. Was it a realistic dream to have that same connection with Mike?

CHAPTER FOUR

When Emily pulled into her driveway, Marc stood next to his car holding a large bag filled with burritos, salsa and chips, and jumbo cups of icy sweet tea, making him an instant hero. As they entered the cottage, Bella greeted them with demanding meows, clearly disapproving of the late dinner service. Appeasing her came first, then they carried their food to the outside dining table. In between mouthfuls, Emily and Anthony took turns filling Marc in on the sequence of events that led up to finding the body.

"Do the police know what happened?" Marc asked. Not that long ago, he'd watched as Anthony and Emily had their lives upended after becoming embroiled in their first murder case. His tense facial expression made it clear he was worried about history repeating itself.

"I don't think so," Emily said. "They're still gathering evidence at Marilyn's house."

Marc grabbed a few bites of salsa and chips from Anthony's plate before saying, "I assume you didn't see it tonight, but the local TV channel reported on the scavenger hunt. Looks like they found another one of Tiki's treasure clues at Save Our Seabirds Wildlife Sanctuary in Sarasota."

"I think the avian veterinarian there was a few years ahead of me at school," Emily said. "I've read about her in our alumni newsletter."

"They interviewed the director for the story. It seems they set a record for donations today," Marc said.

Anthony smiled. "I'm sure that was Marilyn's plan all along—to bring people, press, and awareness to these struggling wildlife centers. I checked, and so far, all the locations in the scavenger hunt are nonprofit places, always in need of cash. Most of them operate with volunteers, but it's expensive to care for all the birds and animals. Some of them do rescue, rehab, and release, but they also provide permanent homes for parrots and seabirds that can't be returned to the wild."

Emily's phone buzzed, alerting her to a message. "It's Mike. He's going to drop by in an hour." She felt both anxious and excited at the prospect of seeing him again.

"Yes." Anthony fist bumped with Marc. "You should have seen the two of them tonight—like watching nervous high school kids at the big dance."

"Stop," Emily laughed. "I don't know why it was so awkward."

"Duh, I do," Anthony replied. "It's because you like him so much. You two need to talk. We'll stay until he gets here, but then you're on your own."

"Thanks, guys," she said before standing. "Make yourselves at home. I'm going to freshen up."

Emily rushed through a shower—her mind moving at the speed of light. Was Mike coming to get her official statement for the police record, or for more personal reasons? Her usual after-work wardrobe included comfy lounging clothes, but she opted for a casual teal-colored sundress and even put on some mascara and lipstick.

Emily looked forward to seeing Mike, but was uncertain what she wanted to say to him. She rehearsed some opening lines before rejoining Anthony and Marc on the deck.

"Here, Em." Anthony handed her a glass of wine. "I found an open bottle in your fridge. I figured we both need a glass after the night we've had."

"Thanks." Emily took a sip as she stared at the ocean. "What a gorgeous night." The sun had set, coloring the sky with shades of blue and purple. Emily inhaled deeply before turning back to her friends who were sitting together watching a video on Marc's phone. "What are you looking at?"

"Just showing Anthony the video from the local news report about Marilyn's treasure hunt." Marc handed his phone to Emily and pressed play. She watched the short broadcast, surprised by the hype surrounding Tiki's latest clue.

"It looks like the momentum is building. I watched a video from last week where Tiki's clue was the word, *Wonder,* and that led the treasure hunters to the Everglades Wonder Gardens in Bonita Springs. They also had a record day for visitors, and it looks like even more people showed up today," Anthony said.

"Do Tiki's videos always post on the same day of the week?" Emily asked.

Anthony searched on his own phone for the answer. "Yes, Marilyn always posts Tiki's treasure clue on a Monday."

"I'm confused," Marc said. "So, Tiki gives the clue about where to go, and then there's a message hidden at that location."

"Yes, each spot has a physical clue hidden somewhere on the grounds. All the clues put together will lead to the final treasure location," Anthony said. "There's a lot of money on the line."

They sat with their own thoughts for a few minutes. Anthony and Emily were more worried than ever about Marilyn. Had this treasure hunt brought someone dangerous into her life? They hoped that wasn't the case, but until she returned, Tiki was their responsibility.

"Emily," Mike called out from the front door.

She sat up straight and ran her fingers through her hair. "We're out here."

Mike joined them on the deck, Emily finding him as handsome as ever. "Hi Anthony. Hi Marc. I didn't mean to barge in."

"Not at all," Anthony said. "We were just leaving." He set his half empty glass of wine on the table and stood, motioning to Marc with his eyebrows it was time to go. "Unless you need to ask me questions about Marilyn and the dead body."

"Duncan is planning to get your statements tomorrow. I'm here on a social call. Just want to make sure you're okay, Em. And you too, Anthony." He moved to sit next to Emily before handing them a bag. "I found this in the cupboard at the house and thought it might help with the parrot."

Anthony took the bag and looked inside. "Perfect. This is Tiki's special pelleted food. The rest of his diet is fruits, veggies, grains, and some seeds, which I can get for him. Thanks, Mike. This helps a lot. Em, I'm going in early again tomorrow, and Marc said he can drop me off on his way to work." Anthony and Marc moved toward the front door, then Anthony turned to face Emily. "We've been through a lot today, but I'm worried about Tiki. What if Marilyn doesn't show up soon?"

"We can handle whatever happens. We always have." She gave him a reassuring hug. Deep down, she realized making a long-term plan for Tiki's care would not be a simple task.

There was an uncomfortable moment after Marc and Anthony left when neither Emily nor Mike said a single word. Then each began talking simultaneously, both breaking into laughter, easing the tension.

"I was happy to see you today, even if it was at a crime scene," Emily said. Mike leaned in for a long, lingering kiss. In an instant, they closed the distance keeping them apart. Mike's kiss left no doubt in Emily's mind about where he stood in the relationship.

"We're both swamped. I get it, but I don't like it," Mike said.

"My schedule has been getting in the way." Emily took a deep breath before continuing. "But I'll be honest. I wondered if you were trying to slow things down between us."

Mike laughed and shook his head. "I thought you were pumping the brakes." He kissed her again. It was obvious neither of them had any interest in slowing down their relationship. "Let's commit to carving out time to spend together."

"I'd rather have plans in place, even if we need to reschedule when something comes up. That's better than going weeks without seeing you." Emily pulled him next to her on the lounge chair, his muscular arms enveloping her in an embrace.

They stayed on the deck until the moon had climbed high in the sky. Bella signaled the late hour when she went to bed on her own, taking her position on her personal pillow. Mike took Bella's hint, committing to call tomorrow to discuss plans for the weekend. After their two-week hiatus, Emily didn't want to wait three more days to see him again.

Mike would be busy with the investigation stemming from their gruesome discovery at Marilyn's house, and she needed the week to work out the details for Tiki's care. She hoped Marilyn would reappear so it would be unnecessary for her and Anthony to put a plan in motion.

The Coral Shores Sheriff's Office was now tasked with finding Marilyn, relieving Anthony and Emily of that burden. Mike and Duncan were excellent at their job, but Emily trusted her own instincts. Her involvement led to conflict with her brother during Mrs. Klein's murder investigation, but she'd also helped solve the case. Circumstances might be different this time, and she had so many unanswered questions. Did Marilyn have other family in the area? Had anyone filed a missing person report for her? The local TV news regularly featured the story about Marilyn and Tiki. All their Flix followers would notice if they didn't post on Monday, making it impossible to keep this under wraps for long.

CHAPTER FIVE

Emily and Anthony were relieved to find Tiki calmly preening his feathers when they arrived at the hospital.

"Morning. Morning. Momo, want some tea?"

"Good morning, Tiki Lulu," they replied in unison. Emily opened the window blinds, then spent the next few minutes talking with the chatty bird.

"Still no messages from Marilyn." Anthony checked both the phone and hospital email accounts before cleaning and replenishing Tiki's cage. The bird pantry Marilyn provided was getting low, so he started a shopping list.

Emily found it fascinating to watch Tiki delicately eat a slice of banana. "He must be missing his morning routine with Marilyn," Emily mused. In the short time she had seen Marilyn and Tiki together, it was obvious how much they loved each other, and it made her sad to think of them apart. "I'll text Duncan to find out if there are any new leads and if he's coming to the hospital today, or wants to meet us after work."

"I'm sure they're searching all her credit cards and talking to friends and family. If Marilyn's disappearance becomes an official missing person case, the police can blast it out to the public," Anthony said.

"There's so much money at stake with this treasure hunt. It could attract unsavory types looking for an easy payout. I assume the police know who the murder victim is, but there was nothing about it on the news this morning." Emily and Anthony didn't need to say it out loud—they were both concerned for Marilyn's safety.

Despite the dark cloud hanging over them, the hospital provided ample distractions from their worries. Jax, one of Emily's favorite patients, was the first appointment of the day. Emily stood next to the reception desk talking with Abigail when the ten-month-old Bernese Mountain Dog bounded into the lobby, dragging his owner, Miss Gallant, behind him.

"Morning. Jax sure loves coming to the vet." His owner caught her breath. "As you can see, he's feeling much better."

Abigail came around her desk to greet them both. Jax wagged his tail with such force, his entire hind end bounced off the ground. "What a good boy," she said, petting his head.

"Hi, Miss Gallant. We're all set up for Jax's X-rays. I'll be back with him in a few minutes, and then we can review his treatment plan." Emily took the giant puppy's leash and led him into the treatment area. He stopped to smell everything along the way, so it took a minute.

Anthony and the technician, Catrinna, were ready and gowned in their protective gear. "I pulled up his last X-rays to compare. We'll be back in a few," Anthony said. Jax happily followed them into the dark room.

His limping began a month ago, first on his left front leg, then on his right. A detailed exam and X-rays confirmed his diagnosis—panosteitis. A painful condition caused by growing pains in young, large breed dogs. After tweaking Jax's diet, prescribing anti-inflammatory pain medicine, and instructing Miss Gallant to rest the active young pup; he seemed to have turned the corner. Indeed, the latest X-rays looked much better.

Jax pulled Emily through the hospital to reunite with his owner who waited in an exam room.

"So, Dr. Benton. How did he do?"

"He's a wonderful patient. Catrinna said that as long as you rub his ears, he sits perfectly still for his X-rays. Here, let me show you the images." Emily turned the screen mounted on the computer for Miss Gallant to see. "We took the X-ray on the left when you first brought him in for his lameness, and the X-ray on the right is from today." Emily pointed at the images to highlight the differences. "This previously inflamed area of his bone now appears normal."

Miss Gallant put a hand on her chest and exhaled. "That's the best news. It's been hard to keep him quiet—he's so full of energy. Does this mean he can play again?"

"Let's start by increasing his leash walks over the next week. If there are no signs of relapse or pain, then you can resume his normal activities. I've refilled a few doses of his pain medicine to have on hand in case he's limping. If anything changes, let us know."

"I will." Jax stood on his hind legs, front feet on the exam table, and leaned across to kiss Emily's hand. He wanted to be part of the celebration. "We'll be back soon for his routine checkup."

When Emily returned to her office, Anthony was waiting for her. "We have a few minutes before the next appointment. Let's make a plan for Tiki."

"Okay. I see you started a shopping list for his food."

"Yes, I'm going to the grocery store at lunch. They should have everything we need. I'm grateful Mike brought Tiki's pellets last night since they're harder to find. Speaking of Mike."

Emily smiled.

"I knew you'd work it out." he said.

"We only talked a little about our dating hiatus, but things seem back on track."

"I'm glad, Em."

"Anyway, back to Tiki. What's the plan for boarding him?"

"Well, I've been thinking about it a lot. He's calm and content right now. Moving him into a large dog kennel provides more space, but I think he's happiest with me in the office. We chat all day long, and when I'm busy, I turn on the Animal Planet or Discovery channel for him to watch. He seems to like that."

"We can decide on a day-by-day basis, but if Marilyn doesn't reappear, we'll need to find Tiki more space. Even if there was someone to care for him, he can't go home since it's a crime scene." Emily looked at her phone. "Still no reply from Duncan."

Anthony nodded. "Let me know if you hear anything. I'm heading out for groceries. Catrinna will keep Tiki company until I get back."

• • •

Her stomach churned as she placed the call.

"Hi, Em. Sorry I haven't got back to you, but I don't have any news about Mrs. Peña."

"Do you mean you don't know where she is, or you can't share any news with me?"

"We don't know where she is. We have some leads, and I'll let you know when I have something to share."

"What about the identity of the dead guy? They didn't mention it on the morning news."

"We have to contact next of kin before we can announce it to the public."

It frustrated Emily to be headed down a familiar path, with Duncan refusing to share any details about the status of the investigation. As far as brothers and sisters go, they were close. Always had been. Their dad died when they were young, so it had only been the three of them for as long as she could remember. After their mom passed away, they became more bonded than ever. That's how she knew he was hiding something from her.

"Do you understand what's involved in the care of an African Grey parrot?" Duncan didn't reply, so she continued. "It's a lot. He's in a small travel cage right now, but he can't stay there forever. I'll need to find him a sanctuary or a foster home. Again, not a simple task. Can't you share something, anything at all, to help me plan?"

"Sorry, no. I've got to go. Can I meet you and Anthony after work to get your statements?"

There was no point in pushing right now. Emily would wait until she could look her brother in the eye. It would be easier to tell if he was being evasive when they were face to face. "Okay. I'll confirm with Anthony. We should be at my place by seven."

With Catrinna's help, Emily worked through a string of routine appointments. As they wrapped up a senior exam on a sweet, tortoiseshell cat named Petal, Anthony returned, his arms weighed down with shopping bags. He had enough groceries to provision a boat for an ocean voyage.

"I didn't know how much to buy." Anthony shrugged and smiled at the surprised looks on their faces. "Believe it or not, I stuck to the list. His diet is so diverse, and I can't buy just a small piece of papaya. I'll take everything home tonight to clean and portion the food so I can bring fresh servings each day."

"What would I do without your parrot prowess? I barely remember the week I spent on birds in vet school," Emily said.

Anthony bowed, accepting her praise before setting his bags on the counter. "Any news from Duncan?"

"No, but I think he knows more than he's saying. He asked to see us together after work to get our statements."

"Marc has a client meeting tonight, so I'm free."

"Great. I'll let him know."

Catrinna helped Anthony unload Tiki's perishables into the staff fridge before each of them returned to the tasks involved with running a small animal hospital. Emily had blood test results to interpret and relay to her clients. Anthony worked on the staff schedule, leaving Catrinna to complete treatments for the hospitalized patients and to prepare the lab samples for pick up. When Emily and Anthony eventually gathered to brainstorm the agenda for an upcoming staff meeting, Abigail called over the intercom.

"Dr. Benton. There's a gentleman here to pick up Tiki. What should I tell him?"

Emily and Anthony turned to each other, mouths open. "Who else knows Tiki is here?" Anthony asked. "Did Duncan speak with any of her family members today?"

"I don't know, but I'm sure he would have told me if he did."

"What should we do?"

Emily tapped her finger on the desk, thinking. "Abigail, please put the gentleman in room one. We'll be there in a minute." She turned to Anthony. "Let's go see what he has to say for himself."

"Em, I'm not giving Tiki to anyone unless it's a request from Marilyn."

"I agree. Just follow my lead."

CHAPTER SIX

Anthony and Emily walked into the exam room and introduced themselves. Anthony's jaw tightened, and he crossed his arms. He was a teddy bear on the inside, but the stranger standing in front of them didn't know that.

The man swallowed hard. "My name's Chad Peña. Marilyn is my aunt, and she asked me to pick Tiki up for her."

Emily and Anthony shared a look, communicating their distrust.

"Mr. Peña, please show us some identification," Emily asked.

The man hesitated, then handed them his wallet. She memorized the address before passing it to Anthony.

"We have a strict hospital policy. We can't release a pet to anyone unless the owner approves them in advance. Your aunt didn't add your name to her list. Can I ask how you found out Tiki was here?"

His face turned red as he shifted his weight. "My aunt sent me a text asking me to pick up Tiki."

Anthony let his anger show through when he asked, "Do you know the police are looking for your aunt, and her home is currently being treated as a crime scene?"

"I don't know what you're talking about. She sent me the text this morning."

"Do you mind showing it to us?" Emily asked.

"Uh, no. I deleted it. Listen, this is my family business. I don't need to show you anything."

"Actually, you do," Anthony said, taking one step forward. The man took one step back. "I'm sorry, but we won't be able to release Tiki to you without Marilyn's consent. You're welcome to leave us your contact info in case anything changes." As he handed the wallet back, the man snatched it out of his hand before turning to leave in haste. Emily grabbed her phone to transcribe his address before she forgot it.

"What the hell, Em. I've got a bad feeling about this."

"Me, too. I'll send Duncan his info. Maybe he can track this guy down before we get together tonight." Emily added a few more helpful details. The nephew's full name was Chad Michael Peña, the Third. He appeared average in every way, including height and build. Somewhere in his late twenties, he had light brown hair, brown eyes, and a narrow face. Emily thought he looked like a weasel, and when he spoke, he whined. A whining weasel.

• • •

After the hospital closed and the staff had gone home, Emily and Anthony checked on Tiki Lulu one last time. Perched on his highest post, he stood on one leg with the other pulled close to his body. He tucked his head into his feathers, signaling it was time to sleep. His ability to lock his toes around the pole and sleep while standing was another miracle of nature. Emily smiled. Thanks to Anthony's knowledge and expertise, she felt more confident about caring for this famous parrot.

With Tiki settled for the night, they tiptoed out of the office. His small, confined space worried them after seeing the luxurious aviary at Marilyn's house. He was accustomed to having lots of freedom to move. Plus, Tiki must be missing his best friend, Marilyn.

Not wanting to be late for their meeting with Duncan, Anthony ordered a pizza to pick up on the way.

• • •

Emily was deep in thought during her drive home, oblivious to the beautiful vistas. Her cottage sat on a barrier island, connected to the mainland by a causeway that afforded views of the Intracoastal Waterway extending to the blue-green waters of the Gulf of Mexico. Locals riding their bikes to and from the beach passed by anglers set up along the walkout areas of the bridge with their chairs, coolers, and shade awnings, patiently watching the tips of their poles for any movement. Everything seemed to move in slow motion. The heat and humidity of late summer kept many of the tourists away. That would all change after Thanksgiving when the snowbirds began their annual migration south, filling up all the local hotels, shops, and restaurants.

While Emily gathered her laptop and work bags, Anthony pulled into the driveway. She smelled the fully loaded pizza as soon as he got out of the car. Working in a veterinary hospital made it difficult to take a proper lunch break. The demanding pace of the day forced her to nibble on snacks, leaving her starving by dinner time.

"Let's eat. It killed me not to grab a slice on the way over," Anthony said.

They walked through the front door, scanning the room for Bella. Asleep on her favorite cat tree overlooking the beach deck, a ray of sunshine reflected off her gray tabby hair, sparkling as if streaked with silver.

"Bella," Anthony said. He set the pizza in the kitchen but returned to scratch under her chin—her preferred location.

"I can hear her purring from over here." Emily portioned their dinner onto plates. "Water or wine? Sorry, those are my only choices."

"Water for now. I may change my mind depending on what Duncan has to say."

Anthony carried Bella to join them outside. Emily finished her last bite, took a deep breath and melted into her beloved chaise lounge. Her mother spent many hours in this same chair during her treatments, and it had become Emily's place to recharge and restore, just as her mother had done during those difficult months. The sound as the waves washed ashore with salty breezes carrying the scent of tropical flowers was a powerful elixir.

"I checked the local news, and there's still nothing about our dead body. Don't you think that's strange?"

She nodded. "Even if they don't know his name, they usually report the crime. Especially if they need the public's help to identify him."

Bella's ears perked up. She was on alert and turned toward the front door. "Duncan must be here," Anthony said.

Her brother knocked once, then let himself in, still in uniform and carrying his work bag.

"We're sitting outside on the deck," she called out to him. "There are a few slices of pizza left if you're hungry."

"Thanks, but I'm good. Hi, Anthony." Duncan sat down at the table. "I know you've both had a long day so thanks for meeting late. This shouldn't take long."

Emily and Anthony exchanged a look, both skeptical this would be a fast and perfunctory conversation. They had questions, too. Duncan documented all the details, starting with Marilyn and Tiki's hospital appointment, finding the body in her estuary, and Chad Peña's attempts to abscond with Tiki. Duncan put his paperwork in his bag and stood to leave when Emily gave him a look. He exhaled and sat back down.

"Okay. First things first. Have you been able to locate Marilyn?" Emily asked.

"No, not yet."

"She's not a suspect, is she?" Emily asked.

Duncan shook his head no.

"Is she an official missing person?" Anthony asked.

"She is."

"Do you have any leads so far? Any credit card activity or insights from friends and family? An electronic breadcrumb to follow?"

Duncan said nothing.

"Is she dead?" Emily inhaled, fighting hard to keep her emotions in check.

"No," Duncan said quickly. "I mean, we don't know. I can't talk about an active investigation. You both know that firsthand."

"Remember the last time?" Emily asked. "Anthony and I helped you solve Mrs. Klein's murder and proved you can trust us with sensitive information. We're directly involved again, whether you like it or not."

Duncan turned to stare at the ocean, fidgeting with the pen between his fingers—clearly uncertain about how to proceed. "Okay, but you both need to promise to keep this confidential." They nodded and he continued. "The victim's name is Dylan Colt. He's a petty criminal with a long rap sheet. Mostly check fraud and robbery, but his latest conviction was for assault. He's only been out of prison for a few months."

"What happened inside Marilyn's house? Was this guy killed there?"

"We just got the DNA back from the lab. Based on the amount of blood, we concluded he was killed in the living room. Whoever dragged his body into the swamp must have hoped an alligator would take care of the evidence."

Emily shuddered as that scene played out in her head. "What about Marilyn? Was any of her blood at the scene? Or other signs of a struggle?"

"Just Colt's blood, but we still have a ton of forensics to process from the house."

They were on a roll. Duncan seemed open to sharing, so they pressed on.

"So, no leads on finding Marilyn?" Anthony asked again.

"No. All the cars registered in her name with the county are still in her garage, and there's been no credit card or banking activity. We found her purse and wallet in the house, but her phone and computer are missing."

"Do you think someone kidnapped her because of the treasure?" Anthony speculated.

"The treasure hunt is complicating things," Duncan admitted. "In theory, the suspect pool includes everyone searching for treasure clues. Thousands of people."

Emily thought about the role her hospital played in all of this. "Marilyn must have suspected something was going on when she left Tiki with us. Her request surprised us that day since she never boarded him at the hospital, but now, I'm wondering if she was trying to keep him safe."

"What about her nephew, Chad the Third?" Anthony said with disdain. "He acted super sketchy today when he tried to check Tiki out of the hospital. Have you talked to him about his aunt's disappearance?"

"No. He's her only relative living in the area, and we haven't been able to find him."

"There's no way Marilyn sent him that text. He was lying one hundred percent," Emily said.

"You might be right, but we have to follow the evidence, one piece at a time. Finding Marilyn is our top priority," Duncan said, making it clear who was in charge of the investigation.

Emily's impatience showed through. Her brother was a great sheriff's deputy, and with Mike on the case, she was certain they would figure out what happened to Marilyn. But, as each hour passed, it was hard not to think the worst. Marilyn had a deep love for Tiki, and Emily believed she would contact them if she could. Before she voiced her confidence in Duncan's skills, he grabbed his car keys and moved for the door.

"I've got to go. I'm trying to get home before Mac and Ava go to bed," Duncan said. "I'll call if anything changes."

Emily had run out of questions. "Thanks. Give the kids a hug for me. Are we still on for Sunday?"

"That's the plan. Night." Duncan turned and walked out the door.

"I don't think I'm cut out for this murder business." Anthony moved to the kitchen to pour them each a generous serving of wine. "So, what's happening on Sunday?"

"The kids are coming over with Elvis for a beach play date, and then Jane and Duncan will join us for dinner."

"Sounds fun. How's Elvis doing?"

"Great. He's so happy. It's hard to imagine it's only been a few months since Mrs. Klein died."

Elvis, a mostly purebred West Highland White Terrier with soft white fur, dark brown eyes, and a tail he carried in a C-shape, had been distraught when Emily found him next to his owner, who was dead on her kitchen floor. From that moment, Emily advocated for both of them, placing Elvis in his forever home with Duncan's family, with the blessing of Mrs. Klein's daughter, Sarah, of course.

Sarah's husband's allergies prevented her from taking Elvis back to her home in California, but her continued connection to Emily, Anthony, and the Coral Shores community ensured regular visits with Elvis. The terrier provided an important link to Sarah's memories of her mom.

"Sarah should be back next week for the design meeting with the architect," Anthony said.

"I'm so excited. Waiting on these final drawings gave us a needed break from the project, but I'm eager to get started again."

"Me, too. If it's okay with you, I want to tell Sarah about our involvement in Marilyn's case and caring for Tiki. With so much going on, I want her to understand why we've been so distracted."

"You're right. We should tell her," Emily said. "She'll know something's off if we're not around to help plan the ceremony."

Mrs. Klein left specific instructions in her will for her beachfront property to be developed into a sea turtle conservation center. She had been a mentor to Emily and Anthony when they volunteered with the Coral Shores Turtle Project in high school. The local beaches were an important nesting ground for the endangered loggerhead and green sea turtles. Volunteers monitored the nests to ensure the turtle hatchlings had the greatest chance to make it back to the ocean. Their efforts contributed to the increasing turtle populations in the Gulf of Mexico and were a genuine source of pride for the community.

Sarah Klein appointed Emily and Anthony as co-directors of the new Eliza Klein Sea Turtle Conservation Center. Funds from the estate, combined with Sarah's vast financial resources, ensured it would become a world-class education center. The hours they spent working on the developmental planning stages were all-consuming and one reason Emily struggled to find time to spend with Mike. It tortured her when she repeatedly had to turn down his offers for a romantic date night. He said he understood and even offered to help with the project, but it caused their relationship to stall right as it was heating up.

"Changing the subject—Mike and I are going on a date Saturday night," Emily said, trying to be nonchalant.

Anthony set his glass of wine on the coffee table and raised his hand, inviting Emily to give him a high-five. "Come on, Em," he said, holding his arm until she obliged him with a celebratory slap. "You two were stressing me out with all your weird energy. I'm happy for you."

Emily nodded and smiled. "I'm happy for me, too. Mike's making dinner at his place, then we're going to Barnacles for their full moon party." Their first date was at Barnacles, a local waterfront restaurant featuring live music and a drum circle beach party coinciding with the lunar calendar.

"Sounds perfect. I've been thinking ahead to this weekend. If we're still caring for Tiki, I don't feel right about leaving him in the hospital. Since we close at noon on Saturday and don't reopen until Monday morning, he'll be alone for a long stretch of time. I think he's done well considering the size of his travel cage, but that's only because there are so many people around to entertain him. He's almost never by himself."

"You're right. We need to assume Marilyn might not return soon, or ever," Emily said, and then paused. "It's horrible to imagine. I hope we're wrong, and Tiki can go home soon."

"I feel sick to my stomach thinking about it. I have a few ideas rolling around in my head, but let me sleep on it. We can talk in the morning." Anthony stood to leave. "I'm wiped out. Get some rest, Em. I'll see you tomorrow."

"Night, Anthony."

He saw himself out, locking the front door with his key as he left. It was going to be another worrisome night. The responsibility of caring for Tiki weighed on her. Emily struggled to pull herself up from her mom's chair and grunted as she lifted Bella to carry her back inside. As she got ready for bed, she flipped on the TV news. Marilyn's missing person status was now public knowledge, and the police had opened a tip line for anyone with information regarding her whereabouts. No wonder Duncan had been willing to share with them tonight. Dylan Colt's murder was the headline story, since violent crimes were a rarity in Coral Shores. The police kept the connection between the murder and missing person case out of the news and held back some details about the crime scene location.

"Bella, the proverbial cat is out of the bag," she said to her feline roommate, who curled up on her pillow, ready for bed. Emily crawled in next to her, falling asleep to the gentle sounds of Bella's purrs.

CHAPTER SEVEN

When Emily walked into the hospital, the sound of Anthony singing made her chuckle.

"He likes Motown music," he said when she entered his office. Tiki bobbed as he stepped in sync with the melody.

"I think he likes your voice most of all."

"Morning. Want some tea, Momo?" Tiki said, taking a break from dancing to nibble on a slice of mango.

"Good morning, Tiki." Emily smiled before turning her attention back to Anthony. "Did you get any sleep last night?"

"Not much, but that's okay. I've come up with a brilliant plan. Check this out." Anthony pointed to a drawing on his desk. "Marc and I were up late talking, and I think we've solved our Tiki problem. We've got that large screened-in deck off the kitchen. It's mostly empty, and we never use it. It would be a great aviary. At least temporarily." The detailed floor plan was drawn to scale, complete with measurements similar to an architectural blueprint.

"Did you do this?" Emily asked.

Anthony turned to look at her with raised eyebrows. "Em, have you ever known me to draw anything?"

"No, I guess not."

"This is all Marc. I told him about the key components of an aviary, and in no time, he figured out how to build it with basic supplies from the hardware store. His engineering brain worked overtime."

Emily took a few minutes to review the drawing while Anthony pointed out where they planned to use lumber and PVC pipe to build a simple, budget-friendly structure.

"This is amazing. Is Marc sure about this? It's an enormous commitment."

"He didn't hesitate. He's been worried about me being worried. I've told him about Tiki's vocabulary, and he's excited to meet him. When we're home, we can open the sliding screen door to the deck to talk with Tiki. It'll almost be like having him in the house."

"What can I do to help?"

"Well, if it's okay with you, I'm going to leave early to meet Marc at the hardware store. If we can start building tonight, I think it will be ready by the time we close tomorrow. Even if I have to keep working on the last details, Tiki can come home with me so he's not alone over the weekend. Plus, I'll have all day Sunday to spend with him."

What an enormous relief. Anthony was not only smart and compassionate, but he always came through for his friends, for Emily, and for the animals they cared for. "Take whatever time you need. I can handle everything here."

"If there's a break in our schedule at lunchtime, I'll run out to the pet store for a couple of feeding stations and toys to string up when we're done. I want to mimic some items I saw in Tiki's aviary at Marilyn's. The more it feels like home, the easier it will be for him to adjust."

Abigail leaned around the corner. "Dr. Benton, your first appointment is here. I'll be happy to sit with Tiki." Star-struck by the famous parrot, the staff continued to jockey for a chance to spend time with him.

"Thanks, Abigail." Anthony motioned for her to sit in his chair, then walked to the lobby to greet the next patient. Dougal Dudick, an eight-year-old greyhound, was adjusting to his new life after retiring from a punishing racing career. The owner, Mrs. Dudick, worked tirelessly with local and national greyhound advocacy groups to shut down the dog track industry. She always stepped up when a senior dog needed a home. The telltale scars visible on Dougal's body resulted from the breed's thin skin and constant risk of injury at the track. Like most greyhounds, he needed a dental cleaning, and today's visit included a pre-anesthetic screening and consultation for the procedure scheduled for next week.

"Hi, Mrs. Dudick. Hi, Dougal." Emily entered the room and smiled before extending her hand for Dougal to sniff. "You are a handsome boy." Since Greyhounds almost never sit down, he crossed the length of the room in two strides to greet her, accepting Emily's gentle pet of his head—demonstrating his calm and friendly personality. Dougal's three-foot height was quite impressive, even for the breed.

"Dr. Benton. Dougal is a true gentle giant. I think he's the tallest greyhound I've ever seen."

Emily completed the exam and removed her stethoscope. "He seems very healthy other than his dental issues. I'm concerned he may have one or two teeth with more advanced disease that will need to be extracted. I'll confirm with a dental X-ray, but he'll feel so much better when we're done."

"Will it get rid of his stinky breath? It's pretty bad."

"Absolutely."

"Wonderful. You do whatever is best for Dougal."

"How's he getting along with Jeebers and Timber?" Mrs. Dudick's other greyhounds were also patients.

"At first, Jeebers wasn't sure about him. He kept taking her squeaky alligator toy, moving it to his dog bed—without her permission, of course. He's since discovered a pink flamingo stuffy at the bottom of the toy basket, and they're now fast friends. Timber gets along with everyone."

Emily smiled. She loved the personality of greyhounds. "Anthony will be back in to collect Dougal's blood sample, and I'll call you tomorrow with the results. Assuming everything is normal, we'll see you both next week. It was nice to meet you, Dougal." She gave him one more pat before she left.

• • •

A mid-morning break in the schedule allowed Emily to dash out to Meyer's Deli. After skipping breakfast in order to get to the hospital early, her grumbling stomach demanded attention. The local deli was a regular stop where she often picked up bagels and cream cheese for the staff. Out and back in fifteen minutes, she pulled into the hospital parking lot and noticed two individuals standing near the front door, and a few more on the sidewalk. Emily didn't recognize them as clients but smiled as she passed by.

"Abigail, are those people outside here to pick up a patient?"

"I don't know. They just showed up and haven't come inside yet."

Emily nodded, then raised the bag of bagels. "I'll put these in the break room. Can you let everyone know to help themselves?"

"Sure, Dr. Benton. Thanks."

Emily smeared two bagels with cream cheese and delivered one to Anthony in his office. "People are standing outside the front door. Do you know why they're here?"

Anthony turned from his computer. "No, but I'll find out."

Emily finished her last bite when he returned.

"I think we have a problem." He pursed his lips and shook his head from side to side.

"Why? What?" she asked. After two decades of friendship, Emily trusted Anthony's instincts. If he thought they had a problem—they did.

"Tiki's paparazzi have tracked him down. After Marilyn's missing person story made the news, her followers have been speculating about what happened. There are some conspiracy theories circulating online, but most of the posts are about Tiki and concerns for his safety."

"Paparazzi?"

"Em, I need you to focus. What are we going to do?"

It took a few seconds for her to compose her thoughts into a coherent question. "Who are the people outside?"

"They're Tiki's followers. Some of them have been taking part in the treasure hunt, but I think a couple are professional bloggers, and at least one has a fancy-looking camera. You know, the kind with a long telephoto lens. When they heard about Marilyn, they began calling around to see if Tiki was at any of the wild bird sanctuaries or local vet hospitals. Coral Shores is small, so it didn't take long for them to find us through the process of elimination."

"You didn't tell them Tiki is here with us, did you?"

"No, of course not, but I don't think I convinced them when I pretended not to know what they were talking about. They asked to tour the hospital. I can't force them to leave but made it clear the reception area is for clients only."

"If we ignore them, maybe they'll get bored and go home."

"Maybe." Anthony did not sound convinced. Tiki had a million loyal Flix followers, and until he and Marilyn were once again posting videos, the social media world would keep searching for them. "I'll let all the staff know Tiki's whereabouts are now top secret."

• • •

It was a relatively quiet day. Anthony left early as planned, so Emily moved into his office, using it as her temporary workspace. An update from the hardware store confirmed he and Marc had all the supplies they needed and were on their way home to start building.

"Hungry. Hungry," Tiki said, surprising Emily once again. Marilyn must have taught him to let her know when he wanted a snack. Anthony had left pre-made meals for Emily to appease him.

"Here you go, Tiki." He nibbled on the medley of broccoli, kale, apple, and one walnut. It was so interesting to sit and watch him eat. He seemed to enjoy the variety of food textures and flavors. Emily turned the TV to *Animal Planet* to entertain him, then focused on wrapping up her day.

The intercom buzzed.

"Dr. Benton, those people are still outside, and a few more have joined the group," said Abigail, sounding worried. "I've watched them take turns making coffee runs. They're very persistent."

Emily walked into the lobby and stood watching the small gathering for a few minutes before deciding to engage Tiki's fan club in the parking lot.

"Hello, I'm Dr. Benton, the owner of the veterinary hospital. Is there anything I can help you with?"

"Hi, Dr. Benton. We're here for Tiki Lulu. Our friends confirmed he's not at any other vet hospital or wildlife center in the area. We know he's here. Can you at least tell us if he's okay? That's all we care about."

They seemed like nice, rational people, but a lot was at stake. "I'm sorry. I can't imagine I can be of any help. Please be considerate of my clients and patients as they come and go. We're closing for the night so you might as well head home." She walked back inside the hospital and locked the doors behind her.

Closing time was stressful as Emily prepared to leave Tiki alone for the fourth straight night. He ate a full dinner and moved to his favorite perch, ready for a good night's sleep, which made her feel less anxious. After the staff had gone, she took one last peek out the front window. Tiki's super fans had vacated the parking lot. She let out an audible sigh. "Crisis averted for now."

• • •

Emily assumed Anthony and Marc would be up late working on the aviary, so the least she could do was bring them dinner and offer to lend a hand. She ordered almost one of everything on the menu from a local favorite, Sunny's Pit BBQ, then drove over to Marc's place, arriving to the sounds of hammering.

"Hi. I come bearing gifts," Emily shouted as she walked into the kitchen. Anthony and Marc were putting the finishing touches on Tiki's primary perch.

"I can smell that BBQ from out here," Anthony said as they both put down their tools.

"Thanks, Em." Marc grabbed some plates, and they wasted no time filling them.

"How's it going?" she asked.

"Great. Thanks to Marc's detailed drawing, we have a clear plan, and it's been easy to build. I now see the wisdom of that old construction rule: *measure twice, cut once*, but that was our only misstep."

"I think we'll have the essentials done tonight so Tiki can move in tomorrow," Marc said.

"I can't thank you enough. It was so hard leaving him at the hospital tonight," Emily said.

Anthony froze. "Is he okay?" he asked, his voice an octave higher.

"He's fine." Emily patted Anthony's hand to comfort him. "I waited to make sure the paparazzi were gone before I left. I talked with them earlier, but they rolled their eyes when I told them Tiki wasn't with us. Did you know Tiki can say *hungry* when he wants to eat?"

Marc smiled. "Anthony told me all about his vocabulary. I can't wait to meet him."

They finished their meal and, despite Emily's repeated offers to help, they convinced her they were almost done for the night. Before leaving, she watched Anthony wrap some hemp rope around sections of the hardwood rod that would become Tiki's main perch. There were three separate perches and two braided rope bridges for him to use. Marc mounted one large and two smaller feeding stations to the sides of the structure, and they planned to finish stringing up his toys in the morning. In short order, Marc's porch became a safe and engaging bird sanctuary. Emily thought Tiki would be happy here, especially after bonding with Anthony. They would all sleep better knowing he had a wonderful new home waiting for him.

CHAPTER EIGHT

Emily's phone defaulted to a *do not disturb* setting when she was sleeping, except for calls from Duncan and Jane, Anthony, and the security alarm company for the veterinary hospital. They would ring through any time, day or night. That's why Emily jumped to a standing position when her phone rang. It was never good news.

"Hello." Her scratchy voice sounded half asleep.

"Is this Dr. Emily Benton?"

"Yes."

"Dr. Benton, I'm calling from Coastal Security. We received an alarm signal from the back door of the Coral Shores Veterinary Hospital. Local law enforcement has been dispatched."

In an instant, Emily was wide awake as a surge of fear engulfed her. "Thank you." She hung up, then pulled a sweatshirt over her pajama top and raced out the door in workout shorts and flip-flops. "Sorry, Bella. Breakfast will have to wait." It was a little after two in the morning and still pitch dark outside. She struggled to keep the speedometer within limits as she drove along the deserted beach road.

Emily understood the pharmaceuticals used in veterinary medicine made animal hospitals susceptible to break-ins. Drug dealers targeted the drugs because of their high street value.

Emily's phone rang again. Anthony was also a primary contact for the security company and would have received the same call.

"Em, I'm almost there." Anthony's place was closer to the hospital since it took Emily extra time to get over the barrier island causeway from the beach.

"I expected this to happen one day, but it's still a shock to receive that call. I'm completely unprepared."

"Me, too. I'm turning into the back alley, and there's a police car at the door. Drive safe. I'll see you in a few minutes."

Thinking about the safety of Tiki and her hospital patients consumed her. Time passed in slow motion as she drove in silence, having decided it would be inappropriate to play any music. Emily had installed a new high-tech security system when she bought the hospital from Dr. Dinsmore. She specifically designed it to employ a silent alarm. Emily didn't want the high-pitched sound to terrorize the hospitalized animals who were often frightened by loud noises. The experts also advised her that in the unlikely event of a break-in, a silent alarm increased the chances of catching the criminal in the act.

Slamming her car into park, she jumped out and ran over to Anthony. He stood talking with a police officer as the officer's partner disappeared inside the open door.

"Hi, Em. This is Officer Susan Garcia." Anthony pointed at Emily to complete the introductions. "This is Dr. Emily Benton, the owner."

The officer nodded. "Dr. Benton. Anthony opened the door for us, and we're almost done with our search. Everything seems secure at first glance. Something must have spooked them before they could get inside."

The damaged back door looked functionally intact. During an exterior search of the hospital, the officers found a crowbar, hatchet, and bolt cutters in some bushes. The heavy steel door and industrial lock had done its job and kept the perpetrators out.

"Can we go inside now?" Emily asked, eager to see for herself that everything was okay.

Just then, the second officer walked outside to join them. "All the doors and windows are secure, and there are no signs of an intruder. Can you both follow me, please?"

Emily and Anthony did a methodical search of every square foot. Nothing appeared out of place, and the few animals in the hospital or boarding in the kennel were resting quietly. Anthony slowly opened his office door and found Tiki sleeping on his perch, unaware of any danger. Emily stood behind him when Anthony reached out and grabbed her hand. "Em, I'm scared to death about something happening to Tiki."

He pulled his door shut then joined the officer in the treatment area, where they accounted for all the opioid pain medicine and narcotics in the lockbox. Nothing was missing.

The officer took down pertinent information in a notebook. "Dr. Benton, there are cameras mounted on the back wall of the building. Are they part of your alarm system?"

"Yes, the security company can access the digital file and provide you with the footage."

The officer handed her a business card and a receipt with the case number listed at the top. "Have them send the video file to the email address on the card. Hopefully, it will help us catch whoever did this."

"We will. And, thank you," Emily said.

Officer Garcia approached them, holding the burglar's tools in an evidence bag. "We'll dust these for prints. Despite all the damage to the frame of the door, the lock itself is intact. I would still recommend you have someone come out to inspect and repair it."

"Absolutely," Anthony replied. "That will be our first call in the morning."

"We'll also have a patrol car drive by on a rotating schedule overnight, even though it would be unusual for them to return to the scene of the crime. What time do you open?"

"At eight o'clock, but I'll be here earlier if you need anything."

The officers nodded, then left through the back door. Anthony and Emily sat down and attempted to compose themselves. "I don't want to jump to conclusions, but I'm worried this has something to do with Tiki and Marilyn," Emily said.

"Me, too. I'm so glad we're moving Tiki later today."

"I won't be able to go back to sleep after all this, but I'm going home to shower and feed Bella. Do you want to meet here around six?"

Anthony nodded. "I may come back sooner, but I'll let you know. It feels wrong to leave right now, but there's nothing else for us to do. Let's double and triple-check the lock first." He put his arm around her shoulder and they walked together to inspect the back door. Convinced the building was secure, they parted ways.

•   •   •

When Emily arrived home, she contemplated calling Duncan but decided against waking him and emailed instead. Until they identified the thief, it would be pointless to speculate about the motive, but she wanted him to be aware of what happened.

Still dark outside, she climbed back into bed with Bella. Sleep wasn't possible, but Emily closed her eyes, allowing the sounds of rhythmic purring and the ocean surf to calm her frayed nerves. She eventually dozed off until she heard a knock at the front door.

After squinting through the security peephole, she swung the door wide and welcomed her visitor inside with a smile.

"Hi, Mike. Is everything okay?" Emily brushed her hair with her fingers and wiped the sleep from her eyes.

"I'm here to ask you the same question." He handed her a cappuccino and warm croissants from her favorite local bakery, Savannah's. "Duncan called this morning after he read your email. He'll be here soon."

The cavalry had arrived. Emily didn't need their help in this matter but appreciated the concern for her safety. Mike's place was a short distance down the beach, and Emily loved he lived close by.

"Thanks for breakfast." They moved to sit at her kitchen island only to be greeted by Bella's demands for food, which Emily obliged.

"We read the police report from the break-in. I'm glad they weren't able to get inside."

With a mouthful of pastry, Emily nodded in agreement. "The officers collected some tools left behind by the thief. How soon will they know about any fingerprint evidence?"

"Maybe tomorrow."

"We'll get the video footage from our security cameras first thing. Hopefully, it will lead to an arrest."

Just then, Duncan walked through the front door, prompting Emily to brew a pot of coffee.

"Is everything okay at the hospital?" Duncan asked.

"Morning. Yes, the back door sustained damage, but the lock was solid."

"I checked and there are no reports of break-ins at other area vet hospitals or medical offices. Sometimes these crimes come in sprees."

"Anthony and I are worried it might have something to do with Marilyn and Tiki. Yesterday, the paparazzi—Tiki's fans—showed up, convinced we had him inside. Nothing we said changed their minds."

Duncan and Mike exchanged a look after hearing this unwelcome news. If the press got involved in Marilyn's missing person case, it would complicate the investigation.

"Let's have our techs dig deeper into the social media posts about this treasure hunt," Mike said before asking Emily, "Do you also have security cameras mounted on the front of the hospital?"

"Yes, there are cameras directed at both the front and back doors. Why?"

"Let us know if the paparazzi show up again. I can't believe I'm using the word *paparazzi* when talking about a parrot." Mike smiled. "Sorry, I can't stay, Em." He reached for his car keys. "But are we still on for tonight?"

Emily touched her stomach to counter the flutter. "Absolutely. I'll be at your place at six." Mike leaned in for a quick kiss before he left.

Duncan grinned at her like only a brother could.

"What?" she said.

"Nothing." Duncan knew about the recent hiccups in Emily and Mike's relationship. "I'm going to stay out of the break-in investigation since the two officers you met last night can handle it. But if you need anything else, let me know."

Even though he said otherwise, Emily thought he would watch over the case from a distance. "I'll see you Sunday when you drop the kids off. Are you and Jane still coming over for dinner?"

"We'll be here. Mac and Ava have sketched plans for a sandcastle dog house for Elvis. They can't wait for their beach day with their favorite aunt." Duncan helped himself to one of Emily's croissants before leaving for the station.

It was after six o'clock, and Emily didn't want Anthony to return to the hospital alone. She composed a text to let him know her ETA, but he beat her to the punch. Anthony confirmed everything was secure, and Tiki was busy doing his normal parrot things: chatting, playing, preening, and eating. Anthony told her to take her time and enjoy her coffee on the deck with Bella.

Emily still planned to arrive early, but took Anthony's advice and savored her coffee outside. Bella joined her, announcing her presence with a solitary, squeaky meow before jumping up and demanding half of the chaise lounge. What a cat wants, a cat gets.

As the sun rose, streaks of orange, red, and yellow painted the horizon, filling Emily with wonder. Bella flicked her tail as a gentle breeze blew through her long, silky fur. Moving to the leeward side of the lounge chair, she curled up for her post-breakfast nap. Emily closed her eyes and listened to the sound of waves breaking on shore. It was hard, but after a few treasured minutes, she pulled herself away from her special space, enticed Bella indoors with treats, then hustled to get out the door and begin her day.

CHAPTER NINE

The hospital was abuzz with behind-the-scenes activities. Technicians completed treatments for the hospitalized patients as the assistants walked the dogs, fed everyone, and cleaned the kennels. Boarding services were offered to their patients with special needs. The diabetic cat or senior dog on multiple medicines benefited from personalized care. The familiar pace of the day created a sense of normalcy—in stark contrast to a police call in the middle of the night.

"A present from Mike." Emily handed Anthony a bag containing the last croissant.

"Mmm. Savannah's." Anthony opened the bag, took a whiff, and smiled. "Wait, did you say, *from Mike*?"

"Yeah, I told Duncan about the break-in, and they both showed up on my doorstep this morning."

Anthony winked after hearing about Mike's early morning visit.

"About that," he said. "I contacted the security company, and they're preparing the video to send to the police starting from closing time until the alarm went off. I'm also downloading an app so we can tap into the live camera feed. Now, we'll be able to keep watch from any location using our phones or laptops."

"Okay, let me know when we can skim through it together. I spoke with Clark Contracting on my way in. He'll have someone here within the hour to look at the door." Emily had a good relationship with Bill Clark, the owner.

After settling into her office, Emily reviewed Dougal Dudick's blood test results. With everything in the normal range, she sent a quick email to Mrs. Dudick to share the good news and to confirm his dental procedure planned for next week. Before moving on to the next file, Abigail called over the intercom.

"Dr. Benton. Anthony. Can you both come here, please?" It wasn't like Abigail to summon them this way. Pets brought in for an emergency triggered a specific series of protocols and code words. If it was an emergency, her request would have a sense of urgency. Plus, the hospital doors weren't open yet. Emily held her breath as she and Anthony walked into the lobby.

Abigail stood in the center of the room, turning to face them as she pointed out the front window. "They're back, and this time they've brought friends."

Anthony sighed. There were close to a dozen people standing together in the front parking lot. A few of them were holding poster-sized photos of Tiki. One sign read, *Where in the World is Tiki Lulu?* "Now, we're in trouble."

They had officially entered uncharted territory. Never in a million years did Emily imagine handling crowd control would be part of running a veterinary hospital. "I'm going to call Duncan for some advice."

For the time being, they agreed to ignore the gathering as long as the people stayed away from the entrance. Abigail and Anthony engaged in a short debate about whether to call them groupies, super fans, or paparazzi, but decided *paparazzi* was more fun to say, even if they didn't appear to be professionals. The doors were now open, and if they disrupted hospital operations, Emily and Anthony would move to Plan B. The only problem—they didn't have a Plan B.

Minutes after sending her text, Duncan called. Emily and Anthony closed the door to the office and put him on speakerphone.

"They're now carrying signs. I'm worried it's going to capture some media attention. What should we do?" Emily asked.

"Don't you share your front lot with the two other businesses across the square?" Duncan asked.

"Yes, an optician and a financial consultant. Thankfully, they're closed on the weekend. A property management company maintains the entire parking lot. Should I call them?"

"I would as a courtesy. If the crowd becomes a problem, I can request a patrol car to swing by. That might be enough to get them to disband."

"Okay. So far, it seems innocent enough. I think they're Tiki's super fans worried about his well-being," she said.

"Tiki's a pretty bird." Apparently, Tiki didn't like being excluded from the conversation.

"Was that the parrot?" Duncan asked.

Emily laughed. "Yes, that's Tiki Lulu. Tiki, say hello."

"Hello."

"Wow, that's cool. I'll have to show the kids his videos tonight. They'll love him." It wasn't like Duncan to become distracted, but Tiki's charm was hard to resist.

"Mike mentioned he wanted security footage of the paparazzi. I can capture a still image of the crowd and send it over," Anthony said. "I'm taking Tiki home with me tonight, but I think we can sneak out the back to avoid the crowd."

There wasn't anything else to do. The hospital closed at noon on Saturdays, and aside from the crowd, the day was routine. They could only hope it would stay that way.

· · ·

"Dr. Benton, your last appointment is here," Abigail called over the intercom.

Tijuana Bob Dodd was an adorable, quirky-looking terrier Mr. Dodd adopted during a recent vacation to Baja, Mexico. Bob took up residence at Mr. Dodd's favorite beach bar, and when it became obvious the friendly, little dog was homeless, he made him part of the family. Bob reminded the bar's owner of a dog he had as a kid growing up in Tijuana, and the name morphed from there. The local vet handled the paperwork and first set of vaccines that allowed Bob to fly to Florida, but Mr. Dodd wanted a complete health checkup and brought him directly to the veterinary hospital the day he landed. Only the best for Tijuana Bob.

During that first appointment, Emily diagnosed Bob with Rocky Mountain Spotted Fever, an infection transmitted through tick bites. At the time of his diagnosis, he had a mild anemia and his platelets were low. After four weeks of antibiotics to treat the infectious disease, Bob was back to recheck his bloodwork to ensure everything had returned to normal.

"Dr. Benton, I thought Tijuana Bob was active and healthy when I met him, but now that we finished his treatment, I can see the difference. He's even more playful, and we started going on trail runs together. He's quite the athlete. At first, I was worried he might chase our cat, Mr. Higgins, but the only thing he chases is butterflies. He never catches them, of course."

Emily smiled at that image. She completed Bob's exam, agreeing that he seemed to be in top health. "It's possible he had this infection for a long time. Ticks can transmit a variety of diseases, but Bob's new preventive medicine will protect him from tick bites in the future."

"I have a monthly reminder on my phone so he never misses a dose," Mr. Dodd said. "I read all the information you sent about this disease. I wondered how Rocky Mountain Spotted Fever caused his illness since he lived in Mexico, but it seems like it's everywhere. And people can get it too."

"Yes, it's widespread throughout North America. I'm going to borrow Bob for his test. The results will be complete within fifteen minutes if you'd like to wait in the lobby."

"Yes, we'll wait. I want to make sure everything is okay before we leave."

Tijuana Bob moved next to Mr. Dodd's leg, reluctant to leave his side. Emily gently picked him up and carried him to the treatment area where Anthony and Catrinna were gathering the supplies needed to collect his blood sample. "When you're done, Mr. Dodd will wait with Bob in the lobby. I'm going to make a few calls." Emily hugged the trembling terrier, then handed him to her team.

On her way back to the office, Emily swung by the lobby to see what was happening outside. The crowd of paparazzi had grown exponentially. She contemplated talking to the die-hard super fans but stuck with Plan A—avoidance. She had so many questions swirling around in her head and a growing urgency to find some answers. Where was Marilyn? Was she okay? Were Duncan and Mike any closer to finding her?

Emily shared the good news with Mr. Dodd that Tijuana Bob's blood test results were perfect. His anemia had resolved with treatment, and there were no follow-ups needed other than his routine annual exams. After Mr. Dodd and Bob left, Abigail locked the doors. The hospital was now closed until Monday morning, and the entire staff gathered in the lobby for an impromptu meeting.

Anthony took the lead. "The crowd of people outside are desperate for information about Tiki. If they ask questions, just say, *no comment.*"

"Today, our clients wanted to know if these people were here to protest something," Abigail said. "I'm worried they'll associate the hospital with some controversy."

Emily shared her concern. "You're right. We need to come up with a consistent answer to put our clients' minds at ease. Thankfully, we have until Monday morning before we have to deal with this again. I'll think about how best to respond before the doors reopen. If anyone has questions or ideas, reach out to Anthony or me this weekend."

"Tiki will come home with me at closing time every night and return in the morning. But I need your help to get away without being seen. If you can all leave at the same time through the front door, I'll leave out the back. I think that will distract his paparazzi."

They all worked quickly to finish end-of-day tasks. Anthony logged into the security camera software and saved a screenshot of the crowd gathered outside to send to Mike. If Tiki's fans had anything to do with Marilyn's disappearance, it was up to the police to figure out what mattered to the investigation. Emily and Anthony wanted to review the security video from the break-in, but they could now do that from home.

Clark Contracting completed the repair to the back door frame and would return to touch-up the paint. The door was secure, and that's all that mattered.

With everyone ready to leave, Emily walked outside to engage the crowd. At that exact moment, Anthony moved Tiki and his cage to a vehicle parked behind the hospital. Marc had borrowed his uncle's van and was sitting in the getaway driver's seat. As they pulled out of the alleyway, Emily approached the paparazzi.

"Dr. Benton. Dr. Benton. Can you give us an update on Tiki?" A man holding a Tiki poster appeared to be the leader of the group. The crowd looked as one might expect of social media-savvy followers—like a bunch of college-aged kids. The only exception was a very tall, thin, older man in the rear. He stood out with his stern and stoic expression. He didn't appear to be having fun.

"I'm sorry. I can't comment on Tiki or his whereabouts. As you know, this is now a matter for the police. You'll have to direct your questions to them."

"We want to know if he's safe," asked another super fan.

It would be so easy to put their minds at ease, but she avoided sharing any details.

"I don't know about his exact location, but I can confirm he's being well cared for."

The crowd erupted in muted cheers.

"The hospital is closed until Monday, so I suggest you all head home."

"Dr. Benton, we're convinced Tiki is inside the hospital. We'll be here every day until Marilyn and Tiki are back together and can speak on their own behalf."

"I understand. I can't make you leave but ask you all to continue to respect my clients and patients." Emily's phone vibrated in her hand to signal a message. Anthony, Tiki, and Marc were safely away. The ruse had worked. "Bye," Emily said to the super fans and walked to her car, hoping they would follow her lead. With access to the security camera from her phone, they would be easy to monitor. She still had time to relax at home with Bella before her date with Mike.

CHAPTER TEN

On hot, humid South Florida summer days, Mother Nature creates an optical illusion. Sea and sky blend, creating a continuous blue-gray horizon that makes it impossible to discern a line between the two. The light surf and bath-tub warm water were perfect for a relaxing swim.

Feeling depleted after the break-in and a sleepless night, Emily decided the best way to recharge was to spend a few hours at the beach, swimming and napping. She grabbed a chair from her storage shed and headed for the water's edge. She melted into the ocean, rising and falling as the gentle surf worked its magic. The stress from the past week ebbed as she allowed each wave to push her closer to shore until she washed up on the beach, toweled off, and plopped into her chair under the shade of a palm tree. It only took minutes of skimming through the latest edition of her veterinary journal before she dozed off. The loud call from a seagull overhead put an end to her nap. Emily checked the time—she'd been sleeping for an hour. With a few things to do before her date with Mike, she gathered up her beach gear and moved inside.

Bella came first. After brushing her out and obliging her with a few of her favorite treats, Emily called to check in with Anthony.

He happily reported Tiki had spent the past hour playing with his toys and exploring every corner of his new home. Everything had worked out as planned.

Both of them now had time to watch last night's break-in video. Emily skimmed through the first few hours but slowed the recording the moment the thief appeared on the screen; time stamped at one forty a.m. The person seemed to be alone. Loose-fitting clothes obscured whether it was a man or a woman, and a hoodie hid their face. They were astute enough to hide their identity, but the crook had no mastery of the tools they brought with them. The thief hacked away at the handle and door frame, switching between the hatchet and crowbar. Emily exhaled and let her head drop when she noticed the thief wore gloves, eliminating any chance of finding fingerprints on the tools.

"Well, that was a bust." Emily called Anthony after texting throughout.

"Maybe not. A car drove by the back door before the attempted break-in. What if it's the thief's car, and they were casing the joint."

Emily grinned at Anthony's choice of words as he mimicked some of his favorite TV detectives. "You're right. Why would anyone be driving back there late at night? It's not a shortcut between intersections."

"Exactly. I'm sure the police have some fancy software to enhance the image and get a license plate number. It'll give me an excuse to follow up with Mike since I haven't heard about the paparazzi photo I sent him. I meant to ask you—did you see an old man in the parking lot?"

"I noticed him, but he didn't say anything, so it was hard to tell if he's part of the main group. The others were talking amongst themselves, but he didn't join in."

"He appears to be alone, which is strange. The others hang out together and act like they're having a blast. I'll keep an eye on him," Anthony said. "I checked the security camera live stream and the parking lot is empty. I'm sure they'll be back when our doors open, unless the police get a break in the case and bring Marilyn home."

"I had planned to call Jane to confirm tomorrow's play date with the kids, but I'll reach out to Duncan instead. He said he would let the officers handle the investigation, but I bet he's keeping up-to-date."

"No need. Duncan will be here soon with Mac and Ava. He called after work to arrange for the kids to meet Tiki Lulu. They spent the morning watching the Flix videos and have been obsessing ever since."

Their enthusiasm for meeting Tiki was no surprise to Emily. Mac was eight years old and a pitcher on his little league team. Baseball was his favorite sport, but after Jane took the kids to a rock-climbing gym, they'd both joined a kid's team. Ava was five and already had an amazing sense of comedic timing. She was the creative one. Both kids had hints of the Benton red hair but were closer to strawberry blondes.

"Are they bringing Elvis with them?" He was the kids' first love and went everywhere they did, but since nobody could predict how a parrot would respond to a dog, it might be best if Elvis skipped this outing.

"No, not this time. Tiki's finally settled, and I want to keep things that way," Anthony said.

"I'll leave it to you to get the latest details out of Duncan—he bristles every time I ask for info. He may have already found the owner of that car since the police have had the video all day. Oh, and see if you can get an update on Marilyn or Chad's whereabouts, and the Colt murder."

"Will do and message me if you learn anything after your date with Mike. I know you, Em. You'll be tempted to pump him for information. Just this once—tread lightly."

She had learned to heed Anthony's advice over the years. Whenever she ignored his words of wisdom, regret usually followed.

"Do you and Marc want to join us for dinner tomorrow night?" she asked. "Elvis will be here with the kids."

"Thanks, but I'm going to lie low this weekend. I want to spend as much time as possible with Tiki. I'm still planning to bring him with me to work on Monday, and we'll see how he handles that transition to and from the hospital. One step at a time."

"He's lucky to have you. Thanks, Anthony. I'd be a mess trying to figure this out on my own."

"Have fun tonight."

• • •

Emily celebrated Mike's move to the beach earlier in the year, since it meant he lived only a short drive away. That proximity made things more difficult these past few weeks as they struggled to connect. Sometimes, Emily would pass by his townhouse on her way home and wonder whether to stop by unannounced. Tonight's date was the do-over she longed for, hoping to pick up where they left off.

Emily knocked on his door, but when he didn't answer, she walked in. "Mike?" she called.

He stepped inside from the ocean-view deck. "I'm out here. Come join me."

Emily's heart skipped a beat. Mike wore a BBQ apron while tending to some ribs on the grill. *Be cool, Em.*

"It smells delicious."

"The sauce is my mom's recipe." He opened the cooler, grabbed a beer, and poured her a glass of wine. As he handed her the glass, he leaned in for a kiss. "Cheers." They clinked glasses and in a single moment, the awkward energy between them disappeared. "I hope you're hungry."

"Always. I skipped lunch."

"I thought you might be wiped out after being up all night and working all day. We talked about going to see the band at Barnacles, but I'd be happy to stay in tonight. It's totally up to you."

Overjoyed to have Mike all to herself, Emily said, "It looks like we're going to have a gorgeous sunset. Let's stay here. I feel okay right now, but I don't think I'm up for a night out."

"What's the latest news on the turtle center?" Mike asked.

"Sarah Klein will be here next week to meet with the architect who's designing the conservation center. Once we sign off on the final drawings and the city approves the permits, the general contractor is ready to break ground."

"That's exciting. I saw Marlon and Sharon last week. They're still trying to recruit me for Turtle Watch. I told them I can't commit to a regular shift because of my work."

"They understand. There will be lots of opportunities to help once the center opens." Marlon and Sharon were founding members of the Coral Shores Turtle Project and would manage day-to-day operations. They were busy with a flurry of activities to prepare for the grand opening.

"I'll help anywhere I can. Being able to witness turtles hatching has been my favorite thing about moving to Florida. Except for meeting you, of course." Mike put his BBQ tongs down and turned to Emily, taking the wineglass out of her hand and setting it on the table. He swept a lock of hair away from her face before they melted together. The sizzling from the grill demanded Mike's attention, and when they pulled apart, they were both out of breath. "I missed you, Em."

"I missed you, too." Emily stepped closer to hug Mike from behind as he brushed on the next layer of BBQ sauce. He put his free hand on her arm and pulled her tight. She heard him take a deep breath before turning to face her.

"I'll be honest. I wasn't sure where we stood," Mike said.

"I know my schedule keeps getting in the way, but I can't tell you how many times I wanted to call you."

"What stopped you?"

Emily shrugged. "I don't know. I thought you wanted to slow things down."

Mike smiled. "Nothing could be further from the truth." He kissed her again, leaving no doubt he meant what he said.

"I promise to do a better job of telling you how I feel. No more mixed signals," she said.

"Same for me. I know the turtle center needs your focus right now. I get it. It just means we'll have to get creative with our time."

Mike's sexy grin was impossible to resist, so Emily closed the distance between them. Kissing the man of her dreams as he held on to BBQ tongs prompted her to peek around his shoulder at the grill.

"I'll set the table so we can eat outside," she said, kissing him once more before letting go.

Their picture-perfect evening included a delicious dinner topped off by a spectacular sunset. Mike's new lounge chair, inspired by her mom's famous chair, had room for both of them. She nestled in Mike's arms as they talked, but when he failed to start a discussion about Marilyn and Tiki's case, Emily broached the subject. She had questions that needed answers.

"Have you looked at Anthony's photos of Tiki's fans?"

"I have, and the lab techs are working on identifying each of the parrot groupies."

"Paparazzi," Emily corrected. "That's what Anthony's calling Tiki's super fans."

Mike nodded. "I know you're worried about Marilyn and the hospital. I can't share the details of an ongoing investigation, but you should know, it's our number one focus."

Frustrated at being kept in the dark, Emily debated whether to keep pushing for more details, but she trusted Mike when he said he was doing everything within his power to solve this case. She hoped Anthony had more success pumping Duncan for information. After deciding to drop the subject for the night, she pulled Mike's arms around her.

Shades of deep purple provided the backdrop to the myriad of stars illuminating the night sky. Emily's eyelids became heavy as her contribution to their conversation faded in and out until she eventually fell asleep. Mike didn't move a muscle for an hour, allowing her to rest. When she woke up and smelled his soap, she turned to hug him tight.

"I think you were dreaming." He kissed her neck.

"I'm so sorry." Emily blushed in response to her dating misstep.

"Not at all. I dozed off myself. It's been a long week."

Emily agreed. Even though she didn't want the date to end, she was exhausted. Mike planned to join Duncan, Jane, and the kids for dinner tomorrow night, and knowing she would see him again so soon made it easier to leave. Within minutes of walking in her front door, Emily and Bella were fast asleep.

CHAPTER ELEVEN

As daybreak transitioned to sunrise, Emily lingered in bed, half-awake, until Bella's demand for food and her need for coffee became the catalyst to start the day. Still reminiscing about last night's date, she traced her fingers along her cheek, recalling Mike's touch before he kissed her. The beep signaling the end of the brew cycle forced her out of her daydream—she filled her mug and moved outside to her mom's coveted chair, followed by Bella. Mornings were Emily's favorite, and she enjoyed Sunday most of all. A moment each week when she could ease into her day.

When she returned to the kitchen for a second cup, a text from Anthony popped up on her phone. He sent a short video of Tiki swinging on a rope bridge and chirping, "Morning, want some tea, Momo?" Emily replied with a heart emoji. So many things might have gone wrong with Tiki this past week, if not for Anthony and Marc.

Emily turned on the local news to check for any recent developments in the murder investigation. It surprised her to see the lead story focused on Marilyn and Tiki's treasure hunt. Their followers were aware of her missing person status, and since the weekly Flix videos all led the treasure hunters to wild bird sanctuaries, they took it upon themselves to search for more clues. Wild bird centers across the state of Florida, from Tallahassee to Key West, experienced record attendance rates. Without a new Flix video to guide them to the next location, the super fans covered their bases and visited them all. Concern for Marilyn and Tiki's wellbeing grew as flowers and parrot-themed mementos, including Christmas ornaments, stuffed animals, and artwork, were placed at the entry gates of bird sanctuaries, creating makeshift shrines.

The outpouring of love wasn't Emily's primary takeaway from the story. She realized the small congregation of paparazzi coming to the hospital each day was about to explode in size. And there were no additional details about Dylan Colt or his connection to Marilyn. Feeling anxious and needing to take action, she made a call.

"Anthony, I think we should get together and make a plan. Is now a good time? I'll bring donuts." Emily knew she'd called too early. Anthony wasn't a morning person.

"What are you talking about?" He struggled to hide the sleep in his voice.

"Channel 2 News just aired a story about Marilyn, Tiki, and the treasure hunt. In the past two days, their super fans swarmed every single wild bird sanctuary across the state. They're trying to find another hidden clue, and since they don't have a Tiki video to guide them, they're visiting every nonprofit bird center. Small shrines to support Marilyn and Tiki's safe return are popping up everywhere."

"Oh. I didn't see that."

"So, can I come over now? We need to get ahead of this and come up with a plan in case a mob of followers shows up at the hospital tomorrow."

"Sure, but I've already done some sourcing in case we need help. When Duncan was here yesterday, he gave me the contact info for a company that provides security and crowd control at concerts and sporting events. They also rent out barricades and signs to contain large groups."

"I can't believe we're having this conversation. Did Duncan share any scoops about the investigation?"

"Not much, but I think there's a lot going on we don't know about. He said nothing specific, but that's my impression. They're working with other state agencies on Marilyn's disappearance. It's not an official kidnapping because there's been no ransom demand. Seems like semantics to me, but they're the experts."

Emily could hear a parrot singing in the background.

"How's Tiki?"

"He's great. Marc is obsessed with him. He pulled his chair up to the screen door last night and sat talking with him till bedtime."

Emily smiled. When Anthony and Marc started dating, she became protective of her best friend. Anthony, who's half Cuban and half Puerto Rican, wore his emotions on his sleeve. She could tell right away he was serious about Marc, and once she got to know Marc, she fell in love with him, too. Marc was as tall as Anthony but had a lean frame, white blonde hair, and blue eyes. He was smart, even-keeled, and thoughtful—a perfect complement to Anthony's more exuberant, fun-loving personality. They were proof that opposites attract. Seeing Anthony this happy made her happy, and when he moved into Marc's place, taking their relationship to the next level, she cheered them on.

"You're still welcome to come by with donuts. I can show you what I found on the security company website. Hiring a security guard could get expensive, but we might not have a choice."

"No, I'll leave you in peace. Send me a link to the website, and I'll look it over. How much advance notice do they need?"

"Twenty-four hours, depending on the order. If you're okay with it, I'll ask them to bring some barricades and signs on Monday morning so we have a way to keep the paparazzi pushed back from the hospital front door and client parking spots. If nobody shows up, the company can pick up the equipment the next day."

"That sounds great. I'll talk with Duncan when he drops off Mac and Ava. Maybe he can continue the police patrols in the area like he did after the break-in."

"Try to relax and enjoy your day with the kiddos. We can handle anything that comes up when we get to work tomorrow. I'm going in early with Tiki to get him set up before the doors open and the fans arrive."

"Thanks, Anthony."

He was right. She needed to focus on the kids today, but with a few hours before they arrived, there was time to do a little sleuthing. Duncan and Mike's unwillingness to share updates about the case forced her to take matters into her own hands. Emily retrieved Chad's address; thankful she had saved the information in her phone when he came to the hospital for Tiki. Palmetto Road was on the south side of Coral Shores—not too far away.

Still thinking about donuts, she made a quick stop for a chocolate glazed before cruising by Chad's place, a modern four-unit apartment complex. She circled the block twice before parking in front of the building. Designated spaces assigned with each tenant's unit number confirmed Chad's parking spot was empty. She walked past his ground-floor windows and when she didn't see any sign of activity, she rang the call button for his apartment. Risky, but worth it. Nobody answered, so Emily stepped back as she decided what to do next. That's when she saw a mother and young daughter coming toward her on the sidewalk. When the mom pulled out her keys to enter the building, Emily took a chance and approached her.

"Excuse me. I'm visiting my friend, Chad, and he's not answering his door."

The lady looked Emily up and down with suspicion. Emily's smile helped put her at ease.

"I haven't seen him for a few days," she replied. "I'm sorry, I can't let you in the building."

"I understand. Thank you." Emily turned to walk back to her car. Out of the corner of her eye, she noticed a dark gray sedan idling at the nearby cross street. It pulled onto the main road, then slowly drove past before accelerating. The tinted windows made it hard to see inside, leaving her feeling uneasy and craving the safety of her own home. The outing wasn't a complete bust, since it confirmed Duncan's report that Chad was in the wind. If he had nothing to hide, why was he in hiding? She checked the time—the kids would be arriving soon and everything else could wait.

• • •

"Auntie Em. Look!" Mac and Ava jumped out of the car with Elvis in tow. The little terrier wore a bright blue, doggy-sized life jacket adorned along the top with a replica of a shark's dorsal fin.

Emily laughed as Elvis whizzed by. "He's the cutest landshark I've ever seen."

Mac followed Elvis into the cottage, but Ava stopped. "Auntie Em, sharks live in the water. Not on the land."

"You're right. They do." Apparently satisfied with her aunt's reply, she ran to catch up with her brother. Emily walked halfway across the front lawn to help Jane with her bags when she heard a crash from inside her cottage.

"Auntie Em!" both kids shouted in unison. "Help!"

Jane dropped her bags and the two adults sprinted into the living room. A large potted house plant lay on its side next to Bella's cat tree. Emily's massive cat stood on the top platform with her back arched like a Halloween cat—her tail puffed out to twice its normal size.

"What happened?" Emily asked.

"Bella started hissing, then she knocked over the plant," Mac said, his eyes as wide as saucers.

It did not deter Elvis. He wagged his tail then bowed down, an invitation to play, but Bella wasn't having any of it. Elvis's exuberant greetings were the norm, but his shark outfit must have scared her.

Emily unclipped Elvis's life jacket and moved it out of sight. Hoping a few of Bella's favorite treats might diffuse the situation, she stood next to the cat tree, gently talking to the distraught cat as she pet her head. Mac and Ava each placed the treats in front of Bella. She sniffed them a few times before accepting their peace offering.

"We're sorry Bella. Elvis won't hurt you," Mac said. "He's a pretend shark." Bella had recovered from her scare and groomed herself—back to acting aloof.

"Why don't we go outside on the deck and give Bella a minute to herself?" Jane scooped up dirt from the overturned plant.

Emily took Elvis's leash, then led them toward the beach side of the cottage. "Kids, Elvis is an excellent swimmer."

"We know. We're going fishing with Daddy's friend and Elvis gets to come. Mommy said we should test his jacket first," Mac said.

Jane shrugged her shoulders and grinned.

Ava sat on the deck next to Elvis, her eyes filled with tears. Emily wrapped her arm around her niece and pulled her close.

"Is Bella, okay?" Ava sniffed as her tears trickled down her face.

"Bella will be fine. I think Elvis startled her is all. She does love him." Emily might be exaggerating that last point. When Jane and Duncan adopted Elvis, the traumatized little terrier found the exact home he needed, with children who adored him, and the best kind of friendship with Bella. It had taken some time for her to warm up to him, but Emily was certain Bella now enjoyed his boisterous visits. "Do you want to come with me to check on her?"

Ava nodded, then held Emily's hand as they walked inside. Bella let out a demure "meow" and purred as Ava stroked her fur.

"See. She's okay now," Emily said.

Ava smiled. "Bella, you're the prettiest. You don't need to be scared of Elvis."

Emily's heart melted. Having the kids run around her home while playing with Elvis was precisely why she took the leap and purchased her hometown veterinary hospital. The original plan after finishing her university internship included moving to a big city and working in a specialty referral hospital. That plan lost its appeal after her mom got sick.

Mac stood at the patio doors next to Jane, who held Elvis in her arms. Emily motioned for them to approach. Elvis wagged his tail but remained calm while Bella sniffed him all over. He snuck in a quick lick of her ear and when she didn't protest, Emily knew all was forgiven.

"Well, it seems things are back to normal," she said. "I was so distracted, I forgot to ask about Duncan. Is he coming?"

"He'll be here soon, but he can only stay a few minutes. He's got to work today."

Emily's shoulders slumped in disappointment. She had to rely on law enforcement professionals to investigate these crimes, but since she'd become involved in a break-in, a murder, a missing person case, and paparazzi crowd control, she needed more information. This case had become personal.

Elvis and Bella occupied the kids' attention, allowing Jane to pull Emily aside for a private conversation. "So, how were things with Mike last night?"

"Great, except for the part where I fell asleep."

"Em, you were up all night. I'm sure he understands. So, where do things stand between the two of you? Romantically speaking, that is."

"They're good, I think. Neither of us wanted things to change. Life just got in the way for a few weeks."

"Phew." Jane executed a dramatic wipe of her brow. "Anthony, Marc, and I were panicking."

"So, you're all continuing to insert yourselves into my love life?" Emily said in jest.

"Well, yes. Somebody needs to keep you focused. He's a catch, Em, but so are you. We want you both to be happy, and we all agree—Mike could be the one."

Emily began to reply just as Duncan walked through the front door.

"Hi, Em," Duncan gave Jane a kiss before greeting the kids. They told him all about Bella's scary shark run-in. Ava's impersonation of Bella, hissing and puffing up, had them doubled over with laughter. When the kids moved outside on the deck to play ball with Elvis, Duncan walked into the kitchen for a glass of water, and Emily followed behind. "Sorry, I have to take a rain check for dinner," he said.

"Jane told me you have to work. Does it involve Marilyn's case?"

Duncan avoided looking at her but nodded in the affirmative.

"C'mon Duncan. I need more than that. Did you see the news this morning? This treasure hunt is getting out of control. I'm worried about the hospital and Tiki."

Duncan took a long drink. Emily thought he was buying time to figure out what to say. She kept silent but continued to stare at him, waiting to make eye contact.

He turned to face her, his eyes narrowed and lips pursed as if debating what to do next. "Walk me to my car." Duncan kissed Jane goodbye, then waved to the kids as he left.

"What is it?" Emily asked once she was outside. "Is she—dead?"

"No, we haven't found her yet. Our lab techs enhanced the video from your hospital break-in. The license plate from the car seen that night belongs to a girlfriend of Dylan Colt. I'm heading to her place with Mike as soon as I leave here."

Emily reached out and grabbed Duncan's arm. This revelation made her head spin. Until now, Marilyn's disappearance and the murder of Dylan Colt were crimes unrelated to the hospital break-in. This new information connected them, and the implications were difficult to process. "I don't understand," she said.

"We pulled the DMV record for the girlfriend, and she's only five foot two inches. The thief in the video is taller, but we need to determine if she played a role as a getaway driver or accomplice. I've got to go. Mike or I will be in touch. I don't think either of us will make it back tonight. He wanted me to tell you he's sorry, and he'll call you."

"Okay. I understand." Her voice trailed off as the news swirled around in her head. "Will you let me know what happens? For Tiki's sake."

He nodded, climbed into this sheriff's car, and sped off. When she walked back into the cottage, Jane immediately questioned her about their private conversation.

"Em, what is it? If you need me to stay, I can cancel my plans."

Blinking hard, she tried to focus her thoughts. She could compartmentalize things when necessary, and the kids deserved all her attention. "No, I'm fine. Duncan is following a lead about the hospital break-in. I've been looking forward to having the kids and Elvis all to myself. You go. I'll see you for dinner." Emily smiled to convince her things were okay.

"All right, but call me if you need me," Jane said before hugging her tight. "Kids," she called out to the deck. "Auntie Em is in charge so remember your best manners."

"We will, Mommy," Mac said, speaking on behalf of Ava and Elvis.

After Jane left, Emily waved for the kids to come inside. "Let's get ready for our beach day. I've got the toys and sunshade set up, but I need help loading our snacks in the cooler."

"Did you bring our boogie boards, too?" Ava asked. "I want to be a surfer, Auntie Em."

"Absolutely."

They packed the cooler with carrots and dip, watermelon slices, cheesy crackers, and water for everyone, including Elvis. The little terrier led the way to the beach where they spent the day swimming, running, and laughing. Elvis loved to chase the sandpipers along the shore. After the kids built him a sand castle, they worked on their boogie-boarding skills. It was a perfect afternoon, but that didn't stop Emily from feeling melancholy as she thought about her mom. She would have loved a day like this with her grandkids. Her absence created physical pain, but Emily realized these happy moments were, little by little, displacing the overwhelming, heavy grief. Hearing the kids' laughter confirmed Emily was exactly where she needed to be. Finishing her day with Jane and the kids over a family dinner would be the perfect way to replenish her energy before a challenging week ahead.

CHAPTER TWELVE

"Tiki! Tiki! Tiki!" chanted the crowd.

Emily drove past the paparazzi to the designated staff parking area, behind the hospital and hidden from view. Anthony had forewarned her after sneaking in the back door an hour earlier. *Welcome to Monday*, she thought.

"Morning. Want some tea, Momo?" Tiki nibbled on a piece of papaya as he watched a documentary about mountain gorillas.

Emily had joined Anthony in his office. "Morning, Tiki. I wish Momo was here, too."

"Now and then, I hear him muttering 'Momo' over and over again." Anthony's brow furrowed as he turned to watch Tiki. "Almost like he's calling for her."

Emily put her arm around Anthony's shoulder. They shared an understanding that no matter how hard they worked to care for this one-of-a-kind parrot, Marilyn would always be his forever person.

Emily shifted her focus to something within her control. "Do you know when the security company is delivering the barricades? I counted almost twenty people out there, and we're not even open yet."

"They'll be here soon and will handle the setup. And, there's one more thing. That same older, tall guy is out there again. When I arrived this morning, I saw him walk out from behind the hospital before joining the crowd in front. I don't like random people sneaking around—not ever, but especially not now. I checked, and he wasn't visible on the security camera, which means he didn't get near the door."

"That's unsettling. I saw him along with some new faces. Let's hope they don't scare off our clients."

The previous night, after Jane took the kids home, Emily called Anthony to update him on the developments involving Dylan Colt's girlfriend and the car license plate. She also told him about her reconnaissance mission to Chad's apartment. He made her promise to never investigate on her own again. Emily had no choice but to agree, since he wouldn't let it go otherwise. They were certain Chad the Third's disappearance had something to do with Marilyn.

"I think we have an even bigger problem. Remember how Marilyn and Tiki's weekly treasure hunt videos posted to her Flix account every Monday?"

Emily nodded and held her breath, waiting for him to finish.

"Well, a new post from Marilyn loaded a few minutes ago. She must have prerecorded a Flix video and scheduled it in advance. I stepped away to watch it because I thought Tiki might get upset after hearing her voice. I didn't want to take a chance."

Emily moved to her office to play the recording, out of Tiki's earshot. Marilyn and Tiki had an extraordinary bond filled with love and watching them together brought tears to her eyes. Imagining Marilyn injured, or worse, became unbearable. She tried to shake off that feeling and concentrate on the clue. The latest video showcased Tiki wearing a pink hat, covered with pink feathers, while balancing on one leg. Other than the over-the-top accessory, he looked the same as he does when he perches to sleep. She watched it one more time, then returned to Anthony's office.

"Do you have any idea what the clue is about?" she asked.

Anthony shook his head. "I've been too preoccupied to think it through."

"This is going to set off a firestorm," Emily said. "The paparazzi are desperate to find Marilyn and Tiki. I don't envy Mike and Duncan trying to work the case with this added media attention."

"I think it's a good thing. All this publicity about her disappearance will increase the chance someone sees something and then says something."

"A double-edged sword, I guess. I'll check with Duncan about the possibility of having regular police patrols through our parking lot. Plus, I want to know more about any connections between our break-in and these other serious crimes."

"The police need to figure this out." Anthony looked deflated as he handed his office mate a piece of spinach to munch on.

• • •

Emily's message to Duncan was forceful—she needed to talk to him. He must have heard the urgency in her voice since he called back right away.

"Sorry, Em. I'm in the middle of something. What's up?"

"What do you mean, *what's up*? A missing person and a murder are *what's up*. Not to mention a break-in and a treasure hunt. Almost two dozen people are outside the hospital chanting Tiki's name. A new video posted on Marilyn and Tiki's Flix account this morning, so I expect more super fans are headed this way."

Duncan said nothing at first. "Did Anthony contact the security company?"

"Yes, they're going to set up barricades and signs to keep the paparazzi away from our doors. Could you send a patrol car by the hospital?"

"I can do that."

"Thank you. Now, what about the girlfriend? Is she involved in the break-in?"

"No, she has an alibi for the time of the attempted robbery. Dylan Colt is her ex-boyfriend, and there's no love lost there. He took her car last week and never returned it."

"Did she report it stolen?"

"No. She thought there was a better chance of getting it back in one piece if she was patient. If she called the cops on him, she thought he would set it on fire or push it into a canal, just to spite her. I think her exact words were, *He's as mean as a snake.*"

"So, where's the car? Colt sure isn't driving it since he's in the morgue."

"We've issued a BOLO for the vehicle. Something will turn up."

After watching many TV detective shows, Emily learned the meaning of a BOLO. *Be on the lookout* was one of her favorite acronyms. The police hadn't found Marilyn after issuing a BOLO for her whereabouts. She hoped it would be easier to find a car.

"I've got to go. You should see a police cruiser within the hour. Let me know if anything changes," then he hung up.

• • •

Catrinna worked with Emily through morning appointments while Anthony dealt with the security company. After strategizing with the company representative, traffic cones and signs were used to identify designated customer parking for the hospital clients. Despite the growing crowd, they were cooperative when asked to stand behind a new set of barricades, pushing them away from the front of the hospital.

The fans bombarded Anthony with questions about Marilyn and Tiki, which he answered with a respectful, *no comment*. Anthony tried to engage with the older, tall man in the crowd, but the man refused to respond to any attempt at casual conversation and stepped away. As they wrapped up, a police cruiser from the Sheriff's office drove slowly through the parking lot. Their presence caused the chanting to stop. Mission accomplished.

Anthony went looking for Emily to update her on the new security protocols and found her and Catrinna occupied with Kizmet Hedden in the treatment area. The ten-month-old kitten had short, black fur and a kink near the tip of her tail. During a play session with her older brother, Kirby, things took a turn for the worse. Mrs. Hedden had been working on a project in her arts and crafts room when she heard hissing, followed by the sound of a lamp crashing to the floor. She raced into the family room and found Kirby fluffed up like a puffer fish and Kizmet hiding behind the couch. Kizmet immediately held her right eye shut, and it teared profusely.

Mrs. Hedden theorized that Kizmet's zoomies upset a much older Kirby who often lost his patience with the kitten. "He must have taken a swipe at her to get her to cool her jets. Otherwise, they're good friends."

"Turn the lights off, please?" Emily asked Anthony as he passed by the switch.

"Everything okay?"

"I'm staining Kizmet's eye to check for a corneal ulcer." Once the room was dark, Emily used the blue light on her ophthalmoscope to look for the telltale green stain. Kizmet had a minor scratch, resulting in an ulcer that required medicated eye drops and close monitoring. Thankfully, the injury wasn't serious and the numbing drops Emily used were working. Kizmet now held her eye open.

"She's such a good patient, especially for a kitten," Catrinna said. "Kizmet purred the entire time." Purring during an office visit is often a stress response in cats and not always a sign of contentment, but in Kizmet's case, she really was that sweet.

Emily rinsed the stain out of Kizmet's eye and returned to the exam room to show Mrs. Hedden how to administer the eye drops. Three times a day would be a challenge, but necessary to heal the injury. After scheduling a recheck exam for the end of the week, Emily instructed Mrs. Hedden to return right away if things got worse.

Once the lobby had emptied, Emily, Anthony, Abigail, and Catrinna stood together to watch the paparazzi. They struggled to devise a cohesive story to tell their clients who inquired about the crowd outside. With the increased media coverage, any made-up story sounded disingenuous.

"My friend, Jacob, overheard Tiki's fans talking this morning. He was leaving an eye doctor's appointment, and a few of them walked past him on their way back from the coffee shop. The scuttlebutt about today's Flix video is that it leads to a bird sanctuary with resident flamingos. There are around a dozen places in Florida with flamingos. I haven't researched which ones are nonprofit," Abigail said.

"That makes sense. Tiki looked pretty cute in that pink hat, and his one-legged impression of a flamingo was spot-on," Anthony said.

"It wouldn't surprise me if they find the next clue right away. There are so many more people looking," Emily said.

"I saw photos of the clues. They're beautiful, hand-painted Mexican tiles, about twelve inches in size. Each one has a single number painted on it with a little image of Tiki in the corner." Abigail moved to her desk to pull up the picture. The tiles were hidden inside the wild bird sanctuaries at locations that forced the guests to tour the whole place. "So far, they've found numbers; eight, nine, zero, and five."

"Does anyone know what they mean?" Emily asked.

"Nope," Abigail replied. "The directors at each of these facilities are tight-lipped about the treasure hunt. None of them are talking to the press."

"I'm sure Marilyn made special deals with each of the bird sanctuaries before hiding the tiles, or she kept the treasure details compartmentalized so each location only had knowledge about their own tile," Emily said.

Abigail replayed today's Flix post. "Nobody knows how many more tiles might still be out there. Especially if Marilyn recorded these videos ahead of time."

Emily and Anthony moved into his office to finish their conversation in private. The staff were already concerned after the break-in attempt, so they wanted to avoid adding to those worries by speculating about the connection to Marilyn and a murder.

"We need to distract the crowd during my getaway with Tiki," Anthony said.

"I'll handle it. Every time I go outside, they bombard me with questions."

Anthony planned to leave early to change up his schedule. He didn't want the paparazzi to predict his movements. "I'm getting a creepy vibe from that older dude. He looks like a character from a black-and-white horror film. It's got to be hard to maintain such a pale complexion when you live in Florida. I'm going to send Duncan a screenshot of the crowd to include Mr. Freaky. It might be wise to figure out who he is after finding him lurking around this morning."

The old man that Anthony named Mr. Freaky, might just be a person who loves parrots, but Emily wanted to be on alert for anything that seemed out of place.

• • •

The paparazzi's chants reached a crescendo until a passing police or sheriff's vehicle temporarily tamped down the volume. Every time Emily looked out the front window, the crowd size grew. It now looked like a tailgate party at a Jimmy Buffett concert. Jimmy's die-hard fans, known as Parrotheads, often dressed up in parrot-shaped hats, t-shirts, and an array of memorabilia—much like those now gathered outside. The only thing missing from this crowd was a blender full of margaritas and Jimmy's music playing in the background.

Abigail expertly diffused questions posed by their clients. She played it off as a social media phenomenon and not associated with the hospital. Anthony was concerned the crowd would frighten the dogs and cats on their way in and out of the building, but so far, the paparazzi were respectful of the patients. It seemed most of the followers were here because of their love for Tiki and Marilyn, and that carried over in their kindness to other animals.

With Anthony prepared to leave, Emily went outside to occupy the crowd's attention. She thanked them for staying behind the barricade. Questions shouted at Emily about Tiki remained unanswered as she tried to change the subject back to this morning's video clue. The crowd, eager to speculate about the treasure, began sharing their theories with Emily, but when Anthony's text confirmed he was safely away, she said good night. The older man Anthony had named Mr. Freaky stood a short distance behind the crowd and watched her with a blank stare. Emily didn't see him blink once. With luck, Anthony's photo of the man would help with his identification.

As she turned to walk back inside, Anthony called. "Hey, I got your text—" she said before he cut her off.

"Em, I need help. I think I'm being followed."

CHAPTER THIRTEEN

"Are you safe right now?" Emily started sprinting for her office.

"I think so." The ambient noise from Anthony's speakerphone did nothing to muffle the sound of fear in his voice. "After we left the hospital, I noticed the same car in my rearview mirror on three separate occasions. I even made a couple of random turns to prove to myself I wasn't being paranoid. The car followed me every time."

"Where are you?"

"Near your house. Beach Road is so quiet and straight, and I thought it would be impossible for a car to blend in and follow me here. I haven't seen them for a few minutes, so it must have worked. It's too risky to go home and take a chance some bad guy traces Tiki to my place. What should I do?"

"I'm leaving now, and I'll call Duncan and Mike to meet us at my place. Keep driving around until I get there."

"Okay, thanks, Em."

Emily grabbed her keys and ran out the door. She fumbled while trying to unlock the car, struggling to steady her nerves before getting behind the wheel. She sent a quick text to Abigail, asking her to lock up the hospital and to reach out if she needed anything. Once Emily was underway, she called Duncan—his phone went directly to voicemail, but Mike answered on the first ring.

"Hi, Em—"

She interrupted him to address the urgent topic at hand. After sharing the details about Anthony's predicament, Emily heard the wail of his police siren. "I'm turning around. I'll be there in ten minutes."

When she arrived home, Mike's unmarked police car was parked next to Anthony's van, and both men were standing in the front yard.

"Are you okay?" Emily ran to Anthony's side, then peeked in the window to check on Tiki.

"I'm better now," Anthony said.

Emily looped her hand around Mike's forearm and leaned in. "Thanks for getting here so fast." He smiled and bent down to kiss the top of her head.

"I don't think you're being paranoid," Mike said to Anthony before turning to Emily. "His description of the car matches the vehicle seen on your security video around the time of the break-in—the one stolen by Dylan Colt."

Emily's jaw dropped as she turned to look at Anthony. "What? Did you catch the license plate number?"

"No, and I didn't see the driver's face because I was concentrating on not getting into an accident. They had a baseball hat pulled over their eyes and the sunshade hanging down. I'm pretty sure there was only one person in the car." Anthony stepped closer to the van to monitor Tiki. "I don't want to leave him in there much longer. What should we do?"

"Duncan's on his way, and he'll escort you home and stay nearby to ensure they didn't follow you," Mike said.

Anthony sighed. "I've never had a tail before. It's more fun watching it happen on TV."

"I have a feeling it's going to be a long week," Emily added.

Duncan soon pulled up to the curb. Mike had updated him on the way over, so he didn't linger to chat. Anthony was eager to get home, and they left right away.

"Since you're already here, would you like to stay for dinner?" Emily asked Mike. "And it's my night for turtle watch."

Mike's eyes opened wide, and he smiled. "Sounds perfect."

Their first date had included a beach walk to check on the turtle nests. Emily's volunteer responsibilities included surveying the nests for activity after sunset, but whenever Mike joined her, the scientific task doubled as a romantic outing. She found it hard to concentrate as they moved from nest to nest, holding hands. Awestruck the first time Mike witnessed a hatching, his authentic enthusiasm made him even more attractive to her. He wouldn't be able to pass up a chance to see this amazing feat of nature.

Using leftovers from her fridge, Emily put together an eclectic charcuterie board for dinner. Her goal of having a well-stocked cupboard and cooking homemade meals seemed out-of-reach. Chicken salad, lettuce leaves for wraps, pickles, cheese and crackers, and fresh berries were tonight's makeshift entrée. After dinner, Bella beckoned them to follow her onto the deck where Emily brushed her as she lay in the sun on the lounge chair.

Picking up where she left off with Mike felt natural, but Emily struggled to understand how her busy schedule allowed them to become so easily estranged. It might be as simple as life getting in the way, but she wanted to be certain it wasn't more than that. For now, she would keep the conversation light.

Emily glanced at her phone; a text from Anthony confirmed he arrived home safely. As she responded, Duncan called Mike to discuss this latest escalation in the case—solving the murder and finding Marilyn was their priority. Emily and Anthony had to focus on a new security arrangement for Tiki.

• • •

"Bella, we won't be long." Emily lifted her hefty Maine Coon off the deck chair and carried her inside to her cat tree. She handed Mike a flashlight, and they held hands as they began their walk up the beach.

"Do you have the final turtle center drawings yet?" Mike asked.

"Our last few changes are being incorporated into the plan, and we're meeting this week with the architect to do a site walkthrough with the builder."

"That's exciting. I'm sure it requires unique expertise."

"Yes, we've consulted and partnered with marine biologists and other turtle hospitals on the Atlantic and Gulf coasts. Turtles requiring hospitalization will be transported to nearby facilities, but we'll have a small treatment area to start their care. The goal of the center is to offer an interactive education for students of all ages, as well as the public, and to raise awareness about sea turtle conservation. We'll also have a new meeting space for the turtle volunteers. Until now, all the training sessions were held in Marlon's living room."

"Are Marlon and Sharon still going to be in charge of operations?"

Emily nodded. "Marlon has decades of experience working at different turtle centers and combined with Sharon's communication director skills—they're a dream team."

"And with you and Anthony at the helm, it will be an amazing success."

"Don't forget about Sarah's resources. She's quite formidable. Industry experts and advisors are donating their time to help Sarah realize her mom's vision for the center."

Turtle nests labeled and roped off by the Coral Shores Turtle Project protected the fragile eggs, and surveillance systems aided in predicting when the hatchlings would break out of their shells and begin the treacherous journey to the ocean. As a volunteer,

Emily's job was to ensure their route from the nest to the water was free of obstacles that could hinder their success. After inspecting the area, they concluded there were no signs of an imminent turtle hatch.

On the way back to Emily's cottage, Mike tightened his grip on her hand. "I really struggled these past few weeks, not knowing what you were thinking or feeling." The tone in his voice caused Emily to pause. He sounded almost sad, but then turned to her with a smile on his face.

She pulled his arm close to her side and leaned into his body. "I'm glad we cleared the air over dinner at your place. Between the hospital and my commitments with the turtle center, I haven't had a spare minute. I know I did a terrible job of sharing my feelings," then Emily paused. "To be completely honest, I thought something else was going on. But instead of asking you about it, I buried myself in work."

"We were getting so close, so fast, like we were on a path, you know—taking things to the next level in our relationship. Working with Duncan every day is a constant reminder of how our lives have become intertwined. I might have used your busy schedule to take some time and think about what those next steps would look like."

Her throat tightened. "Did you come to any conclusions?"

Mike stopped walking and turned Emily to face him. Alone on the beach, he pulled her close, and they melded into an intense embrace. When they stepped apart, Emily's head spun and her legs wobbled.

"I hope that answers your question." He grinned.

Emily nodded, still catching her breath. "I had some of those same feelings. I know one thing for sure. I want you in my life."

"Well, that's good, because I'm not going anywhere."

She wrapped her arms around his waist as they slowly made their way back to her cottage. They both agreed to be more open in the future, but for now, they would enjoy their time together, with no pressure to define the next steps.

Emily didn't want Mike to leave, but she had promised to call Anthony before it was too late. It would not be a quick conversation because they had to make plans for Tiki. That didn't stop Emily and Mike from stretching out their goodbye, finding it difficult to let go of each other. They were making up for lost time. After one last, long kiss, Mike walked to his car but not before confirming their next date.

• • •

"Is Mike still there?" Anthony asked.

"No. He just left. We walked up the beach and, on our way, home, we talked again about the last few weeks."

"That's good. It killed me to watch the two of you acting all weird."

"I know. It's hard for me too. I like him. A lot."

"I'm pretty sure he feels the same way. You should see how he looks at you when you're not watching." Emily enjoyed hearing that.

"Enough about my love life. Is everything okay with you and Tiki?"

She knew Anthony was feeling vulnerable after recent events. Duncan had stayed outside their place for almost an hour, making sure things were quiet before leaving for the night. Getting Tiki in and out of the hospital every day had become increasingly difficult.

"Tiki's fine. He ate well and is now sleeping, but I'm a wreck. Marc left his evening meeting to come home early, and we've been brainstorming how to manage Tiki through the end of the week."

"Any new ideas?"

"Nope. I still want to bring him to work with me each day. I'm not comfortable leaving him alone. Marc's going to be here on Thursday when we meet with Sarah and the Turtle Team." Anthony had named the group of consultants bringing the turtle center to fruition the *Turtle Team*.

"I can continue to play interference with the paparazzi when you take Tiki home each night. If it's easier to leave earlier in the day, do that," Emily said.

"I might. I'll continue to come in the morning before the staff. I'm going to ask the property manager for approval to barricade the alley behind the hospital so nobody other than you or me can get close to the back door. I'll keep the van parked there. Plus, it should deter fans from wandering."

"Won't the barricades draw attention to that area?"

"Don't think so," Anthony said. "Tiki's fans are gathering to create a community. It's a social media phenomenon, and most of the people are there for their own needs and to post selfies. I think they're genuinely worried about Marilyn and Tiki—it doesn't feel like they have any malicious intent. Does that sound naïve?"

Emily thought for a moment. "What about Mr. Freaky? I don't think he's part of the core group."

"He stands out for sure. I sent his picture to Mike, and he passed it on to Officer Garcia and her partner to check him out."

"Mike told me the likelihood of getting a hit on the BOLO for the car went up after tonight. At least we know the car isn't sitting at the bottom of a canal. Assuming it was Dylan Colt's girlfriend's car, the more it's on the road, the easier it will be to track down the person who followed you."

"I hope so. I have a bad feeling things are escalating out of control. It doesn't help that the news media is focused on Marilyn's disappearance and the treasure hunt. If the crowd at work continues to grow, we might want to consider hiring a security guard. They would need to be discreet so our clients feel safe, but their presence could deter any disruptive activity by the paparazzi."

Even though Tiki's super fans conducted themselves peacefully, they were a real problem. Keeping Tiki Lulu's whereabouts a secret was essential, but not as important as finding Marilyn. Duncan and Mike were tight-lipped about the investigation, leaving Anthony and Emily to make plans in isolation. With a treasure hunt added to the mix, it had become an investigatory quagmire.

CHAPTER FOURTEEN

The new normal was far from normal. Over the next few days, the Coral Shores Veterinary Hospital became ground zero for everything associated with Tiki Lulu and Marilyn, including the missing person investigation and the treasure hunt. Media vans, food trucks, and paparazzi filled the parking lot of the hospital and neighboring businesses. Tiki's fans camped out in RVs or under portable shade tents, many with large grills for cooking. Outdoor TV viewing areas became central gathering spots. Someone painted a likeness of Tiki Lulu on a cornhole board, and a tournament appeared to be in full swing. An all-ages affair more reminiscent of a tailgate party at a championship football game than a veterinary hospital.

As the crowd size ballooned, the police dispatched an officer to be stationed in the parking lot, eliminating the need for Emily to hire a private security company. They spent most of their time directing traffic, but that constant presence kept things safe. Duncan likely had a role to play in that decision, and she was grateful.

Concerns the media circus would deter their clients from scheduling appointments were unfounded. The opposite happened. The number of Tiki's followers on Flix doubled in the past week, now approaching two million. That level of engagement included many of Emily's clients who did not want to miss out on the festivities.

Head receptionist, Abigail, convinced Anthony to add a second receptionist to the shift, as curious clients who came in to buy food or refill their pet's heartworm and flea medicine added to the busy appointment schedule. These routine purchases provided legitimate cover, allowing Emily's clients to check things out without appearing nosy.

"I spoke with the property manager this morning," Anthony said. He and Emily took a moment in their day to eat lunch and strategize.

"I hope they understand this is all out of our control."

"They do. As long as the police are here to keep the customer parking accessible for the other businesses, they're willing to ride it out. And, they're fine with letting us block off the alley."

"I've told the crowd multiple times Tiki isn't here, but they just ignore me."

"Online conspiracy theories are growing every day. It's riskier each time Tiki and I move between the hospital and my place. The paparazzi are going to figure it out."

Emily and Anthony were quiet for a few minutes as they watched Tiki preen himself. He used both his bill and his feet to stroke every feather from its base to its tip. Tiki's plumage was beautiful. Grooming was a normal behavior, but Anthony voiced concerns that Tiki had been talking less often over the past few days. Emily hadn't noticed the change, but Anthony spent more time with him, and she trusted his observations.

"Em, I think we should contact the wild bird centers taking part in Marilyn's treasure hunt. A few of them provide permanent homes for parrots. Since Marilyn already endorsed them, we should trust them, too." Anthony choked up. Relinquishing Tiki to a sanctuary instead of returning him to Marilyn was difficult to contemplate. Emily hated seeing her friend so distraught.

"I guess it wouldn't hurt to call and find out what's involved with re-homing a parrot, but let's put off making any decisions. If we can manage until the weekend, we'll then have time to collect our thoughts. We need a break from all this drama and chaos." Emily wanted to sound strong for Anthony, but when she turned to look at Tiki, she felt a lump in her throat. It had only taken days to build a strong, emotional bond with this amazing parrot.

Anthony pushed his shoulders back and sat up straight. "Okay. I'll wait till Monday to make the calls. On a lighter note, did you see Otter is coming in this afternoon?"

"I'll never get used to calling her that—she's still Susan to me. We had to wait until the moons were in alignment to repeat Sara Lee's blood work," Emily said with a grin. Otter always lifted her spirits, and they all needed some celestial good karma to get through the day.

"I'm leaving early to get Tiki settled before our meeting with Sarah and the Turtle Team. Marc is working from home this afternoon so he can stay with him."

"Tell him—thank you. The meeting is at Marlon's house, and he's arranging dinner for us. After, we're all going over to Mrs. Klein's house to walk the site with the contractor."

"I know we need to call it the Eliza Klein Sea Turtle Education Center, but for now, it's Mrs. Klein's cottage. It must be hard for Sarah sometimes. It hasn't been that long since her mom died."

Emily nodded. The overwhelming grief after losing a parent never goes away and often comes in waves, set off by the smallest cue. That became magnified for Sarah, who lost her mom to a violent crime. Right after Emily's mom died, she would break down in sobs when she sat in her mom's chaise lounge or put on a pair of her mom's favorite flip-flops. Emily cherished her mom's extensive collection of flip-flops and could not part with them. When she closed her eyes, she pictured her mom wearing every pair of them. Only with time did the memories become less painful.

• • •

"Hi, Otter," Emily said as she entered the exam room. Sara Lee's tail wagged at lightning speed. She struggled to contain her excitement and performed her own version of doggy tap dancing, shifting her weight from foot to foot. Emily bent down to pet her. "Hi, Sara Lee."

"She loves the attention," Otter smiled. "But mostly we both love coming to see you, Emily. I've been following Marilyn and Tiki's story on the news. How are you doing?"

"As well as to be expected. We're worried for Marilyn."

"It's a circus out there. Reminds me of a recent Arts and Psychic Fair I attended."

Emily tried to imagine what goes on at a psychic fair, but she was at a loss. "How's Sarah Lee doing?"

"She's wonderful. She loves her new food and no more tummy troubles. The moons are in alignment, so we're here to recheck her blood work. I feel good about this."

Once Emily completed Sarah Lee's exam, they collected the blood sample to submit to the lab. Sarah Lee had regained the weight she lost during her illness, which was a good sign.

"The results will be back in a couple of days," Emily told Otter as they walked to the lobby. It was difficult to avoid looking out the front window, but Emily needed to compartmentalize her workday from the ongoing chaos. She faced away from the banners and signs to focus on her patients and staff. As she started toward her office, Otter pulled her aside.

"I wasn't going to say anything, but I can see the worry on your face. I had a premonition when I walked through the parking lot before our appointment. It was brief, but I saw Marilyn Peña and her parrot, Tiki Lulu, reunited. An aura of joy, love, and peace surrounded them."

Emily didn't believe in psychics or fortune tellers, but she believed in Otter. Her mom, who was also a skeptic, shared many stories about moments when Otter—she was Susan back then—

predicted a future outcome. Whether some people were more intuitive or had *the gift*, who was Emily to say otherwise?

"I needed to hear that right now," she said before hugging Otter. "Let's hope your vision comes true."

• • •

With Anthony prepared to leave with Tiki, Emily walked into the front parking lot. Her presence no longer provided a diversion, as the crescendo of activity took on a life of its own. The original group of paparazzi were still front and center, being interviewed by a local TV news reporter. Emily scanned the crowd and noticed Mr. Freaky standing alone under a coconut palm tree. His appearance had changed. He now looked gaunt and unwell. Emily watched him for a few minutes until he turned his head ever so slightly in her direction and stared. They held each other's gaze for a moment before Emily did an about-face and walked back into the hospital. Something was off about that guy. She wanted to know if Duncan had any information about his identity, but it would have to wait. Emily rushed to finish her day so she could get home to change before the turtle meeting.

• • •

"Emily." Sarah jumped out of her chair to greet her with a hug. The two had become close friends. When they first met, they bonded over Elvis and their shared grief after losing their mothers. That connection blossomed during their time working together on the turtle project.

"Hi, everyone. Sorry I'm late," Emily said.

Sharon stood to welcome Emily to the meeting. "You're not late. We're early. Just couldn't help ourselves. This is so exciting."

Sharon and their host, Marlon, would run daily operations at the Turtle Conservation Center. Their decades of work protecting sea turtles made them an ideal choice.

"Let's eat first before we start the meeting," Marlon said, then waved for them to follow. Luis Ruiz, the architect, joined Sharon, Marlon, and Sarah as they helped themselves to pasta and salad. Emily stayed back, motioning over to Anthony. She wanted to talk with him in private.

"Is everything okay with Tiki?" Ever since Anthony shared his thoughts about Tiki's quiet demeanor, it weighed on her.

"Marc prepped him a whole smorgasbord of tasty treats. When I left for the meeting, he was enjoying his snacks and talking up a storm—he's happy in his new home."

Bringing Tiki to work each day wasn't a practical or long-term strategy, but at least for now, they breathed easy.

"Speaking of snacks, I'm starving." Anthony walked to the kitchen and filled his plate.

The Turtle Team gathered in Marlon's Florida room, where he passed cannoli around for dessert. As they reviewed the most recent changes to the architectural drawing for the Eliza Klein Turtle Conservation Center, everyone agreed they were about to embark on a life-changing project. Building a world-class center was beyond their wildest dreams.

Sarah glanced down at her watch, then stood. "Marlon, thank you so much for arranging this delicious meal. It's time to make our way over to my mom's place to meet the contractor. Emily, could you drive with me? I can bring you back to your car when we're done."

"Sure." Emily assumed Sarah had something to discuss, but otherwise thought nothing of it.

• • •

"We're excited to have you back in town. How long are you staying?" Emily asked Sarah during the short drive to the beach.

"Only a few days this time, but I'll be back more often once we break ground. I've been struggling with the impending demolition of my mom's place in order to clear the land. Now that Luis figured out a way to incorporate the bones of her cottage into the new welcome center, well, my heart is whole. Mom would love this design."

"I agree. It's perfect." Mrs. Klein's murder had shocked the community, but her legacy would now carry on for future generations.

"Emily, I've been following the local news, and after Anthony filled me in on all the details—I'm worried about both of you. How are you handling everything?"

"I have to admit, it's a lot. It's stressful enough caring for a parrot, but the treasure hunt and media attention are getting out of control. Anthony and Marc built a new temporary home for Tiki Lulu, but we have to face the reality that Marilyn might not be coming back."

"I hope you're not mad, but I called Duncan. When I heard you discovered another murder victim, I got scared." Sarah worked with Duncan and Mike on her mom's murder investigation and helped to see the killers brought to justice.

"Oh." Emily tried to hide her surprise even though Sarah came from a place of concern. "Technically, Anthony found the body this time. It was a shock, but we've been there to support each other."

"That's what he said too when I asked him before you arrived tonight. Your friendship is something we all aspire to have. If you want my help with anything, please ask. I have an army of media specialists I can enlist to help with publicity or whatever else you need."

"Thanks, Sarah. I appreciate the offer. I hope Duncan and Mike will find Marilyn soon, and this whole thing will settle down." Emily didn't sound very convincing.

As they pulled into Mrs. Klein's driveway, they saw the Turtle Team huddled together in the front yard with the building contractor. Luis Ruiz held the site plans to lead their walk-through. Emily didn't see Anthony standing with the group, so she began scanning the property. When he popped out from behind a truck, frantically waving his phone over his head, panic covered his face. Emily jumped out of the car as he ran toward her.

"Em, it's Marc. Something's wrong. We have to go."

CHAPTER FIFTEEN

Sarah turned to Emily. "Go. We can handle things here."

Emily sprinted to catch up to Anthony, who already had his car in reverse. He began driving down Beach Road before Emily pulled the door shut. Her hands shook as she struggled with the seat buckle.

"What's going on?"

"Marc and Tiki Lulu were enjoying a quiet evening at home when Tiki suddenly became agitated. He started flapping his wings and screeching, *Chad! Chad!* Marc couldn't calm him down, so he called me."

"I don't even understand what that means. Was Tiki referring to Chad—Marilyn's nephew?"

"I don't know, but Marc swore he saw someone moving in the shadows outside the aviary. Most of the screened-in porch faces a row of bushes and some trees. That's why he picked that townhouse. It's in a quiet area of the neighborhood. He called out to them, but they'd already disappeared. Tiki Lulu is very smart. If he said it was Chad, it was Chad."

There was no arguing with his logic. Why else would Tiki shout out that name? He'd shared his vast vocabulary with them over the past week, but not once had Tiki said Chad's name. Not anything even close to it. Not a *chance* or *champ* or *channel*—not even a *had*. When parrots learn new words, their early pronunciation is often a work in progress, but since Marc had been vehement about what he heard, there could only be one conclusion—it had to be Chad.

"I told Marc to call Duncan," Anthony said.

"You did the right thing. We've suspected Chad the day he tried to take Tiki home from the hospital. Marilyn's missing person story is big news, so why hasn't he come forward as a concerned family member? And why is he hiding from the police?"

The ramifications of tonight's latest twist set in as they spent the last few minutes driving in silence. Anthony's white-knuckled grip on the steering wheel added to the tension. When they entered the parking lot at Marc and Anthony's place, they saw a police vehicle parked in front of the townhouse. Anthony pulled to the curb and jumped from the car, leaving the engine running and the driver's side door wide open. Emily took a moment to secure his car, then raced after him.

Anthony and Marc stood next to the screen door, watching Tiki.

"Is he okay?" Emily asked as she joined them.

"He is now," Marc replied.

"Where's the police officer?"

"He's walking around the property. I doubt he'll find anything." Marc adjusted the makeshift TV stand he had created for Tiki by repositioning their breakfast table. "When Tiki got upset, I first tried offering him his favorite foods, but that didn't help. He only settled down when I turned on a show about panda bears."

"Did you get a good look at the person?" Emily asked Marc.

Marc shook his head. "It was too dark, but they were standing near the porch on this side of the bushes."

"Maybe it was a kid in the neighborhood, snooping around," Emily said.

Both Anthony and Marc turned to look at her. "You don't believe that, do you? If I remember correctly, you told me more than once when we were investigating Mrs. Klein's murder that you don't believe in coincidences," Anthony said.

He had her there. She didn't believe in coincidences, which meant Tiki's reaction to the intruder had to be taken seriously.

Anthony patted his pants pocket for his car keys, prompting Emily to hand them over. "Thanks, Em. I have to tell you, I'm on my last nerve."

Between the growing spectacle in the hospital parking lot and another break-in attempt, their lives were teetering on a precipice. They needed to catch a break, clear their heads, and work on Plan B as it pertained to Tiki's long-term care.

Emily's phone vibrated in her pocket. "It's a text from Sarah. She wants to know if we're okay. They finished the site walk-through, and she'll update us when we're ready."

"I feel bad running off the way I did," Anthony said.

"They'll understand. I told her we're fine, and we'll fill her in later." Emily turned toward voices coming from outside the front door. Marc walked over to check it out and returned with Duncan.

"Hi," Duncan said.

Emily smiled. His presence brought her great peace. He was a successful sheriff's deputy, but he was also her big brother. They always had each other's back, and now that he was here, she could breathe easy.

"Thanks for coming. I'm sorry we called you at home. I panicked," Anthony said.

"No worries. You can call me anytime. Officer Baker searched the immediate area, and nothing seems out of place. He found some footprints in the dirt outside Tiki's porch, but that's all."

"I'm telling you, Duncan, Tiki knew it was Chad lurking outside. There's no other explanation," Anthony said.

"I don't doubt you, but what can I do when the eyewitness is a parrot?" The question hung in the air for a minute. "I've ordered Officer Baker to make regular swings through the parking lot during his overnight shift. Are you taking Tiki with you to work tomorrow?" Emily and Anthony nodded. "Okay. Let me know if you change your plans since it affects patrol routes. You all look tired. Why don't you try to get some rest? You'll be safe tonight."

Duncan was holding something back, but Emily decided not to press him right now. Marc and Anthony moved their armchairs next to the porch to sit beside Tiki, who seemed content and calm as he began his nighttime sleep routine.

"If it's okay with both of you, I'm going to head home," Emily said. "Duncan, I drove here with Anthony and left my car at Marlon's house. We were meeting about the turtle center when everything went sideways. Can you give me a lift?"

"Sure," he replied, then they both said their goodbyes.

She waited until they were in Duncan's car before asking questions. As they pulled onto the road, she noticed him turning to look up at security cameras aimed toward the entrance of the townhouse complex.

"I'm surprised how seriously you're taking the words of a parrot," Emily said. "What's going on here, Duncan? Do you know something about Chad?"

He kept driving, eyes forward. Emily was wise to wait until they were in a confined space to get some answers. Duncan had no escape route.

"Em, this investigation has a lot of moving parts. I can't talk about it."

"I don't know why we keep ending up in this situation. I need information to help keep Tiki, Anthony, and Marc safe. They did a wonderful thing bringing him into their home, and now I'm worried that decision is putting them all at risk. You need to help me out."

It was a reasonable argument, and after a moment, Duncan relented. He pulled his car to a stop on the shoulder of the road and turned to Emily. "What I'm about to share with you is confidential, and keeping it that way is critical to the investigation. But first, is there something you want to tell me?"

Uh oh, Emily thought, before feigning innocence. "What do you mean?"

"Em, I know you went to Chad's apartment. I think you owe me an explanation."

She needed to tread lightly. "I'm stuck in the middle of a murder case, and neither you nor Mike will talk to me. How did you find out?"

"We have an undercover officer staking out Chad's place. Do you know how embarrassing it was to find out you were there from the investigative team? But that wasn't the worst part. What if he'd been home? What if he hurt you?"

Now, the gray sedan made sense to her, but she hated hearing the disappointment in her brother's voice. "I'm truly sorry. I should have told you." Duncan accepted her apology when she promised not to do it again. "You can trust me."

"I know I can, but what about sharing information with Anthony and Marc?"

"They don't count. We're all one entity. They're my family too but not a word beyond the three of us."

Duncan thought about it, then nodded before pulling back onto the road. "Chad Peña's DNA was on Dylan Colt's body. His prints were all over Marilyn's house, but that's expected. He had been staying there until recently. That's how we got his DNA—off a toothbrush."

"Where's he living now? I talked to his neighbor, and she hadn't seen him in days."

"We're trying to track him down. He hasn't yet returned to his apartment. He's an only child, and both his parents are deceased. Marilyn is his only relative living nearby. We issued an arrest warrant for Chad, but right now, we don't have any leads. Chad Peña is an underachiever. He dropped out of college and can't hold down a job. He was helping his aunt until she cut him off four weeks ago. After burning through a trust fund left to him by Marilyn's husband, he's broke."

"Does he have a criminal record?"

"Nothing more than a few parking tickets."

"It's the third time someone's tried to get their hands on Tiki Lulu. I'm taking a leap and assuming Chad attempted the break-in at the hospital. Why would he want Marilyn's parrot?"

"Someone is logging in to Marilyn's email account. We assume it's not her since there have been no requests for help. It's possible he stole her password and is looking for something related to the treasure hunt. It's the only link between Tiki and the money."

"Anthony and I planned to contact some wild bird sanctuaries about the possibility of moving Tiki into a new home. I can't put anyone else in the middle of this—not if Tiki is in danger. What am I going to do? I can't afford a security detail for him."

"I think you're all safe when you're at work, and we can begin night patrols at Marc and Anthony's place. At least until we get Chad Peña into custody."

"What about Marilyn? Do you have any leads?"

Duncan shook his head. "And still no ransom demand. We think finding Chad will lead us to Marilyn."

As Duncan pulled into Marlon's driveway, the entire Turtle Team, minus Luis Ruiz who had left for the night, spilled out into the front yard. They had waited to see for themselves that Emily was okay.

Duncan left her in caring hands. "I promise to let you know if anything changes." Emily took him at his word.

She didn't have the energy to rehash the entire sequence of events with the team, beginning with Marilyn's veterinary appointment for Tiki's nail trim. They understood her reluctance to share and just wanted to make certain she and Anthony were safe. It took some convincing, but they eventually agreed to let Emily drive herself home. Sarah wouldn't take no for an answer when she proposed bringing dinner to Emily's tomorrow night. It would give them a chance to catch up and review the turtle plans. And, of course, Anthony was invited.

Emily's only thoughts were about climbing into bed and putting an end to this day. After a quick refresh of Bella's food and water, she changed into her comfiest pajamas. As she lay her head on the pillow, Mike called.

"Hi, Em. Duncan filled me in on everything. I can come over."

The thought of falling asleep in Mike's arms was tempting, but Emily had nothing left to give. "Thanks, Mike. Bella is on protective duty as my bodyguard, so I think I'm okay. I'm exhausted. Can I take a rain check?"

"Sure. How about Saturday night?"

"That would be great. Sarah Klein is coming over tomorrow evening to talk about the turtle center plans, and Anthony and I have some stuff to work out for Tiki's care, but otherwise, my weekend is free."

Hearing Mike's voice was the perfect remedy after a difficult day. Dealing with the harsh reality surrounding Tiki and Marilyn's safety would still be there in the morning, but there was nothing she could do about it right now. Bella's gentle purring provided the white noise she needed to ease her mind and, within five minutes, Emily was fast asleep.

CHAPTER SIXTEEN

"Oh no," Emily said to herself as she watched the morning news. "It never ends."

To ensure this outburst didn't interfere with the delivery of her breakfast, Bella let out a demanding, "Meow," then pranced into the kitchen, prompting Emily to follow.

"Here you go, Bella." Emily set the savory salmon paté on the floor.

With her coffee machine in the middle of a brew cycle, Emily executed a deft move to swap her empty mug for the pot, then once her mug was full, she returned the pot without spilling a drop. One sip was all she needed to face the day.

Her mom's ocean-view chaise lounge provided a place of comfort to counter the stress from the outside world—but not this morning. The rising sun reflected off the water, casting a red glow. The surf was eerily calm, and the air seemed thick. Without a breeze, the palm trees stood motionless. Even the chirping ocean birds were quiet. *Red sky at night, sailors' delight. Red sky at morning, sailors take warning.* Her mom always swore by the accuracy of that old sailor's weather forecast.

The weighted air and ominous sky contributed to Emily's anxious state. It was hurricane season, so she would be wise to monitor the weather, to make sure nothing was churning in the Gulf. After watching the breaking story about Marilyn and Tiki's case, Emily avoided the TV news, opting to check the weather app on her phone. Hopes of carving out a few minutes of quiet time vanished in an instant. There were five texts and two missed calls from Anthony.

• • •

"Hi, Em," Anthony said when he answered her call. "Did you see it?"

"I did." A reporter had been broadcasting live from the hospital parking lot in front of a large group of people. "I sort of tuned out when I saw the crowd, but I caught the part about another treasure clue being found at Flamingo Gardens in Davie."

"Makes sense after the video posted of Tiki in the pink feathered hat, standing on one leg. My granny took me to Flamingo Gardens when I was a kid. It's a great place."

"What number was on the tile this time?"

"Number one. That makes five numbers so far: eight, nine, zero, five and now, one. Do you know how many numbers are in a latitude and longitude GPS location?"

"Six or more digits for each, but I'm just guessing."

"I thought if all the numbers were part of a geolocation, it might lead to the buried treasure. *X marks the spot.*"

"That makes sense. Did Marilyn ever announce how many clues she hid when she launched this treasure hunt?"

"I don't think so. I'm about to leave for the hospital. Marc said he could take the day off work to stay home with Tiki, but I know he has an important project deadline. Since Tiki seems okay this morning, I'm going to bring him with me. Let's hope the paparazzi are oblivious to our arrival."

"I'll be there soon. I think it might be a good idea to call all the clients with scheduled appointments through closing on Saturday to let them know what's going on. Just as a courtesy."

"Good idea. I'll get Abigail started on that when she comes in. Bye."

• • •

Emily stopped at Savannah's bakery on her way to work to pick up a dozen of their decadent gourmet donuts for the staff. Everyone had been doing an amazing job at maintaining business as usual despite the distractions swirling around them. Given the demands of the week, the pastries were her way of saying "thank you." After setting the box in the lunchroom, she brought Anthony's favorite maple bacon donut to his office.

"Yum. Thanks, Em. After watching the news this morning, I forgot to eat breakfast."

"I lost my appetite, too. The crowd out front looks bigger than yesterday."

"Whatcha doing? Momo. Momo. Want some tea?" Tiki bobbed up and down on his perch. He then sorted through the food items in his feeder and selecting a slice of apple. Emily found his culinary habits fascinating.

"How is he?" she asked. "And don't candy-coat it for me."

"Overall, he seems fine, but I still think he's quieter and maybe a little less active. He's used to that fancy, huge aviary Marilyn built for him. We're trying to compensate for the smaller space by ensuring someone is always there to keep him occupied."

"But that's not sustainable. Not for you and Marc, or Tiki."

"I know, but we're handling it for now, and we can work on a plan this weekend. Since Saturday is a half day, I thought I'd work from home. I have some paperwork to catch up on, and I'm worried about moving Tiki for a few hours."

"I like that idea. We can survive the morning without you, but just barely." Emily hugged her friend. "I was so distracted last night after Tiki's *Chad-shouting* fiasco, I forgot to ask Duncan about Mr. Freaky. He's already back under the coconut palm. I'll bring it up the next time I talk to him." Emily moved to her office, turning her attention to the day ahead.

It became increasingly difficult to ignore the circus-like atmosphere outside the front doors. By mid-morning, an additional police cruiser arrived to assist with crowd control. The banners were getting bigger, and the parrot outfits worn by the super fans were more elaborate. Red tail feathers accented parrot wings crafted from a variety of materials. African grey parrot-shaped hats were the hot ticket item. Glancing across the lot, it looked like a sea of parrot heads, bobbing to the beat of the music. Someone had created a playlist of songs with lyrics about birds. Nelly Furtado's "I'm Like a Bird" played on the loudspeaker.

After speaking with most of their clients, Abigail informed Emily some had opted to reschedule for the following week. Emily couldn't blame them. Routine checkups weren't urgent and could wait a few days. For clients with pets experiencing a medical issue, the crowd wouldn't keep them away. Their pet came first.

One of those patients was Boo Boo Taylor, the Yorkie. His owners named him after Yogi Bear's sidekick, which was fitting because he looked like a teddy bear. Boo Boo was eleven years old and despite his kidney disease being well managed with a special diet, he'd developed high blood pressure, a common complication. It always shocked her clients when they found out their pet had hypertension. For Mr. Taylor, it became a bonding moment with his little terrier since he was also being treated for high blood pressure. After Boo Boo started a new medicine last month, this appointment had been scheduled to recheck his pressures.

"Hi, Dr. Benton. Boo Boo is taking his pills like a champ. I don't want him to eat extra salt by hiding the pill in a piece of cheese, so

I steamed some baby carrots, and it's easy to push the little pill inside. And he loves them. I hope his readings today are better than last time."

"That's a great way to hide his medicine. We're going to check his pressures here in the room with you. Boo Boo is very calm in your arms, and that will help us avoid artificially high readings caused by stress. I'll do his exam after we're done."

Anthony carried in the portable machine, and after a quick hello to Boo Boo and Mr. Taylor, he attached the tiny blood pressure cuff to Boo Boo's front leg. The machine cycled through three separate readings, and they recorded the average in his medical record. Boo Boo's pressures were consistently in the normal range. The medicine had worked—great news for Mr. Taylor and his beloved pup.

"Those are almost the same readings I had on my last trip to the cardiologist," Mr. Taylor said.

"Yes, people and dogs have the same normal values."

"Interesting. He's so little, I assumed his pressures would be lower."

"Boo Boo's medicine dose is based on his eight-pound weight, but that's the only difference. We'll recheck the readings when I see you at his mid-year senior checkup."

"Sounds like a plan. I'll book that next appointment before I leave. Let's go Boo Boo. I saw a vegan food truck in the parking lot. Time for an early lunch. Bye, Dr. Benton. Bye, Anthony."

Anthony and Emily walked together as they returned the blood pressure machine to the surgery room. "You know how much I love food trucks," Anthony said.

"I do." Emily smiled. "In high school, you dragged me all over Coral Shores and to the beaches to get your favorite fish tacos from Taco Zone. Now, that was a great food truck."

"Those were amazing tacos. I noticed a chicken and waffle truck this morning. They're getting a lot of hype on social media. I think I'll check them out. Your donut was delicious, but now I'm sugar-crashing."

"Might as well take advantage of the only upside of this media circus. Grab two of whatever you order. I didn't bring my lunch."

"Sure. I'll be back soon."

•   •   •

Anthony reminded Emily good food takes time when he returned with their order. It was worth the wait. They didn't say a word until they finished their meal. With the TV tuned to The Discovery Channel, a program about dolphins captured Tiki's attention. His entire head fluffed up as he flipped his tail up and down—a sign of excitement.

"I've never seen him do that before," Anthony said. "He likes this show." The documentary examined the sounds dolphins made to communicate with each other. Every whistle, click, and squeal had meaning. Emily and Anthony's jaws dropped when Tiki mimicked the sounds he heard coming from the TV.

"How does he do that?" Emily asked. "Can he replicate those sounds after only hearing them once?"

"I think it takes more time than that." All three sat watching the program together. Tiki repeated every dolphin sound with perfect accuracy, but his favorite was the whistle dolphins used to communicate with each other. "Marilyn must have introduced him to dolphins."

"That's amazing." Emily was in awe. "I want to sit here all day and watch shows with Tiki, but duty calls."

•   •   •

The number of clients coming into the hospital dwindled during the afternoon, so it wasn't a shock when the last two appointments of the day called to cancel. Emily took advantage of the break in the schedule to catch up on paperwork. The highlight of her week was reporting Sara Lee's perfect lab test results to Otter. She forwarded the report in an email and received an immediate text from Otter filled with happy face and heart emojis.

After she cleared her desk, she called Duncan but failed to connect. She assumed he would update her if there were important developments, but nobody enjoyed being kept in limbo, especially Emily. After last night's discussion, she wanted to hear his voice. It would be easy to tell if he truly forgave her for telling a white lie. Disappointing her brother didn't feel good, even if she had everyone else's best interests at heart.

Anthony walked to Emily's office and leaned on her door. "If you're good here, I'm going to head out with Tiki."

"Give me a few minutes, and I'll leave with you. I want to follow you home, just in case. Abigail can close for us. And I texted Sarah to reschedule for tonight. She understood and said we can go over the plans the next time she's in town."

Anthony didn't say so, but Emily knew that Tiki's care, on top of the chaos surrounding the hospital, had worn him down. Parrots were sensitive to change. Maintaining a consistent routine would help minimize their stress, but that took effort and planning. They were all worried for Marilyn's safety, and as each day passed, it became harder to envision a happy ending.

As the crowd outside focused on their own festivities, providing a distraction during Anthony's covert getaway became unnecessary. Anthony left first with Tiki and parked at a nearby office complex to wait for Emily to pull in behind.

Once they arrived at the townhouse, Anthony parked in his designated spot while Emily waited opposite the front door. He rolled Tiki and his cage across the lot, then mouthed a "thank you" before disappearing inside.

Emily had pulled out of her parking spot when she noticed a car turn the corner at the far end of the row of homes. It matched the description of Dylan Colt's girlfriend's car from the hospital break-in video; the same car that followed Anthony home earlier this week. She was too far away to see the driver, so on instinct, she began her pursuit, then called Anthony.

"Call Duncan for me. Keep texting him and calling him until he picks up. I need to talk to him," Emily said.

"Why? What happened?"

"I think someone was waiting outside your townhouse, but you came home early and messed up their plans. It's the same type of car that followed you last time. Double-check Tiki's screened-in porch to make sure it wasn't tampered with. I'm tailing them right now, and I have to concentrate. That's why I need you to call Duncan."

"Em, don't do this. Let the police handle it. It's a common car—you can't be sure it's the same person."

"You know I hate coincidences. There's no way I'm letting them get away again, but I'll be careful. Promise. Wait, they just turned onto the causeway heading south. I've got to go. Call Duncan," she said before hanging up.

CHAPTER SEVENTEEN

As a fan of all TV crime dramas, Emily had seen her fair share of stakeouts and picked up a few pointers about how to follow someone without getting caught. At least how actors on the screen did it. Odds were, it was more boring and technical than portrayed, but Emily did her best to channel her inner detective.

"Don't get too close," she said to herself. Keeping the car in sight on the open causeway was easy since there were no intersections, so Emily followed in the adjacent lane to stay out of their rearview mirror. It got trickier when the car signaled to exit onto a more congested side street. Dixie Highway, a four-lane road with lots of traffic lights, was home to every fast-food chain and car dealership. After she ran a yellow light to keep pace, the next light turned red, forcing them both to stop. Emily loosened her grip, shaking her hands to release the tension. So far, she was confident the person driving Colt's girlfriend's car didn't know they were being followed.

"Duncan, thank goodness." Emily answered her phone and put it on speaker. "I'm on Dixie Highway heading south, just off exit ten—"

Duncan cut her off. "What are you doing? Did you even see the license number?"

"I'm not close enough to see the plate."

"I know you want to help, but this has to stop. Pull over and let me handle it."

Duncan's tone made it clear he wasn't fooling around. Emily's eyes narrowed, and she drew her lower lip between her teeth, taking a moment to think before replying. *In for a penny, in for a pound* popped into her head. "I'm being careful and staying out of sight." Emily braced herself in anticipation of what came next.

"You're not going to listen to me, are you?" His voice had an angry edge.

"I always listen to you, but you forget I'm a responsible adult and not just your little sister. I promise I'm being safe."

"I'm texting with Mike. He's headed to your location, so stay on the phone with me until he can take over pursuit in his unmarked car."

"Are there any officers nearby?"

"We don't even know if you're following the same car from the break-in. I can't call it in based on a hunch."

"Trust me—it's the same car." Emily was emphatic. "But we don't want to spook them."

After driving through four more traffic lights, the road cleared and the area became less developed. Emily had dropped a few cars behind but got nervous about losing the target.

"I'm south of the main business area, heading towards Edgewood. Wait, they're changing lanes."

"Can you see the name of a cross street or a business?"

"No, I passed an orange grove on the left. There are no signs." Within minutes, Emily approached the next intersection. "They're turning right on Catcher Road, and I see a billboard for Alabaster Acres."

"I know that place. It's an oyster farm on the back bay. I think it's open to the public. You've gone far enough. It's time to back off."

"Where's Mike?"

"He'll be there soon. His lights and siren are on to clear traffic, but he'll turn them off when he gets close. If you see the car turn into a residential neighborhood, do not follow them. Don't risk it."

"What else is around here? All I can see are a few homes and some orchards."

"Let me check." After less than a minute, Duncan came back on the line. "Dead-end roads on the left back onto canals leading out to the bay. To the right, it's mostly farmland."

"I just passed Alabaster Acres. Wait, they're turning left. It's about a half mile past the oyster farm."

"Turn around and wait for Mike."

"But what if we lose them? I'm so close to finding out who's behind this."

"Emily." Duncan never called her by her full name, and it didn't go unnoticed. "Wait for Mike."

For a split second, she considered pulling onto the shoulder of the road, but changed her mind. It was a good thing too, since she would have missed the car turning into a driveway.

Emily decreased her speed as she contemplated whether to risk a drive-by. The small cul-de-sac would allow her to turn around without stopping, in case she had to leave in haste, so she went for it. After passing the first house, water views of the bay opened on both sides. All the homes had private docks in their backyards, with direct water access. As Emily approached the suspect's property, she sped up to avoid suspicion, driving past as if her destination was farther down the road.

"Mike is less than five minutes away," Duncan said.

She saw the suspect's car parked behind a ranch house that appeared to be deserted with its overgrown yard. She turned around and pulled to a stop in front of a neighbor's house before dropping a pin to the location on her phone and sending it to both Duncan and Mike.

"I told you to wait at the farm," Duncan said, after receiving her message.

"The car's in the driveway, but I can't see anyone." Already knowing what he would say, she quickly added, "I'll call you right back," then hung up. Mike would be arriving any minute, which emboldened Emily to check things out on foot.

A row of trees along the border of the property provided enough cover for her to see the side door and into the backyard. Emily inched closer until someone bolted from the back of the house toward the water, forcing her to drop to the ground behind a large bush. Since peeking through the branches offered no view, she contemplated moving closer, but a little voice inside told her to stay put. Engines roaring to life prompted Emily to stand, but it was too late as she watched the boat pull away from the dock. "Crap."

Unsure if anyone else was inside the house, she took a chance and ran toward the water, hoping to identify the driver. The boat reached the end of the canal and turned toward the back bay. "Double crap." They were getting away.

The sound of an approaching car forced Emily to run for cover along the tree line until she reached the front yard. Once she saw it was Mike's car, she waved her arms to get his attention. He screeched to a stop before jumping out.

"Are you okay?" he shouted.

"I'm fine," she said after running to meet him. She grabbed his hand, pulling him toward the dock. "They're getting away by boat." She led Mike into the backyard and pointed toward the departing vessel. "Is there a police marine unit that can go after them?"

Mike turned her to face him. "Breathe, Em."

"But we have to stop him." Frustration and adrenalin collided, threatening to overwhelm her. Mike's calm energy helped soothe her rising panic. He took both her hands into his, forcing her to look at him. "Okay, I'll breathe."

"So, there's only one guy driving the boat?" he asked.

"Yes, but I didn't see his face."

"I'll check to see what resources we have in the area."

Emily nodded as she attempted to gain control over her emotions.

Mike stepped away to speak in private. When he returned, he said, "Backup is on the way. Will you stay in my car while I check things out?"

Emily gave him a look, communicating her intent to follow him during the search. "I won't get in the way, and I'll stay close."

Mike tilted his head and squinted at her, as if assessing her credulity. "I need to confirm the license plate number. If it's a match to Colt's girlfriend's car, I can get a search warrant for the property and the house." They walked to the driveway, and Mike used his phone camera to capture the plate details. It was a match. He sent the picture to Duncan so he could get to work on the warrant.

"Em, I'm going to knock on the front door. I need you to stay in the car for a minute. I can't concentrate on my job if I'm worried about you."

She didn't want to risk anyone's safety, especially Mike's, so she held back. After repeated authoritative knocks at the door went unanswered, he returned to wait in his car with Emily.

"Did you see a name on the boat?" he asked.

"No, it was too far away. It's one of those sport fishing boats with a canopy in the middle and two outboard engines. I'll search on my phone to see if I can find a picture that looks similar. It looked new."

"Good idea." Mike read a text from Duncan. "The property is owned by a Sandra Bleecher. Does that name ring a bell?"

"Nope. Never heard of her. Did he say anything about looking for the boat? Isn't there a Coast Guard station nearby?"

"That would be jumping the gun—we need more evidence. Sorry, Em. I know you're worried about Anthony, Marc, and Tiki."

"And Marilyn. Where is she?" Emily spoke to no one in particular and didn't expect Mike to answer.

"We asked for support from the Florida Department of Law Enforcement. The media attention elevated the profile of this case. The FDLE has additional resources to help with the investigation, since the treasure hunt involves multiple counties across the state."

"What about the FBI? Can't they help too?"

"They'll get involved in kidnapping cases, but until there's a ransom demand, we're treating this as a missing person case. That may change though."

Emily rested her head on the seat back and closed her eyes. How did all of this fit together? Evidence of Dylan Colt's girlfriend's car on the hospital security video and again at Anthony and Marc's place had been the only connection between Colt's murder and subsequent attempts to get to Tiki. With Colt in the morgue, who's driving the car? It had to be Chad. Was he Colt's partner, or his murderer, or both? Emily's gut told her Chad, definitely not an innocent bystander, was the top suspect in Tiki's attempted abductions. She opened her eyes to find Mike staring at her. "What?" she asked.

"You're beautiful when you're crime solving." He smiled, then took her hand in his and kissed it. "Your instincts are always spot-on. What are you thinking?"

"What's the connection between Colt and Chad Peña? The person driving away in the boat fit the general physical description of Chad the Third."

"Chad the Third?" Mike asked.

"That's what Anthony calls him. He's Chad Michael Peña, the Third. We read it on his driver's license when he tried to pick Tiki up from the hospital."

"So far, we haven't been able to figure out the origins of their relationship. Colt's a low-level career criminal, and Peña's a washed-up frat boy living off his family's money. They run in different circles."

"There has to be a connection somewhere," Emily said, then turned her attention back to her internet search for photos of fishing boats. She scrolled through images until she saw one that looked like a match. "Here." She handed Mike her phone. "I'm pretty sure this is the boat. A twenty-eight-foot Boston Whaler."

Mike whistled. "She's a beauty. Expensive, too. There's no way Colt, or Chad for that matter, could afford one of these." His phone rang. "It's Duncan." Mike listened for a few minutes, interjecting occasionally to ask questions before hanging up.

"He's on his way with the warrant. Sandra Bleecher is Dylan Colt's maternal grandmother. She died two months ago after a long battle with cancer, and Colt was her only living relative. She died without a will, so the estate is in probate. Colt must have been staying here."

"That still doesn't tell us who's been driving the car and using his grandmother's boat dock."

"No, but the warrant covers the car and the house. This is a big break, Em."

She should have been elated but none of it lessened her sense of urgency for finding Marilyn and dealing with Tiki's long-term needs. The clock was ticking.

CHAPTER EIGHTEEN

It took Duncan over an hour to get the search warrant. Under normal circumstances, it would be excruciating for Emily to wait before taking action. Not this time. Sitting alone with Mike gave them an opportunity to talk. They both wanted to make up for lost time and confirmed their plans for Saturday night.

Duncan arrived, followed by an officer from the sheriff's department. Emily stood back from the group, but eavesdropped on their discussion. She hoped they wouldn't notice when she followed them inside—but no chance of that happening.

"Em, you'll need to stay here so we can execute the search," Duncan said. Before she replied, he added, "It's not negotiable," and walked with the officer to the front door.

Mike turned to her. "There are protocols to follow. I'll be back as soon as we're done." He ran to catch up.

Emily owed Anthony an update, so she returned to her own car to make the call.

"Is everything okay? I'm struggling to keep it together over here. I should have been with you."

"You don't have to worry. I'm fine. Mike and Duncan are here."

Anthony shouted to Marc, who had rushed home when Emily began her pursuit of the car outside their townhome. "She's safe."

"I did it. I tailed the car to a house in Edgewood, but unfortunately, the driver got away by boat."

"That's disappointing. Great job, though. But, one more thing—can you promise me to never do that again? Seriously, Em. Duncan was beside himself when I called him."

"I didn't have a choice unless I wanted them to get away."

"I know, but still. It's so dangerous. How would you feel if Duncan showed up at the hospital and tried to help you with a surgery? You wouldn't be happy about it. It's the same thing."

Emily had never thought about it that way. Anthony always said the right thing to bring clarity to any situation.

"There's one important distinction. Neither of us asked to be involved in this case. After being thrown in the middle of it, we've had to deal with all the consequences. Between the growing mob at work and caring for Tiki—that's all on us."

"So, what's happening now?" Anthony asked, changing the subject. "I'm putting you on speaker so Marc can hear."

Emily updated them both on her pursuit, finding Colt's grandmother's house, and the getaway boat. "I'd bet money the person I followed was Chad."

"Chad the Third? Marilyn's useless nephew?" Marc asked.

Emily laughed at his description. "Yes, him. I'm staying here until Mike and Duncan finish their search. Wait—a tow truck just pulled up to the house." An officer walked outside to confer with the driver.

"I bet they're going to take the car back to the crime lab," Anthony said.

"Coral Shores has a crime lab?" Marc asked.

"I don't know. I just assume they do. That's what happens on TV shows." Anthony and Marc continued conversing about their favorite CSI crime drama as if Emily wasn't on the other end of the line. She enjoyed listening to their exchange before reinserting herself into the conversation.

"How's Tiki doing?"

"Did you tell her?" Marc asked.

"Tell me what."

Anthony spoke up. "After you told me to check Tiki's aviary, I inspected every square inch, inside and out, and I found an opening in the screen. The precision cut had to be made with wire cutters. I know it wasn't there when we built the structure for him."

"Whoever I followed must have been trying to break-in. Or they were creating an opening and planned to come back after dark. I'm glad you left work early."

"Me, too."

"When you called, I was about to leave for the hardware store. I can fix the screen, and I'm going to buy a few motion-activated outdoor flood lights. If anyone tries to sneak behind the bushes next to Tiki's house, they'll be lit up like a Christmas tree," Marc said.

"And we're going to sleep next to the porch in shifts tonight," Anthony added. "Nobody is getting anywhere near him. Not on our watch."

Emily was grateful to be part of the team, like the Three Musketeers. They had power in numbers, especially when they were unsure about what they were up against.

"I can help with the overnight shifts," she said. "You don't have to handle this all on your own."

"Thanks, Em," Anthony said. "You've had a big night already, and it's still not over. Go home to Bella and try to get some rest. You'll be doing double duty tomorrow at work since I'm staying home with Tiki."

"I'll be home tomorrow, too. In case you need Anthony's help for anything," Marc said.

"Thanks, guys. Oh, wait. Duncan's coming out of the house. I'll call you back."

• • •

As he approached, Duncan looked relaxed. She hoped that meant he forgave her for disregarding his instructions. Since there were no signs of strain on his face, she also assumed Marilyn's body was not inside the house, and she exhaled.

"What's happening?" she asked.

Duncan held her stare for a few long seconds before answering. "You and I need to have a talk about a few things, but not now."

Emily started to say something, then caught herself, opting for silence. He was right, not tonight. "I know we do. What did you find inside?"

"The house is empty, but there's evidence someone was held against their will." He pulled his phone from his pocket. "One bedroom door had been bolted shut using two heavy-duty locks mounted on the outside."

"Oh." Emily looked at the picture and agreed the locks had only one purpose—to keep someone trapped inside the room.

"We think they held Marilyn here."

"How can you tell?" Duncan flipped through additional images, then handed her the phone. Scrawled in red was the word *CHAD*. "Where was this?"

"Inside the locked room, behind a painting mounted on the wall."

Her head spun. "But what does it mean?"

"Whoever wrote this was trying to send a message or hide a clue. The kitchen is stocked with fresh food, which means someone's been staying there after Colt's murder. We called the crime scene unit, and they'll be here soon. The car will be moved to the lab for processing."

"Why are you telling me all this? I thought I was in the proverbial dog house after following the car."

"You'll have to thank Mike for that. He made me realize you were doing what any of us would have done. I know I can be overprotective sometimes—"

"Sometimes?" Emily smiled.

"Okay, most of the time. I can't help it. If anything happened to you, I'd never forgive myself." Duncan turned away to compose himself.

He'd taken on the role of her protector ever since their mom died. She understood they were each processing their grief in different ways, and she needed to be more understanding when he acted like this since it came from a place of love.

"And I promise I'll never put myself or anyone else in danger."

"It's not always that simple, Em. Things can turn for the worse in an instant."

She updated him about the tampered porch screen at Anthony and Marc's place, but stopped mid-sentence when she had an epiphany. "Can you show me that last picture again?" Duncan opened his phone for Emily to scrutinize the image. "This looks like the same red color of Tiki's tail feathers. Was this written in lipstick?"

"It's possible, but I'm no expert."

"Is there a chance I can go inside to see it up close?"

"Why?"

"When Marilyn brought Tiki Lulu to the vet hospital, she wore a shade of red lipstick that had to be custom made. It was a perfect color match to Tiki's tail feathers. She wore the same lipstick in all the videos—it's her signature color."

"Aren't all red lipsticks basically the same?" Duncan asked.

"Absolutely not. Trust me. Anthony and I noticed her lipstick shade that first day."

"Okay, give me a minute." He went into the house, likely to confer with Mike, and when he returned, he said, "The crime scene team will be here soon. Once they're done collecting evidence, you can put on protective gear and go inside. Promise me you won't touch anything and you'll follow all my instructions."

"I promise."

Emily waited alone outside while the forensic team came and went from the house, carrying bags of evidence. Mike spoke with the lead CSI technician before he turned and walked toward her, with gear in hand.

"Great catch about the lipstick. If you can put on the coveralls and gear, I'll take you inside. Duncan's getting the team started on processing the car so the tow truck driver can move it to the police garage."

Emily pulled on the white jumpsuit, booties, and gloves, transforming into a billowy marshmallow. "Don't even," she said, forcing Mike to stifle a laugh.

"I'm trying," he said. "Let's go."

Emily followed him into the house. The air closed in around her, but it might have been the effect of wearing a jumpsuit on a sticky, hot Florida evening. The décor matched that of an older lady. Floral patterned arm chairs and curio cabinets full of figurines were visible in the living room. The tidy kitchen had been well maintained, but dated by its avocado green appliances and linoleum flooring. Mike led her down a hallway, past a bathroom and a small bedroom. After reaching the end of the hall and seeing the two deadbolt locks, she fought hard to avoid retching on the crime scene. Emily took a deep breath before entering the room, mindful to avoid touching anything on her way inside.

"During our search, I noticed a crooked painting." Mike walked over to the painting and, with gloved hands, lifted it from the wall. Written in block letters on the peeling wallpaper was the name *CHAD*.

Emily moved closer to examine the evidence before speaking. "That's it. That's Marilyn's lipstick."

"How can you be sure?" Mike asked.

"It's such a distinct shade of red. If Tiki were here, you'd see for yourself—it's an exact match to his red tail feathers."

"Okay. The crime scene techs will analyze the substance used to write the letters."

"I'll check with Anthony, but Marilyn may have filled out some paperwork when she admitted Tiki for boarding after her appointment at the hospital that day. Can you use that to compare the handwriting to this clue?"

"We can if we need confirmation. We also have handwriting samples from the papers we collected at her house." Mike led her out of the room.

Emily struggled to contain her emotions as she stepped into the front yard. The jumpsuit felt like a straightjacket as she frantically pulled off the protective gear. Once she was free, she bent at the waist, resting her hands on her knees as a sob escaped her lungs. It became impossible to contain the overwhelming wave of emotions after finding proof Marilyn had been alive in this house. Even though she never admitted it out loud, Emily wondered if she'd been murdered on the same day Anthony found Dylan Colt's body, then dumped somewhere deep in the Everglades, never to be found. Mike moved next to her, resting his hand on her back.

"Em, are you all right?" he asked.

She stood up and wiped her face with the jumpsuit she held in her hand and nodded. "That horrible room made me think about how scared she must be. I can't even imagine what she's been through. And to have the wherewithal to leave us a clue. She's a tough lady. And smart."

"She's all those things," Mike said.

"Where is she now? What if the kidnapper panics?" Duncan joined them on the front lawn. "It's her, Duncan. I know it."

He acknowledged her declaration with a nod. "We're doing everything in our power to find her. We'll be here late, so why don't you go home. I'll check on you when we're done," he said. "And, Em. It's because of you we have all this evidence. We're that much closer to finding Marilyn and catching the murderer. You did good." He patted her shoulder, then turned to walk back into the house.

Emily was speechless. Being included in the investigation signified a big breakthrough, but more importantly, her brother trusted her instincts and appreciated her help. Mike smiled, then wrapped his arm around her shoulder as he walked her to her car. Harmony in the Benton family was good for everyone.

CHAPTER NINETEEN

The adrenalin surge Emily experienced during her pursuit of Colt's girlfriend's car, followed by the discovery of Marilyn's captivity, had waned. Her defenses cracked, leaving behind only sadness and anger. Under normal circumstances, she would reach out to Anthony for friendship and support, but he was bearing the full burden of Tiki's care, and she didn't want to add her issues to his list. But then again, she owed him a phone call.

"Em, we've been waiting to hear from you. Where are you?"

"I'm driving home. I have some good news and some bad news." She heard Anthony inhale, preparing for the worst.

"Duncan and Mike found proof inside the house that Marilyn had been held there.

"Oh no. Wait, is that the good news or the bad news?" he asked.

"It's the good news. We know she's alive—or was alive. The bad news is we don't know where they took her. They let me go inside the house, and I know I'm an amateur, but I didn't see anything resembling a struggle or a crime scene."

"What makes them think Marilyn had been there?"

"Well, there were two deadbolt locks on the outside of a door to a bedroom. On the wall of that same room, behind a painting, they found the name *CHAD* written in red lipstick. In her red lipstick," Emily said with the emphasis on *her*.

"Oh, wow. That's so smart. I knew it was him. Spineless creep."

"Duncan cautioned me about jumping to conclusions. Just because Chad's name is on the wall doesn't mean he's the bad guy. She might've wanted the police to find him. Maybe he's in trouble, too."

"But why would Tiki shout out his name if it wasn't Chad sneaking around our house?"

"Good point. It surprised me that the kidnapper would let her keep any belongings, but then I got to thinking. My nan always put her lipstick inside her bra if she didn't have access to her purse. She went nowhere without it. What if Marilyn did the same thing?"

"Yes, I remember my auntie doing that, too. So, what's next?"

"I don't know. I'm sure the forensics lab will be busy processing all the evidence from the house and the car, but I feel Mike and Duncan are holding back some information. They kept walking off to talk in private. This investigation may be further along than we thought."

"Marc asked if you want me to come over. He said he can handle Tiki over-watch by himself."

"Aww. That's sweet, but I'm okay. I think we're all safe tonight. No one would risk coming back to your house, not after their daring escape on the water."

"You might be right, but I won't let my guard down. If they're desperate, it makes them dangerous."

That thought lingered as they said good night. Emily pulled into her driveway, grateful to be home. As soon as she walked into her cottage, Bella meowed at her in rapid succession, then ran to the kitchen.

"I'm sorry, sweet girl." Despite her own hunger, Emily fed Bella first. There would be no peace until her very bossy cat was satiated. Opting for a fast meal, she popped a frozen entrée into the microwave, then poured herself a glass of wine.

After one of the longest weeks of her life, she still had to get through Saturday without Anthony by her side. She doubted whether he or Marc would get much sleep since they were on edge after the events of the day. At least Anthony could stay home tomorrow and regroup.

Strings of lights filled the beach deck with a soft glow. A gentle, tropical breeze had replaced the oppressive morning air, making it a comfortable place to finish her day. Bella announced herself with a demure cooing sound, prompting Emily to scoot over. Her gentle purr, combined with the sound of the surf breaking onshore, became the perfect antidote after a stressful day.

Emily struggled to stay awake. In a preemptive move, she texted Duncan and Mike to let them know she was home and heading to bed. They would be working until late in the night, and she didn't want them concerned when she failed to answer their calls.

"Come on." Emily prompted Bella to follow her inside. "Time for bed." It wasn't long before vet and cat were sound asleep.

• • •

The early morning sun streamed into the bedroom, nudging Emily awake. Recharged after a nine-hour sleep, she could survive a short day at work. Bella slept on her favorite pillow at the head of the bed, but as soon as she sensed movement, she was up and ready to eat. As Bella enjoyed her seafood medley, Emily poured a cup of coffee and climbed back in bed, taking a moment to transition into her day. After a few sips to clear the cobwebs, she turned on the TV.

"...Coming up next, breaking news in the missing person investigation of Marilyn Peña and her beloved parrot, Tiki Lulu. Stay tuned to Channel 2 News."

That was fast. Hoping he might be awake, she texted Anthony to turn on the TV so they could watch the news together. Before the end of the commercial break, he called. "Have you heard from Duncan or Mike?"

"No, but I crashed right after getting home. I assume everything was quiet with Tiki. No more trespassers?"

"Totally uneventful, but we still slept in shifts," he said as the news broadcast resumed.

Marilyn's missing person case had escalated to a kidnapping, and the police were asking for the public's help to find her. Multiple law enforcement agencies, including a spokeswoman from the FBI, held an early morning press conference outside the Sheriff's office. Emily saw both Duncan and Mike standing with the group behind the podium. They looked tired.

"Em, I think I should come to work today. The super fans will be in overdrive after this news breaks."

"The police will be there to deal with the crowd outside, and I can stay inside the hospital, in our little bubble. I have a feeling it will be quiet, anyway."

"Will you promise to ask for help if you need it? I'm only a few minutes away."

"I will."

• • •

Navigating the hospital parking lot took some care since the news vans, vendors, and paparazzi dressed in parrot paraphernalia expanded to fill the lots of the neighboring businesses. The police were on scene, providing a calming presence. Driving slowly through the area, Emily saw the original group standing together, flying flags featuring a picture of Tiki Lulu. That didn't take long. Tiki merchandise was everywhere.

Once again, Mr. Freaky stood alone on the outskirts of the activity, under the coconut palm. Even from a distance, his drawn appearance concerned her. After last night's break in the case, Emily found it hard to believe he had any involvement with Marilyn's kidnapping based on his age and frail appearance. *But who was he, and why was he here?* she wondered.

She moved the temporary barricade used to block access to the back of the hospital, then parked next to the door before darting inside. Once she settled at her desk, Emily texted Duncan and Mike—eager for any news after the search of Colt's grandmother's house and the car. Only an hour had passed since the press conference, so she didn't expect to hear from either of them right away.

"Morning, Dr. Benton." Abigail was the first employee to arrive at work. Her handling of the clients and the chaos over the past week helped maintain normal hospital operations. Without being asked, she picked up extra shifts to manage the foot traffic and phone calls. Emily made a mental note to talk with Anthony about giving her a bonus in her next paycheck. A small token to recognize her commitment and hard work. "I checked the messages, and there were a few more cancelations."

"I figured that would happen." The news coverage about Marilyn's abduction changed things—scaring away clients who may have been curious at first but were now growing concerned. Emily kept last night's car chase to herself for now.

"We received an urgent appointment request, and I've scheduled it first thing," Abigail said. "It sounds like Moose Englewood may have a hotspot."

That did not surprise Emily, since Moose, a happy, healthy chocolate lab with an active lifestyle, was a frequent patient. His last visit turned into a surgical emergency to remove a fishing hook from his upper lip. Emily loved seeing Moose, so it was a perfect way to start her day.

• • •

Hotspots weren't serious, but they flared up quickly, becoming painful and itchy. Despite the extensive area of inflamed and infected skin on Moose's left chest and leg area, he wagged his tail and showed off all his tricks to earn treats after she walked into the exam room.

"I swear, Dr. Benton. It wasn't there yesterday. It looks bad." Mr. Englewood's face tightened as he looked down, shaking his head. "Neither of us got any sleep last night. Not with all his licking and scratching."

"Moisture on the skin is often the cause, and hotspots occur suddenly. Has he been swimming lately?" Emily asked.

"Daily. We've been out fishing, and he loves to jump in the ocean off the back of the boat. His hair is so thick, he takes all day to dry."

Emily nodded. "That will do it. The most important thing is to shave the entire area so the infected skin can stay open to the air. He'll need medicine for the next week and an Elizabethan collar to keep him from licking."

"Oh, no, not the cone. He hates that."

"In a couple of days, his hot spot will be healing and dry. You can take his collar off as long as you're around to watch him. If he licks, you'll have to put it back on and try again the next day. Keep him out of the water this next week, and in the future, towel dry him after he swims to make sure you get all the moisture out of his fur."

"Will do. And thanks for fitting us in on short notice. I can see you have your hands full with the antics going on in the parking lot. I've been following the story on the news. I hope they find that Marilyn lady soon."

"So do we, Mr. Englewood. I'm going to borrow Moose for a few minutes. We'll meet you in the lobby when we're done."

Moose bounced his way to the treatment area of the hospital. Wounds were always larger than at first glance, but Moose was a trouper as Catrinna clipped, then cleaned the hotspot. Fitting him for his cone collar became a little more challenging. He kept walking into cabinets and door frames on his way back to the lobby. They assured Mr. Englewood that Moose would get better at navigating with the cone.

Soon after the Englewoods left the hospital, the leader of the super fans came running in the front door, waving his arms wildly. "Help! Help! We need a doctor," he shouted, motioning for them to follow before running back into the parking lot. Emily and Catrinna didn't hesitate for a second before racing after him, knowing emergencies often require care to be provided in an owner's car, especially if an injury or illness limits the pet's ability to walk.

CHAPTER TWENTY

Emily scanned the parking lot for a frantic pet owner as she followed the paparazzi leader toward the large coconut palm tree. When Emily and Catrinna caught up to him, prepared to help a cat or dog in need, it shocked them to see a group of people gathered around Mr. Freaky, who lay unconscious on the ground. His pale face looked gray-white.

"I'm a veterinarian," Emily said to the super fan who had summoned them, as she bent down next to Mr. Freaky to check for a pulse. It was weak and thready. His respirations were shallow but stable, and his skin was hot to touch.

"I know, but you're the only doctor here. We called 911."

When Mr. Freaky collapsed, he fell away from the shade of the palm tree and into full sun.

"What's your name?" Emily asked the paparazzi leader.

"Franklin."

"Okay, Franklin. I need your help. Can you move your tent over here to provide him with some shade? Gather something we can use to prop up his feet. I need a towel and a bottle of cold water." Emily turned to the crowd at large. "Does anyone know this man?" They all shook their heads *no*.

She checked his left wrist for a medic alert bracelet, but his right arm rested behind his back. As she gently pulled it forward, she bumped against the wallet in his back pocket. Uncertain about the protocol for invading his privacy under these circumstances, she pulled it out. The EMTs would need his identity. Archibald Sherman, aka Mr. Freaky, was eighty years old, and according to the address on his driver's license, he lived nearby.

Franklin returned with all of Emily's requested items and took charge, moving to protect Mr. Sherman from the elements. Catrinna elevated his feet while Emily used the cooling towel on his neck and head. She didn't know if this was a cardiac event or some other medical emergency, but it wasn't a stretch to assume dehydration and heat stroke could be a factor after standing vigil for days in the hot, humid Florida weather.

As sirens approached, Mr. Sherman blinked. He appeared to be regaining consciousness.

"Mr. Sherman, help is on the way," Emily said.

He attempted to sit up but was unsuccessful. Emily caught his head and shoulders before they fell back to the ground.

"Where am I?" His weakened voice made him barely audible.

Emily held his hand and spoke in a calm, gentle tone. "You're at the veterinary hospital. You must have fainted. Just rest until the ambulance gets here."

His lips moved, forcing Emily to lean closer to hear him. "Dr. Benton. Is Tiki safe?"

The surprise at hearing her name caused her to sit back, and while she decided how to answer, the ambulance and a police car arrived. Franklin cleared a path for the vehicles to pull up next to Mr. Sherman. As soon as the EMTs were at his side, she stepped away.

The officer assigned crowd control duties had left the parking lot after being dispatched to a more pressing call, but returned in response to Franklin's 911 emergency. Officer Sandra Garcia, the police woman Emily met on the night of the hospital break-in, walked toward the group of spectators, taking charge as she moved them back a respectable distance. After acknowledging Emily with a nod, she joined the EMTs, who lifted Mr. Sherman onto a stretcher. They hooked him up to monitoring equipment and started IV fluids. Emily thought his color already improved with their supportive care. After being loaded in the back of the ambulance, he offered Emily a weak smile.

"Okay, people. There's nothing left to see here," Officer Garcia said, forcing the crowd to disperse to their previous posts at food trucks, merch tables, and lawn chairs. Since Mr. Sherman's emergency hadn't scared them off, Emily was certain they were here for the long haul.

"We better go back inside now," Catrinna said. "I think I saw Mrs. Alonso arrive. She has an appointment for Cookie's suture removal."

"Sure. Thanks for all your help just now. That was scary," Emily said as they walked toward the hospital.

"My hands were shaking at first, but then I saw how calm you were. I've never dealt with a human emergency before. What happened to him?" Catrinna asked.

"No idea. I'll try to get an update from the hospital before we close."

Abigail opened the door for them. "I was so worried it was one of our patients until a paparazzi person told me a man fainted. Is he okay?"

"Yes, thanks to Dr. Benton." Catrinna smiled.

"The EMTs are taking him to get the care he needs," Emily said.

"That's terrible. I hope he'll be all right," then she handed Emily a medical record. "Cookie is in room one waiting for you. Mrs. Alonso wanted you to check the incision to make sure it's one hundred percent healed. That's what she told me—it has to be one hundred percent or she would keep worrying."

It would be an understatement to label Mrs. Alonso as a very concerned pet parent. If Cookie sneezed once, Mrs. Alonso scheduled a checkup. An unintended outcome of all those vet visits was Cookie, an adorable, senior toy poodle, loved coming to the hospital. Unlike many dogs and cats, who were fearful of going to the vet, Cookie viewed the visit as a play date.

During Cookie's recent dental cleaning, Emily removed a small cyst-like mass, the size of a pencil eraser, from the skin of her front leg. It looked like a benign lump common in older dogs. Mrs. Alonso called every day after surgery for the results even though Emily told her the biopsy took three to five days to come back from the pathology lab. As soon as the report had been completed, Emily shared the good news. The tiny, benign mass was not a cancer, and after being fully removed, no further treatment was needed. To express her elation, Mrs. Alonso sent the hospital a big box of gourmet chocolate chip cookies with a thank-you card from Cookie.

Catrinna carried the affectionate poodle to the treatment area, receiving a face-full of dog kisses along the way. After the stitches were removed, Emily reassured Mrs. Alonso that Cookie's half-inch incision met her threshold of being one hundred percent healed. It became even more challenging to convince her the hair would grow back, and there would be no visible scar.

"Thank you, Dr. Benton. Cookie means everything to me. She needs to be okay, or better than okay."

"I understand. I feel the same way about my cat, Bella."

Cookie pranced back into the exam room with Catrinna holding her leash. "As usual, Cookie wins the prize for best patient of the day." Mrs. Alonso beamed with pride as they returned to the lobby.

• • •

Saturdays were usually the busiest day of the week, despite closing at noon. Condensing a full day's work into a half-day schedule was challenging. But not today. Clients who were nervous about the continued media circus outside canceled their pets' routine medical appointments, causing a negative impact on hospital operations.

Emily updated Anthony on Mr. Sherman's medical emergency. At least now he could stop calling him Mr. Freaky. She tried twice to call Duncan but ended up sending a text. It should be a straightforward task to look into Archibald Sherman now that they knew his name. She couldn't imagine this frail man had anything to do with the case. There had to be an innocent explanation for his continued presence at the hospital.

"Dr. Benton, I'm getting ready to leave and wondered if you spoke with anyone at the hospital about Mr. Sherman?" Catrinna and Abigail appeared together outside Emily's office.

"No, but I'll call them now."

She introduced herself as Dr. Emily Benton in order to get an update on Mr. Sherman's status, but failed to mention she was a veterinarian. The nurse confirmed his admission to the hospital in stable condition, but any other details would have to come directly from his attending physician. Visitors were welcome. Emily advised she would call back since she wanted to get off the phone before they figured out she was a Doctor of Veterinary Medicine, not a "people" doctor.

"Thanks," Catrinna said. "We thought something terrible happened to him. I feel better now. Do you need anything before we leave?"

"No. Thank you both for everything. I know this week hasn't been easy, and I appreciate all your help."

• • •

Once the hospital became quiet, Emily had a moment to think. Duncan was too busy or not interested in pursuing Mr. Sherman's background check, and while she was tempted to ask Mike for help, she didn't want to pull either of them away from focusing on the case. Marilyn took top priority, but she was tired of waiting. Since she had rendered first aid to Mr. Sherman, it would be natural to check up on him in the hospital. Any kind-hearted citizen would be concerned. His weakened condition eliminated him as a physical threat, but she thought it would be wise to bring a witness to corroborate their conversation. Emily had only one partner in crime, so she called to invite Anthony to join her.

"I'm in," he said after Emily updated him in on her plan. "Marc can stay here with Tiki."

"Great. I'll pick you up in fifteen minutes."

• • •

They didn't know what to expect after checking in at the visitor's desk on Mr. Sherman's floor. A nurse told them he finished his lunch and had a great appetite. She instructed them to keep their visit short since he needed his rest.

Emily and Anthony tiptoed into his room. The partially drawn curtain provided some privacy, but they could see Mr. Sherman sitting up in bed using headphones to watch a show.

"Oh, Dr. Benton. Hello." He removed his headphones and turned off the TV.

"Hi, Mr. Sherman. My name is Anthony. I work at the veterinary hospital with Dr. Benton."

"Nice to meet you, Anthony. Please call me Archie. I've seen you outside talking with Tiki's friends."

"We were worried about you and wanted to see how you're doing. Is there anything you need?" Emily asked.

"Oh, I'm a little embarrassed. Thank you for helping me earlier. The doctor told me I fainted from dehydration. I guess the heat got to me. My wife would have scolded me for being so careless."

"Is your wife here, or do you want us to call her for you?" Anthony asked.

Archie lowered his gaze, and he seemed to drift off in thought.

Emily and Anthony shared a confused look, uncertain what to say next since he declined to answer their question. Emily got right to the point. "Mr. Sherman, do you mind me asking why you come to the hospital every day? You don't appear to be with the social media followers camped out in our parking lot."

Archie wiped away a tear, cleared his voice, then looked them both squarely in the eye. "My wife of fifty-eight years passed away in February. Margaret and I were high school sweethearts." Archie smiled, as if recalling some happy memory. "The only reason I survived these past few months was because of our beloved African Grey parrot, Bonkers. We hand-raised Bonkers as a chick, and he was the joy of our lives."

"We're so sorry about Margaret. I'm sure it's been hard." Anthony's voice cracked as he struggled to control his own emotions.

"I thought I was handling things okay on my own. That is until Bonkers died."

Emily gasped. Dealing with such a profound, back-to-back loss was too sad to contemplate. When the death of a pet followed the death of another family member, the grief often magnified exponentially.

"How old was Bonkers?" Anthony asked.

"He was fifty-five years old. His birthday would have been last Monday. We adopted him after Margaret and I learned we weren't able to have our own family. He was our boy." Archie wiped away another tear.

Saying, "I'm sorry," seemed inadequate, but that's all they could offer.

"Do you have any pictures of Margaret and Bonkers?" Anthony asked.

"Oh, yes." Archie turned to his bedside table and opened the drawer. He pulled three photos from a pocket in his wallet. "This is Margaret and me on our fiftieth wedding anniversary. This is Bonkers in his aviary, and this is one of the three of us together."

Emily looked at the pictures, then passed them to Anthony. Bonkers was the spitting image of Tiki Lulu. Archie's presence at the hospital now made sense.

"Is that why you come every day? Were you hoping to get a look at Tiki Lulu?" Emily asked.

"I'm not sure what I thought would happen. I saw the story about Tiki on the local TV news, and he looked exactly like Bonkers. I've been so lonely. I just needed to be there. All those other people who love Tiki Lulu made me feel connected to something again. And the thought of him being without Marilyn, his best friend—I didn't know if he was grieving, too. I realize it's not logical."

"It's perfectly logical," Anthony said, then smiled as he returned the photos. "The only part I don't understand is why you stopped taking care of yourself."

"My doctor and the nurses have read me the riot act, and I know better. I won't let this happen again."

"You need time to rest and regain your strength. If we see you there next week, you better have a water bottle in your hand," Emily said.

He nodded in agreement. "There is one thing you can do for me. Can you tell me if Tiki is safe?"

Anthony exchanged a look with Emily, confirming it was the right time to divulge some details. "Tiki's doing great," he said. "We're caring for him, and he's eating well and talking up a storm. I can tell he misses Marilyn, but so far, we're able to keep him entertained."

Archie smiled for the first time. "That's the very best news. I can rest now that I know he's okay. Thank you for that." His eyes closed, which was their cue to leave. Archie's story was both heartbreaking and heartwarming. Emily and Anthony had done their good deed for the day, happily removing Archie from their suspect list.

CHAPTER TWENTY-ONE

"Marc sent me a grocery list. He wants to cook for you tonight," Anthony said as they drove out of the hospital parking lot.

Knowing Marc's reputation as an outstanding home chef made turning down his offer more difficult. "Oh, no. I can't. Mike and I have a date."

"Give me a second." Anthony texted Marc. "He's inviting both of you and wants to include Duncan, Jane, and the kids. We've avoided leaving the house for Tiki's safety, and I think Marc's getting antsy."

The look on Anthony's face made it clear this was important to them. They all had sacrificed, but Marc more than any of them. Emily and Anthony had a built-in obligation to Tiki as his veterinary care team, but Marc had stepped up to build him a beautiful home and took time off work to parrot-sit. If Marc and Anthony wanted her to be there, she planned to show up.

"I'll confirm with Mike, but I'm sure he's flexible. Tell Marc that sounds great. Let me know what I can bring."

"He says, *just yourselves*. Based on the length of his shopping list, I think he has everything covered."

"Is this the first time the two of you have hosted a party since moving in together?"

"Sort of." Anthony shrugged. "One of Marc's coworkers came over for dinner one night when they were working on a project."

Emily nodded, doing her best to play it cool. Hosting their first party as a couple was a big deal, even though Anthony hadn't said so.

"Drop me off at my car instead of the front door. Tiki gets a little worked up when we come and go, so I'll head straight for the grocery store."

Once she was alone in the car, Emily texted Jane with a heads-up. She knew Marc would contact Jane directly, but she wanted to make sure Jane understood the importance of the invite. After sending the message, Emily realized the kids were in their afternoon swim lessons, but she received a thumbs up emoji in reply. They would be there.

Mike was next. It was strange she hadn't heard from him since last night. He usually checked in to confirm their dates. She left him a short voicemail, and when she pulled into her cottage driveway, he called.

"Hi, Em. Sorry I missed you. Are you doing okay after last night?"

"I'm good, just tired. Have there been any big breaks in the case? Any leads on Marilyn?"

"That's why I didn't reach out until now. I can't share the specifics, but a lot is happening, and you can take all the credit for that." Then he changed the subject. "Are you still up for a night out?"

She loved receiving recognition for her amateur police work, even if he kept the latest details to himself. Duncan always discouraged her involvement at every turn, for her own safety, which meant he rarely complimented her when she uncovered a lead or a clue. He avoided emboldening her investigatory activities at all costs.

"About that. Marc and Anthony invited us, Jane, Duncan, and the kids for dinner. They don't want to leave Tiki alone, especially after everything that's happened."

"Sounds perfect to me. Plus, I'm excited about meeting Tiki. I'll pick up a couple bottles of wine. What time is dinner?"

Emily smiled. Mike was the real deal, and she couldn't be happier about the status of their relationship. "Dinner's at seven, not too late for the kids." Mike planned to come by early and spend time with Emily. That left her with a few unscheduled hours—a rare occurrence.

• • •

The ocean had always been Emily's go-to place to clear her mind. Perched on her tree, Bella accepted a few treats before resuming her afternoon nap, allowing Emily to leave the cottage without feeling guilty about abandoning her feline roommate. She grabbed her swim fins, mask, and snorkel and beelined it to the water. The bath-tub warm ocean and flat, calm surf created perfect conditions for a swim along the shoreline.

Emily effortlessly covered a large distance thanks to all the training laps in the pool during high school swim team practice. After making the turn at her midway point, she noticed a stingray cruising through the shallows. It was black and covered with white polka dots—a spotted eagle ray. Even though things looked larger under water, it must have been eight feet wide. To Emily, the majestic ray appeared to be flying. She kept a safe distance and kicked hard to snorkel alongside. When it turned toward deeper water, Emily popped her head up to check her location, then finished her swim with a leisurely stroke.

Moving back to Coral Shores after vet school had been a simple decision when her mom got sick, but during moments like this, Emily realized her good fortune to live near the ocean. Tourists flocked to the area every winter to enjoy the tropical climate, but the natural beauty in and around the water was the real draw for her. Only a few people got to experience the joy of swimming next to a stingray. Her work with sea turtle rescue, including the construction of a new conservation center, fulfilled a childhood dream. She didn't want to live anywhere else.

After drying off, it became too hot to sit in the sun, so she moved into the shade on her beach deck. Bella, now awake from her siesta, joined her on her mom's chair for some undivided attention. Everything else on the to-do list could wait.

• • •

Emily rarely fussed with her hair and make-up, but this counted as a special occasion. Anthony and Marc's first dinner party signified a step forward in their relationship, so she picked a bouquet of hibiscus from her garden to bring as a gift.

Running behind at work, Mike called with an update. "Sorry, Emily. I still have to pick up the wine, but I'll be there soon."

"No worries. We have time." It wasn't like Mike to be late, but she didn't mind, since she assumed it involved Marilyn's case. She turned on the local TV channel to check for any late-breaking news. They replayed the morning story, so she concluded nothing had changed. As the meteorologist wrapped up the weekend weather forecast, Mike pulled into the driveway.

"Hi." He leaned in to kiss her when she opened the door, then took a step back. "You look beautiful."

"Thanks." Her denim sundress, paired with her mother's royal blue flip-flops, were beachy-chic.

"I didn't have time to run home and change. Do you mind if I splash some water on my face before we go?"

"Of course. Come on in."

Bella jumped down from her cat tree to greet Mike. She shamelessly swooned for him. Emily heard her purring as she flopped on her side, allowing him to pet her belly.

"I barely get a side-eye from her when I come home." Emily laughed.

While Mike washed up, Emily grabbed her bouquet to be ready to go. She thought he looked more tired than he did during the morning press conference. Tired or not, he always looked handsome. When he joined her in the kitchen, she handed him a large glass of water, which he drank all at once.

"Thanks. It's been a day."

"You can tell me all about it on the drive over. Let's go."

• • •

It wasn't a surprise when Mike avoided sharing any investigatory details. Emily reminded him she helped to break things wide open in the case, but even then, he declined to comment. As they pulled into the townhouse complex, she dropped the subject for the time being. This evening was all about Marc and Anthony.

"Mike, Em, come on in," Anthony called out. "We're in the kitchen."

"Whatever you're cooking smells great," Mike said as he handed over the wine. Emily found a vase for her flowers, filled it with water, and set it on the table.

"Marc's making his auntie's famous seafood paella. He visited her in Spain during high school, and he's even using an authentic paella pan she sent him from Valencia. I wasn't sure if Mac and Ava would like it, so we made them a kid-friendly meal just in case."

"Hello. Whatcha doing? Hello," Tiki said from his perch.

Anthony handed them each a glass of sangria. "Why don't you visit with Tiki. We're almost finished in here. Em, I talked with Jane, and she's going to bring Elvis. We agreed if having a dog in the house upsets Tiki, she'll take him back home. I thought Tiki might enjoy meeting him."

"We'll find out soon enough," she replied. Elvis loved everyone and everything, but it was an unknown.

Emily sat next to Mike's chair, which was positioned beside Tiki's screened-in porch. Marc and Anthony had created a comfortable seating area that made it easy to interact with the parrot, complete with a TV for his viewing pleasure. Mike became transfixed as he watched Tiki eat an almond. "This is amazing. They built all this?"

Emily smiled when she noticed the additional toys and perches. "Yes, Marc designed it, and they built it together."

Soon after, Jane and Duncan arrived with the kids. Elvis ran to greet Mike and Emily in his usual manner. Lots of spinning and wagging before rolling over for belly rubs. Elvis always looked like he had a smile on his face. Emily held his leash as Mac and Ava instructed their adorable terrier to sit. He obeyed on first command.

"Auntie Em, we've been practicing. Mommy said he has to use all his manners tonight. We don't want him to scare Tiki Lulu," Mac said.

Occupied by the humans in the room, it took Elvis a minute before he noticed Tiki, who had shimmied across his perch to get a closer look.

"Woof. Woof. Woof," Tiki said, mimicking the bark of a dog. Anthony and Marc ran out of the kitchen with their jaws hanging open. Elvis whipped his head around to face the parrot. He stopped wagging his tail and pulled his ears flat to the side of this head. Everyone held their breath, waiting to see what came next. Elvis's ears turned forward, and he began crawling, inching his way next to the aviary, as his tail resumed its happy wag. Dog and bird were instantly enamored with each other.

"Good boy, Elvis." Mac continued to pet his head as Tiki moved down to his lowest perch, now only a few feet away, but still separated by the porch screen. Anthony placed pillows on the floor so the kids could sit next to their dog.

"That went better than I thought it would," Jane said, keeping a close eye on Elvis. Mike stood to give Jane his chair, then joined Duncan in the living room. The two men had their backs turned and were whispering. Emily kept glancing over, straining to catch the odd word.

"Em, let it go. I know you're involved in another murder case, but leave the police work to your brother and Mike. Duncan keeps talking about how the Feds are trying to take the lead in the investigation. It sounds dangerous and serious to me."

"It is, but they keep forgetting I'm wrapped up in all this. Anthony, too. We're going to be forced to decide what to do with Tiki, and it's hard to plan things when they refuse to share the details surrounding Marilyn's abduction."

"I get it, but please be careful."

• • •

When Marc and Anthony emerged from the kitchen, they carried a large metal pan filled with the aromatic paella and set it in the center of the table. "Dinner is served," Marc declared. Anthony motioned for Mac and Ava to follow him into the kitchen. He wanted them to know Marc also made his special homemade mac and cheese with a side of buttery carrots. They decided to try the fancy food first, but seemed relieved to have a backup plan.

After many celebratory toasts, the room became quiet as they savored their meal. Marc received an enthusiastic two thumbs up from almost everyone seated at the table. Mac loved the paella, but Ava picked through her plate with a skeptical look on her face. Anthony snuck away to the kitchen and returned with the mac n cheese, causing Ava's face to light up. Now, it was unanimous. After dinner, the kids returned to watch Tiki, and Emily volunteered to walk Elvis while everyone cleaned up.

Elvis resisted being pulled away from his feathered friend, but once they were outside, he enjoyed all the unfamiliar smells as he led Emily around the outskirts of the townhouse complex. She was preoccupied thinking about what came next for Tiki, which was why she failed to notice a white sedan turn from the side street behind Marc's row of homes. She looked over her shoulder at the car as she guided Elvis away from the curb, but then stopped cold in her tracks. Chad the Third was behind the wheel.

Without thinking, Emily stepped onto the road to block the car from leaving. Chad sped toward them. With only one exit out of the complex, he had to get past. Not wanting to play a game of chicken with a moving vehicle, Emily scooped Elvis up and jumped out of the way, narrowly escaping the impact of the car's bumper. Chad squealed his tires as he turned onto the main road, getting away once again.

"Help," Emily yelled. She knew they would hear her through Tiki's open porch. "Mike, Duncan. Come quick!"

CHAPTER TWENTY-TWO

Duncan and Mike burst through the front door, racing to Emily in the parking lot. They turned left and right, scanning the area for threats.

"What happened?" Duncan asked.

Before she answered, Jane and Anthony came charging behind, looking much less composed

"Em. You're okay. You're okay," Anthony said, repeating the affirmation for his own benefit after realizing she didn't appear injured. He clutched his chest, trying to catch his breath before he and Jane enveloped her in a group hug.

Elvis acted oblivious to the threat as he wagged his tail and wriggled his way between their legs. Jane leaned over, letting him lick her hand. When they stepped apart, Jane asked, "Why were you screaming for help?"

"I saw Chad the Third."

"Are you sure?" Duncan and Mike asked in unison.

"Positive. He drove by in a sporty, white BMW. I tried to stop him, but he gunned it and almost ran us over trying to get away. I was worried about Elvis, so I didn't catch his license plate number. Sorry." Mike and Duncan exchanged a quick look, then Mike stepped away to make a call.

Jane scooped Elvis up in her arms and hugged him tight. He kissed her face, a good sign he had survived the event unscathed. "The kids are worried. I'm going to let them know everything is okay." She started back inside with Elvis.

Emily felt horrible about scaring Mac and Ava. "I'm the worst aunt," she said to no one in particular.

"No, you're not," Duncan said. "But trying to stop a moving car with your body is not so smart." He walked over to join Mike, who was still on the phone.

"You know. This is the second time you and Elvis narrowly escaped being the victim of a hit and run," Anthony said.

"Trust me. I know." Emily experienced PTSD, recalling when Mrs. Klein's murderer tried to run them over. It was less menacing this time. Chad didn't swerve to run them down. Instead, she'd stepped onto the road. Of course, Chad should have stopped, but he didn't. "Sorry I ruined your party. I'm quite the dinner guest."

"You'll always be my favorite dinner guest." Anthony smiled. "Marc will be beside himself. Are you okay out here?"

"I'm fine. I want to find out what's happening. I won't be long."

Anthony turned to walk inside, leaving Emily alone. Feeling uncertain about whether to insert herself into Duncan and Mike's phone conversation, her face flushed as she clenched and released her fists. Anger surged within her about the situation. Anger towards Chad. Anger about being kept out of the case. She marched over, intent on getting some answers.

"What's the plan?" she asked Duncan. He held up a finger to his lips. Mike was on speakerphone, so she stood quietly to listen in.

"Thanks, Daniel." Mike hung up.

"What's that all about?" she asked.

"I updated the FDLE agent about Chad and the car. They're searching for him now. Em, Duncan and I have to go."

"Don't worry about me," Emily said. "I'll get a ride with Jane."

Mike kissed her and promised to make it up. Pressed for time, Duncan called Jane to pass along their apologies to Anthony and Marc for abandoning the dinner party, and then they were gone.

Emily put her hands up in the air before letting them drop to her side in dramatic fashion. It didn't feel good being relegated to the sidelines, considering she had been integral in providing another lead in the case. If only she'd driven her own car, she'd be tempted to follow them. Emily walked back inside to find everyone sitting next to Tiki's aviary. Mac and Ava flanked Elvis, each with one hand on his back.

Emily mouthed a message to Jane. "Everything okay?"

Jane walked over and pulled Emily into the kitchen to talk.

"They're fine. We told the kids you saw a gigantic spider, and that's why you screamed. They were proud to learn that Elvis wasn't afraid of spiders," Jane said. "A little white lie goes a long way."

"Thanks. I feel horrible about scaring them."

"Kids are resilient. I assume Duncan will be out late, and that was enough excitement for me. I can take you home on my way." Jane moved to gather her stuff.

"I want to stay for a bit, so I'll get myself home," Emily said before joining the others. Elvis and Tiki exchanged the occasional bark, which sent the kids into fits of hysterical laughter.

"Auntie Em," Ava said. "It's okay to be scared of spiders. I am a little, too." She hugged her aunt for support. Emily struggled to hold back a smile.

"Okay, kids. Time to go." Jane attached Elvis's leash.

"Mr. Anthony. Mr. Marc. Can we bring Elvis to visit Tiki again?" Mac asked. "They're so funny."

"Sure. Tiki would love to see you again," Anthony replied. The kids jumped up and down in celebration. It took twenty minutes to get them out the door.

Once things were quiet, and Tiki had perched to sleep, the three of them retreated to the living room to finish their sangria.

"What the hell, Em?" Anthony said. "Why does Chad want to get at Tiki? It doesn't make any sense."

"I don't know. We're missing something," she said.

"I've spent the past two days and nights with Tiki. Now and then he says something new, at least it's new to me. Do you think Chad is trying to get Tiki in order to silence him?" Marc asked.

They mulled it over for a minute. "That seems far-fetched, but you never know. We need to consider all possibilities. Tiki only repeats things he's heard before. Has he said anything controversial, or a clue?" Emily asked.

"No, he made those dolphin sounds again this afternoon when we were watching an Ocean Voyager show, but he clearly can mimic other animal sounds—like a dog bark. It's hard to imagine it means anything important." They all agreed there had to be another reason for Chad's behavior.

It was late, and Emily could tell Marc and Anthony were struggling with their exhaustion after sleeping in shifts for the past couple of nights. Wanting to be a polite guest and let her hosts get some rest, she opened the app on her phone to call for a ride.

"Take my car, Em," Anthony said. "I don't need it since I'm driving the van back and forth to work. I'll get it from you sometime this week."

"Okay," Emily replied, accepting the keys he handed to her. "Marc, thank you for making your aunt's delicious paella. The entire night was amazing—until Chad showed up."

"He's definitely an unwanted visitor, but Tiki loved having Elvis and the kids here." Marc gave her a hug.

"I'll walk you out," Anthony said. Once they were alone, he turned to her. The muscles in his face tightened, and when he spoke, he didn't mince words. "Things are getting out of hand. I can't put Marc or Tiki in harm's way any longer. I'm going to contact the wild bird centers on Monday to find out about re-homing Tiki." His voice cracked as he continued. "It breaks my heart, Em, but it's what we need to do."

"I know. You're right. We'll face this decision together on Monday. I love you."

"Love you too. Night."

• • •

Emily sat in Anthony's car, thinking. Not only were they faced with a tough decision about Tiki Lulu, but the odds of finding Marilyn alive were fading. Tiki seemed happy, but the experienced people at a wild bird center could provide an enriched environment and a chance to bond with another parrot.

She was still sitting there when a police car from the sheriff's department cruised through the parking lot. She watched as the vehicle made two trips around the complex before leaving through the main entrance. If she had to guess, Duncan and Mike had ordered patrols in their absence.

Where were they right now? Had they found Chad? Her unanswered texts didn't ease her worry, which is why she staked out the townhouse, at least until she heard from either of them. Chad had already gotten away twice, and she didn't plan to give him an opportunity for a third. Despite the addition of federal law enforcement agents to Marilyn's case, Emily had tracked him down. She refused to chalk it up to luck, preferring to believe it resulted from her fine-tuned observational skills. It would be risky for Chad to return, but she wanted Anthony and Marc to be safe. If it meant she didn't sleep, that was okay. She could nap all day on Sunday.

Unlike the exciting TV crime dramas, Emily found the waiting boring and uncomfortable. Actors never had to deal with mosquitoes during their stakeouts as she batted away the biting insects. The cooler evening air allowed her to sit in the car without the engine running, as long as the windows were down. She reclined the seat to be more comfortable while monitoring the townhouse.

Headlights caused her to sit up and look at the clock. She'd never make a living as a private detective by falling asleep on the job. It was after three a.m. and a police cruiser drove through the townhouse complex, completing their hourly loop. Anthony and Marc were safe with this continued law enforcement presence, and her contribution to their security detail was questionable. The police car finished its route and turned back onto the main road when Emily decided to go home.

As she reached into the center console for the car keys, something in her left field of vision caught her attention. On instinct, she scooched down in the seat to hide. A car driving without its lights slowly moved out of the shadows and pulled from the side street closest to Marc's townhouse, turning to continue past his front door at a snail's pace. The darkness obscured the driver's face, but the white BMW was unmistakable. Despite the hot, muggy night, the hair stood up straight on Emily's arms. Chad the Third was back.

CHAPTER TWENTY-THREE

"Be cool," she said under her breath after a moment of panic. Once Chad cleared the row of homes, he turned on his headlights and picked up speed. "Oh, no you don't. Not this time." Emily started the car and pulled out of the parking lot, driving without lights until she reached the main road. She didn't want Chad to see her, so she stayed back a safe distance. Forced to concentrate, Emily held off calling Duncan and Mike. The neighborhood streets merged into four-lane roads as they headed east toward the interstate highway. With so few cars on the road at this hour, she easily maintained Chad's car in her line of sight.

After they passed the Coral Shores city limits, the choices were to either merge onto the main highway or continue to the Everglades. He moved into the right-hand lane, signaling his turn for the ramp to Interstate 75 south. Emily checked the console—she had a full tank of gas. It would ruin her reputation as an amateur detective if she ran out during a pursuit. *Where is he going?* she asked herself. There was only one way to find out.

Emily sat forward in her seat with both hands on the steering wheel, her body rigid. She expected Chad to turn off the highway at any minute, but after they'd driven for almost two hours, roadside signs welcomed her to Naples. Completely unprepared and without a plan, a feeling of dread crept in. Soon the interstate would make a sharp left turn. This stick-straight section of road known as Alligator Alley crossed the state, connecting the Atlantic and Gulf coasts, opening up limitless destinations.

Dawn was a welcome sight. Adrenalin kept Emily alert during her pursuit, but she felt her eyelids getting heavy. After coming this far, there would be no turning back. She pushed through the exhaustion.

With little warning, Chad pulled into the exit lane for Collier Boulevard and turned south. She decreased her speed to stay out of his rearview mirror as she adjusted to follow his move. Directional signs showed they were nearing the Tamiami Trail, giving Emily pause. She preferred the safety of the open interstate, since this two-lane, deserted stretch of highway crossed through the heart of the Everglades, with only a few pull-offs before reaching the outskirts of Miami. It would be Emily's choice if she wanted to avoid scrutiny even though Alligator Alley provided a much faster route across the state.

As the sun peeked above the horizon, it became easier to track him over the next sixty miles of remote highway. Dropping back to increase her safety buffer, Emily decided it was time to call for help. As every mile ticked by, her anxiety grew. She was on her own.

Anthony and Emily tagged each other's phone numbers as favorites so their calls overrode the *do not disturb* feature. They had to reach one another in case of an emergency.

"Em," Anthony's voice croaked since she had woken him from a deep sleep.

"Hi. Did I wake you?" Dumb question, but she was stalling. Telling him what she had done would not go over well.

"What do you think? It's still dark outside. What's up?"

"I'm on the Tamiami Trail, heading east across the Glades. I'm following Chad the Third." Emily heard banging sounds followed by Anthony's cursing. He must have dropped his phone, but when he came back on the line, he sounded wide awake.

"What the hell are you doing?"

"Well, it's a long story."

"And? I'm not going anywhere. Not yet, anyway," Anthony replied.

Emily took a few minutes to update him on her stakeout of their townhouse and spotting Chad's car. She justified her decision not to call sooner because she had to pay attention to the road, but Anthony wasn't having any of it.

"I can't believe you did that without talking to anyone. Or should I say, *are doing that*? What's your plan? What are you going to do once he gets to wherever he's going?"

"I don't know. That's why I called you. He could lead us to Marilyn. Isn't that worth the risk?"

"How can I answer that? It's not all or nothing, Em. There are a dozen different choices you could've made last night, and none of them would put you in danger." Anthony turned to speak with Marc, who was now awake. "She's in the Everglades, following Chad across Florida." Unable to hear Marc's response, she imagined it was much like Anthony's. "Have you called Duncan or Mike? Please say, yes."

"No."

"Em." Anthony's voice teetered on shouting. "Do you want to call them or should I?"

"I'll do it, but it won't be pretty. Listen, can I ask a favor?"

After an extended silence, he said, "Yes."

"I left some dry kibble out for Bella last night, but could you go over and check on her and feed her breakfast? She's going to be mad at me when I get home."

"Of course I can, and I'll brush her out. She loves that."

"Thanks, Anthony. Listen, I'm almost in Miami and need to focus on what I'm doing. I don't want to lose Chad in traffic, or miss a turn. I'll be safe. I promise."

"I want you to call me back. Even if you can't talk, I want the phone line to stay open."

"That's a good idea. Once I know which way he's going, I'll call." Emily hung up before he renegotiated. Given the long night and her fatigue, she needed all her resources for the task at hand. If Chad kept driving east, they would end up in the Atlantic Ocean at Miami Beach, but before that point, they would cross the Florida Turnpike, running north to Orlando and south to the Florida Keys. As they approached the interchange, Emily tightened her grip on the steering wheel.

She was about six cars behind Chad when he changed lanes to merge onto the turnpike, heading south. Emily knew this part of the road, having vacationed in Islamorada as a kid, and from road trips to Key West for college spring break. Anthony didn't have a SunPass transponder in his car, but with the state's updated TOLL-BY-PLATE system, she didn't need to stop at a toll booth.

Chad settled at a consistent speed, allowing her to relax a little. Unable to put it off any longer, she called Duncan. The early morning timing of her call was out of the norm, which might have been the reason he answered on the first ring.

"You're up early," he said.

"Actually, I haven't been to sleep yet. That's why I'm calling. I need your help." She imagined his response would include a mix of confusion, frustration, anger, and fear.

"Are you in your car? What's going on?"

"I'm in Anthony's car. I stayed behind last night and sat in the parking lot outside the townhouse for a few hours. I wanted to make sure Chad didn't come back. Anthony and Marc have been sleeping in shifts to watch over Tiki, and I wanted them to get some rest."

"I arranged for regular patrols around the townhouse all night for everyone's safety. You didn't need to sit there."

"Yes, I did. I saw your officers make their routine checks, and I was about to head home around three a.m. when Chad drove past

Marc's with his lights off. He didn't see me follow him out of the lot, and I've had him in my sights ever since."

"That was over three hours ago. Where are you now?"

"We crossed the Tamiami Trail and are now heading south on the Florida Turnpike, almost to the start of the Keys near Florida City."

"Damn it, Em. What makes you think it's okay to follow him on your own?"

"I was thinking I didn't want him to get away again, and I'm hoping he leads me to Marilyn. That's what I was thinking. It wasn't easy following him in the dark, so I had to concentrate on the road."

"That's no excuse. You could have called anytime—"

Emily didn't want to engage in a debate.

"Well, I'm calling now. I want to know what to do when he gets where he's going. The highway dead ends in Key West, so he'll eventually pull over."

It took a moment before Duncan spoke again. "The entire Keys are under the jurisdiction of the Monroe County Sheriff's office. I have some contacts there, and I'll call them. Are you sure he doesn't know you're following him?"

"Pretty sure. I stayed way back since it's fairly easy to follow a white BMW without traffic on the roads. I have the license plate info now. It's BIRDLDY, and it's a special design, but I can't make out the details. It's like the one Mom used to have that said *Helping Sea Turtles Survive*, but this one has different colors. It must be Marilyn's car, but I thought you accounted for all her cars after you searched her house."

"We did. All the ones registered in her name."

"So, what should I do?" she asked.

"If I thought you'd listen to me, I'd tell you to turn around and come home. Since that's not likely to happen, I'm going to make a call to the Monroe sheriff and to Mike. If Chad pulls in anywhere, drive on past and let the police handle it. As your brother, I don't ask you for much, but just this once, stay in your car. Don't put me in a position where I need to have you arrested for obstruction."

Duncan's words stung. It wasn't his style to use guilt or threats to get her to agree to something—a clear sign he was worried about her safety and doing everything to convince her to follow his advice. For a second, Emily regretted her decision to pursue Chad on her own, but when she pictured Marilyn locked up at Colt's grandmother's house, concern for her own safety seemed inconsequential. She loved her brother, so for now, she agreed to his request.

"Okay, I'll stay in my car." Emily opted to keep the peace instead of negotiating exceptions to the plan. "Anthony will be on the line while I'm driving, but let me know as soon as you get more details. If Chad pulls over, I'll call you right away." Duncan made her promise one more time, then hung up.

• • •

After Emily passed through Key Largo, the first major stop on the Overseas Highway, the land narrowed, exposing sections where the Gulf of Mexico and the Atlantic Ocean touched either side of the road. The blue-green color of the water was unmatched anywhere else along the coast of Florida. She loved driving through the Keys, but this morning, she focused her gaze on Chad's car and ignored the surrounding tropical vistas.

She called Anthony so he could listen in as she maintained her pursuit. She would have preferred him to be sitting beside her but appreciated the remote support. They talked little, but she took comfort knowing he was there if she needed him.

"I'm passing by Lorelei's restaurant," Emily said. Her stomach growled, and she desperately needed a restroom break.

"I love their fish sandwiches," Anthony replied. "Remember our road trip after high school graduation? That was so much fun."

"It was. We should do that again when this is all over." She resumed driving without talking since discussions of food and vacations were distracting. "Duncan's calling. I'm going to keep you on hold and I'll be right back." She switched callers.

"Are you still driving?" Duncan asked.

"Yeah. I'm in Islamorada. What did you find out?"

"Mike and I are on our way. I started driving right after your call, but Mike is a few minutes behind. If Chad stops, send me the address, and the Monroe County sheriff will dispatch officers to the scene. Don't do anything on your own."

"I won't. Let me know when you reach the Keys."

"I'm almost at Alligator Alley. We'll be there soon."

That was music to her ears. She hadn't thought about all the possible pitfalls when she started following Chad. With only eighty miles to go before they reached the end of the road at the southernmost point in Key West, he could make a turn at any moment. Emily desperately wanted to find Marilyn before it was too late. She had to focus.

CHAPTER TWENTY-FOUR

When Emily resumed her call with Anthony, she heard his coffee machine sputtering to signal the end of a brew cycle. "What I wouldn't give for a cup right now."

"Good. You're back. I'm making Tiki's breakfast, then I'm heading over to feed Bella. What did Duncan say?"

"He and Mike are on their way. Wherever and whenever Chad gets to his final destination, they've arranged for the local sheriff to handle things until they arrive."

"So, you won't follow him on foot. Right?"

"I'll wait for help." Anthony said nothing, so she added, "Pinky swear."

• • •

When she entered Marathon in the Middle Keys, the traffic increased, forcing her to navigate more frequent stop lights. Worried about getting separated from Chad, she passed a few cars to close the distance. Without warning, he pulled into a gas station on the right. Unable to follow him without raising suspicion, she turned into the next driveway and sat idling in the parking lot of a realtor's office. Through her rearview mirror, she watched Chad fill his tank before he disappeared inside the building. He returned carrying two bags, then merged back onto the highway. Emily slipped in behind him.

"Chad just gassed up and bought some groceries," Emily said.

"He has to be stopping soon."

"I'm almost at the Seven Mile Bridge. I've got to call in an update, but I'll be right back."

• • •

On speakerphone with Duncan, she heard high-pitched police sirens. He and Mike were approaching the start of the Keys after making record time crossing Alligator Alley—a reassuring sign they were getting closer.

"I'm in constant contact with the Monroe County Sheriff Ron Wheeler," Duncan shouted to be heard over the sirens. "His deputies have been briefed and are prepared to respond."

She told him about Chad's recent pit stop.

"He must be close to his destination," he said. "I've gotta go, but remember to stay in your car and do not approach him. Because you're my sister, and it's our murder suspect, Sheriff Wheeler's been more than cooperative. But he made it clear—he doesn't want you anywhere near this case. If you see a sheriff's car, pull aside and let them follow Chad. Got it?"

Emily didn't have a chance to respond before he hung up.

• • •

"Morning. Want some tea, Momo?" Tiki's salutations were audible when Anthony put the phone on speaker.

"I'm here," he said. "Why don't you tell me when you pass landmarks or make any turns. I have a street map of Marathon pulled up on my laptop so I can track you."

"Good plan. I just passed the stoplights at Key Colony Beach," then Emily yelled, "He's turning. He's turning."

"Where?"

"Left on Sombrero Beach Road. Can you text Duncan and let him know?"

"Sure. I'll give both of them the play-by-play." Anthony forwarded the latest GPS location for Emily. "There's only one way in and out of that neighborhood. It looks to be mostly residential. I think this is it, Em."

She didn't answer, instead focusing on Chad.

"He's turning right on Avenida Primiceria," she said. "Right again on Isla de Palmas. It looks like the street ends at the water. I'll hang back so I don't get stuck on the dead-end road. The homes on this street are huge, waterfront mansions. Wait, he's braking. He's turning into the driveway on the left. It's the last home on the street. And it's the biggest."

"I've got it on street view maps right now. Is it a white house?" Anthony asked.

"Yes."

"Bingo. It's 110 Isla de Palmas. I just dropped a pin to Mike and Duncan's phone. I think you should turn around now."

"I will in a second. I want to see if anyone comes out to meet him. Damn. The car pulled into a garage, and the landscaping blocks my view."

"Em, turn around." Anthony's stern voice grabbed her attention. "Don't even think about it."

It was as if he was reading her mind. She considered walking up to the property to peek through the fence, but if anyone spotted her, it would ruin the element of surprise for any next steps the police might take.

"Tell Mike and Duncan I'm going to park in the lot at Sombrero Beach. I'll call them in a minute. Chad can't leave this neighborhood without passing by me. I'll be back soon."

Emily chose a spot next to the road and backed in. The beach was quiet and deserted when she called her brother. "Where are you now?"

"An hour away. Anthony sent me your location and someone from the Monroe County Sheriff's office should arrive soon to execute a wellness check at the house. We're waiting on a warrant to get inside."

"How long will that take?"

"Depends. You've been up all night, so why don't you get some breakfast before driving home?"

"Are you kidding me? I've come this far, and I'm not going anywhere until you're here and can see what's in that house. I'll be waiting."

Despite the ambient noise from the speakerphone, Duncan's exhale was audible. "I'll call you when we're close."

Emily checked in with Anthony so he didn't worry. She needed a break and got out of the car to stretch her legs and perform a couple of jumping jacks to counteract the lack of sleep. The public restrooms for the beach were close by, and she had no choice. She had to chance a break in her surveillance. Another thing they never discussed during TV stakeouts, she mused. In record time, she came back outside, certain she would have heard a car drive by at this early hour.

Thirst and hunger were getting real, but she figured she could tough it out for a while longer. A local resident out for some exercise passed by and waved. Back in the car with the windows down, the only sounds Emily heard came from the gentle cooing of the mourning doves. Their rhythmic calls lulled her into a sleep-like state. It would feel so good to close her eyes, just for a minute.

A police vehicle with Monroe County Sheriff's Office emblazoned on the side came into view. "It's about time," Emily said to herself. The cruiser followed her previous route, turning right at Avenida Primiceria. Time passed slowly as she waited for word about the house search. Twenty minutes later, the same cruiser drove by, heading back toward the main road.

Feeling frustrated and defeated, she called Duncan and had to fight hard not to raise her voice. "Why are they leaving?" His refusal to answer her question led her to believe he already knew the reason.

"I'm expecting to hear from the sheriff. I'll get back to you as soon as I can," then he hung up.

That would not work for Emily, who thought it was essential to gain access to that house, and she didn't care whether the search was legal. Marilyn's life hung in the balance.

Still stewing over the slow pace of law enforcement, Emily noticed a car heading in her direction. As it approached, she ducked to hide from view, but only after identifying it as the white BMW with Chad behind the wheel, on his way out of the neighborhood. Now she had to decide—follow Chad or take this opportunity to check out the house. In the end, there was no choice. Marilyn came first.

She texted Duncan with an update on Chad's movement and then turned the phone to "do not disturb". She didn't wait for his reply, since she knew what he would say. *Stay put.* Emily started her engine and pulled onto the road. After turning right on Isla de Palmas, she pulled to the side of the road and continued on foot.

The lavish waterfront homes she passed paled compared to the estate at the end of the street—a white, Spanish-style mansion reminiscent of Marilyn's place in Coral Shores. She moved closer, using the decorative iron fence and tropical landscaping for cover. After reaching the driveway, she peered from around a palm tree, checking for movement outside. The custom-made front door had inlay wood carvings of parrots in a jungle setting. *If Marilyn owned the place, why didn't it show up in an earlier search?* She pushed that question to the back of her mind in order to concentrate.

She darted toward the front of the house, then dropped behind a mound of Mexican petunias. Inching along the wall, she saw a row of ground-floor windows. Emily stifled a scream when a small lizard ran across her shoe. Taking a minute to compose herself, she began moving one step at a time. After reaching the first window, she stopped. This was the best vantage point, but anyone inside could see her. A calculated risk she was willing to take.

Emily pressed her face to the glass, shading her eyes to counter the glare. The sunroom, dining room, and kitchen were empty. She moved toward the rear of the house, peeking in each window until she could see the Atlantic Ocean. An ornately framed, outdoor aviary filled most of the backyard. The tall enclosure contained topical landscaping and outdoor seating, but all that foliage blocked the view of the dock and the opposite side of the yard.

She'd be a sitting duck if she continued around the perimeter of the aviary, since she didn't know what was on the other side. The noise from the engines of a large boat cruising nearby made it impossible to hear any sounds coming from within the house, so she took a moment to think through her next steps.

Once the boat reached open water, things quieted and Emily resumed her search. She assumed the doors were locked, but it was worth the risk to double-check. She tiptoed toward the access point for the aviary, then froze when she heard a car approaching. She closed her eyes and held her breath to listen. The car pulled into Marilyn's driveway, and the door slammed shut, followed by the beep of the alarm—her worst-case scenario come true.

Diving behind a large bush-like palm tree for cover, she curled up and made herself as small as possible. There was no way to get off the property without being seen, but unless someone came out the door on her side of the aviary, the tree hid her from view. She pulled her phone from her pocket to check for messages. Only one from Duncan, warning her to stay in her car. Too late for that. She contemplated texting Anthony with the details of her current predicament, when the sound of another door slamming startled her, and she dropped the phone.

There must be a door on the opposite side, she thought. The screened-in structure made it impossible to move and maintain her cover. She picked up her phone and lifted it over her head, snapping a photo toward the door—hoping to capture an image of the perpetrator. No luck. She now had an out-of-focus picture of a palm leaf.

Two beeps caught Emily's attention, followed by *vroom vroom*, as engines roared to life. The telltale *clunk* as they shifted out of neutral revealed the boat was already on the move. With nothing to lose, she ran from her hiding place toward the water. As she passed the far corner of the aviary, a boat pulled away from the dock, with Chad at the helm. The same boat she saw leaving Colt's grandmother's house only a few days ago. Chad looked over his shoulder and locked eyes with Emily. She was too late. Within minutes, he'd be on the open water of the Atlantic Ocean, with countless escape routes.

Emily cursed under her breath. Once again, the weaselly Chad the Third had gotten away. She picked up her phone, took a breath, and called her brother. He'd eventually forgive her for ignoring his instructions, and she needed his help. They had to get into the house, and fast.

CHAPTER TWENTY-FIVE

"Duncan, he's getting away. Does the local sheriff have a marine unit?"

"Where are you?"

Here goes, Emily said to herself. Duncan listened without interruption as she updated him about Chad and the boat.

When she finished, he asked, "Are you sure nobody else is there?"

"I've been around the entire place, even checked for an open door." Emily's frustration over Chad's repeated escapes had peaked. "Why didn't the sheriff go inside when they called at the house? He'd be in custody now."

"Nobody answered the door, and we don't have a search warrant. Stay put, and do not go into the house."

That went better than expected, she thought. He didn't admonish her for acting outside the law. Emily walked toward the boat lift, taking a seat on top of the dock box. Staring out at the teal blue water of the Florida Keys helped calm her nerves. A sandbar and small island were visible across the bay where mangroves sprouted from the shallows. The sun had risen high above the horizon and the temperature soared.

Minutes passed without hearing from anyone. She texted with Anthony until he convinced her to call and put him on speakerphone. She didn't feel like talking, but appreciated him acting as a virtual backup. Listening to Tiki and Marc's conversation put a smile on her face.

Sirens grew louder—they were on their way.

"Anthony, I can hear the police cars. I'm going to hang up now, but I'll call back if I learn anything about Marilyn."

"I hope she's there, and she's okay."

"Me, too," Emily said.

To avoid being mistaken as an intruder, Emily met them outside the front driveway. Two vehicles with their lights flashing pulled to the front of Marilyn's house. An officer stepped out of the first car and checked his phone before approaching her.

"Are you Dr. Emily Benton?" His voice was formal but calm.

"Yes, sir. My brother is Deputy Sheriff Duncan Benton. He'll be here soon."

"My name is Sheriff Wheeler. He asked me to tell you to wait for him. But I'm going to need you to move away from the property. You're welcome to sit in my vehicle."

Emily pictured herself behind a cage screen in the backseat of a police car—with doors that don't open from the inside. "Thank you, Sheriff. My car is parked down the street. I'll wait there."

He nodded, then turned to his fellow officers, motioning for them to follow him to the front door. He looked back in her direction and hesitated, waiting for her to leave before he executed the search warrant.

Emily's brisk walk back to her car morphed into a run. The air conditioning offered a temporary reprieve from the relentless humidity. She drove slowly down the street, passing by Marilyn's driveway, before turning around in the cul-de-sac. From this angle, she saw part of the boat dock and two officers walking away from the water, toward the front yard. She wanted to avoid getting in their way but was eager to find out what was happening inside.

At long last, Duncan's car, followed by Mike's, turned into Isla de Palmas. Awash with relief, Emily walked to the bottom of the driveway to meet them. Duncan parked, then stepped onto the road. Emily moved toward him, but his piercing stare and clenched jaw stopped her in her tracks. She watched him turn and walk away, which is why she didn't see Mike until he stood in front of her.

Mike waited for her to make eye contact then studied her face for a few moments before speaking. His tired eyes narrowed and he exhaled. "Em. Are you all right?"

She fought back her tears. Exhaustion, hunger, and thirst amplified the impact of Duncan's cold greeting. "I'm fine." She lied.

"Give him a few minutes to cool down." Mike looked in Duncan's direction. He put his arm around Emily's shoulders, and she leaned in, grateful for the comfort. "Thinking something terrible could happen to you scared him to death. He wouldn't even wait for me so we could drive here together."

She stepped back and squared her shoulders. "I've never seen him this angry. I apologize for not calling sooner, but I will not apologize for following Chad. This isn't about me. It's about Marilyn."

"I don't disagree, but that doesn't mean you have to handle everything all by yourself. Em, the thought of losing you—" He touched the side of her face. An intimate moment meant just for the two of them. "Can you wait here? I need to speak with Sheriff Wheeler."

Emily nodded.

Duncan emerged from the side of the house, talking with an officer as Sheriff Wheeler walked out the front door to shake Mike's hand. The four men huddled in conversation until they turned around and looked in her direction. She couldn't hear what they were saying, but their relaxed body language made it obvious that Marilyn was not inside. Duncan broke away from the group and walked in her direction.

Emily didn't know what to expect. She and Duncan were close and always looked out for each other. This ongoing tension strained their relationship, and she didn't like it.

"Is there anyone inside?" Emily was the first to speak.

"No, the house is empty." Duncan's voice sounded more distant than angry. She would have preferred anger.

"What happens now?"

"We're searching the house for evidence, and we alerted the Coast Guard and marine patrol units throughout the Keys."

"Listen, Duncan. I know you're mad at me, but I didn't have a choice—"

Duncan cut her off before she finished. "That's bull, and you know it." His voice trembled with anger. "You always have a choice. But you keep choosing to ignore my advice."

Emily's shoulders slumped. It would be futile to defend her actions until he calmed down. "Duncan, I wanted to—"

He put his hand up, signaling her to stop. "Not now. Sheriff Wheeler has been very helpful, but he won't appreciate you meddling in this case, not in his backyard. Go home, Em. Go home. And call Anthony. He keeps on texting me for updates." Duncan turned and walked back to the house.

Feeling dejected, her pursuit of another lead had jeopardized her relationship with her brother, and once again, she had come up empty-handed. As Duncan disappeared inside the house, Mike returned.

"Have you had anything to eat or drink since last night?" he asked. She shook her head, lacking the energy to muster the words. "Why don't you find a place to get some breakfast, and I'll come meet you within the hour?"

Emily didn't answer. She stared out toward the water, feeling numb. To have come so far and still not be any closer to finding Marilyn was depressing.

"Emily," Mike said, trying to draw her back into the conversation.

"Okay, good idea. Thanks, Mike. I'm glad you're here."

There was nothing else to do, so Emily returned to her car and phoned Anthony and Marc to update them about the empty house. They shared in her disappointment and since she didn't feel like recounting her conversation with Duncan; it was a brief call.

After pulling onto the Overseas Highway and driving south into Marathon, signs for a t-shirt and sandal shop caught her attention. Hot, sticky, and in need of a change of clothes, the polar temperature of the air-conditioned store provided a break from the summer heat. She bought the first tank top, shorts, and flip-flops she thought would fit and asked to use a restroom. The clerk took pity on her and offered the key to the staff room. Emily splashed cold water on her face and used a wet paper towel to wipe down her arms and legs. She changed into her new tourist outfit, shoving her old clothes in the bag. The store clerk recommended a favorite local spot for breakfast, Porky's Bayside, only a few miles down the road. It sounded perfect.

• • •

A casual open-air waterfront restaurant next to a marina, Porky's had a tiki-style thatched roof to shade the tables, and cooling fans for comfort. Paraphernalia adorned the ceiling and walls, including out-of-state license plates and a variety of Keys knick-knacks. Presented with a carafe of coffee, Emily inhaled the aroma before drawing her first sip. After her second cup, the caffeine circulating in her system made her feel human again. Emily sent Mike her location but didn't wait before ordering Porky's monster-sized western omelet with hash browns, wheat toast, orange juice, and a large glass of water. She needed time to decompress as she waited for her food.

Several fishing boats moved past the restaurant, heading toward Florida Bay with their charter full of tourists looking for that trophy fish. As she stared out at the water, her server seemed to recognize her need for solitude, only coming near her table to refill her drinks.

During the overnight pursuit of Chad, she hadn't thought about what came next. She never expected to end up deep in the Florida Keys, and now she faced a five-hour drive back home. A post-breakfast nap might be in order.

As her food arrived, Mike joined her at the table. "That looks delicious. I'll order the same thing, please." The server placed a second cup of coffee in front of him. "Why don't we eat first, then we can talk about last night?"

Emily nodded her agreement as she took her first mouthful. After finishing half her plate, she shared the rest with Mike. It didn't hinder him from cleaning his own plate when it arrived. They both leaned back in their chairs, taking in the setting.

Mike set his drink on the table and took Emily's hand into his. "Let's come back here again sometime soon, just the two of us."

She set down her coffee and reached for his free hand. "I'd like that. Duncan and I spent a lot of time in the Keys when we were kids. I'd love to show it to you."

Mike squeezed her hand, then let go. He sipped his coffee, watching her over the rim of his cup. He appeared to be contemplating something serious. Mike's brows tightened. He dropped his arms to rest on the table and leaned forward, staring directly at her.

"I'm going to leave it up to Duncan to talk with you about your decision to follow Chad. I don't have to tell you how risky it was—you already know that. You scared me. As we raced across the state to get here, all I thought about was what I would do if something happened to you. I never want to feel that way again."

Taken aback by his intensity, Emily reflected on her actions. She didn't think she was in danger during her pursuit but understood Duncan and Mike's concerns. The nature of their careers meant they often saw the worst-case scenario play out in a violent crime. It was their job to protect others.

"I'm sorry. Really, I am. I didn't mean to frighten you or Duncan, but you need to know I can handle myself. I wouldn't put anyone at risk. Plus, Anthony was on the phone with me the whole way."

"But you were chasing a murder suspect. What if he realized you were following him and pulled off in a remote location? You could have been attacked or killed."

"Point taken," Emily said. "I wish I handled it differently."

Mike smiled, letting her know he wasn't angry.

"You realize my actions helped you track Chad—once again." Emily held her open hands in front of her, a gesture to punctuate her point. "I'm an asset to the investigation."

Mike nodded, acknowledging she had played a pivotal role.

"So, what happens next?" she asked.

"We keep searching for Chad until we find him. We ran the Bird Lady license plate through the toll booth system. He's traveled between Coral Shores and the Florida Keys at least three times in the past week, not including the one boat trip we know about. The toll booths heading south stop at Florida City, so until you discovered his location in Marathon, we were in the dark."

"When I saw the aviary, I just knew it had to be Marilyn's place. Is the property in her name?" Emily asked.

"We're working on that. The property is held in a separate trust so it didn't show up in our initial searches. I'm hoping there's some evidence in the house to lead us to Marilyn."

"Was there a locked room, like the one at Colt's grandmother's house? Or any other signs he held Marilyn there?"

"Not at first glance."

Emily's voice cracked when she asked, "Be honest with me. Do you think there's a chance she's still alive?"

"I try to avoid speculating, and there's been no evidence of her death. We won't stop until we find her. I promise, Em."

For now, she agreed to leave things to the professionals. Emily had to be at work in the morning, and it's not like she could call in sick. Her clients and patients depended on her. She dreaded the drive home, but putting it off wouldn't make it any easier. At least now, she was fully caffeinated. Mike paid the bill, and they both left the restaurant together.

"Will you call me when you get home?" he asked.

Emily opened her car door and turned to him. "I will. Will you call me if you have any news to share, good or bad?"

"I will. It's hard to say when we'll be heading back. It depends on what we find."

They both stopped talking when Mike moved closer. He kissed her softly until she moved forward, pressing her body against his, needing to feel connected. Mike wrapped his arms around her waist, guiding her back against the car. The high drama of the past twelve hours channeled into their embrace. Emily wished they could run away to Key West for a romantic escape, but reality came into view. Mike stepped back to allow Emily to get in the driver's seat. He leaned inside for one more gentle kiss before they parted ways. She had a long, lonely drive ahead, and Detective Mike Lane had to find Chad and continue the search for Marilyn. The stakes couldn't be higher.

CHAPTER TWENTY-SIX

After a stop for gas, Emily checked in with Anthony. He had more questions than she had answers, which was frustrating for both of them.

"When you get back, do you want some company?" he asked.

"Thanks, but all I want is sleep. Are you going to work from home tomorrow? I think you should stay put with Tiki."

"I'm coming in, at least for the morning. Marc can stay with Tiki, and I have stuff to do. Tiki seems happy at home, and we can juggle things until they find Chad and put his butt in jail."

That was the first time Emily heard Anthony referring to Marc's custom-made aviary as Tiki's home. She wondered if they were considering permanently adopting him. It might be premature to have this discussion with Marilyn still missing, but in case it became a possibility, she hoped Anthony would hold off contacting the wild bird sanctuaries.

"Do whatever you think is best. We can tweak the schedule if we have to. If Tiki's paparazzi fill the parking lot when we get to work on Monday, it will be another quiet day in the hospital."

"Let me know when you get home. Until then, I'm going to keep worrying about you. Oh, and I don't need my car back since I'll be driving the van this week."

• • •

Emily arrived at her cottage feeling grateful to her mom for leaving her such a warm and wonderful place to live. When she stepped inside the front door, Bella uncharacteristically raced over to greet her, squawking her objection to being left alone.

"I'm sorry, Bella. I promise to make it up to you." Emily scooped her up, giving her a hug before setting her down on the couch. Once Bella had her fill of chin rubs and pets, she jumped down and ran to the kitchen, checking to ensure Emily followed her—a few extra servings of her favorite cat treats and all was forgiven.

After a quick shower, Emily changed into her softest pajamas and climbed into bed with her hair still wet. She let Anthony, Duncan, and Mike know she had made it home safely, and within minutes, she was in dreamland.

• • •

Emily woke before her alarm, feeling refreshed. Nothing like a fifteen-hour sleep to clear the mind. After feeding Bella, she brought her morning coffee back to bed and turned on the local news.

Within minutes of seeing the lead story, she texted Anthony to call her ASAP. Another prerecorded video posted to Marilyn and Tiki's Flix account, this time announcing the end to the treasure hunt. All the clues hidden at the wild bird sanctuaries formed a number puzzle, like an anagram. The solution to the puzzle would lead to an actual street address. The news channel played the entire video, including Tiki's clue about the address. As soon as she heard Tiki speak, she knew exactly what it referenced. The dolphin sounds he mimicked were the same ones he made watching the nature TV program about dolphin language.

The news anchor broke away to a field reporter broadcasting live from the veterinary hospital parking lot—already overflowing with people. "Marilyn Peña's whereabouts are still unknown, but the sheriff's office confirmed they are following some promising leads. For now, Tiki Lulu and Marilyn's fans are rallying their support for her safe return. Earlier this morning, I spoke with Franklin, the head of Tiki's local fan club..." said the reporter.

Emily listened as Franklin, the paparazzi leader who helped her when Archie fainted, hypothesized that Tiki was being cared for by the staff of the veterinary hospital. He wore a tie-dye t-shirt imprinted with a photo of Tiki and Marilyn and stood surrounded by a group of fans holding WE ♥ TIKI signs. He urged the public to help find Marilyn and committed to maintaining their vigil. The camera then panned through the crowd. Emily saw Archie in his regular spot under the coconut palm, with a water bottle in hand. An enormous improvement. Food trucks were pulling into the lot as the crowd chanted. "Tiki! Tiki! Tiki!"

She muted the TV and opened the Flix app to rewatch the video. The five numbers; eight, five, zero, nine, and one combined to form a street address. Trying to figure out the correct order of the numbers was the tricky part, even when using Tiki's dolphin impersonations as a clue. The lucky winner had to take a selfie standing in front of the secret location and text the picture and their name to a phone number that flashed across the screen. The first person to send the photo would win the grand prize of two hundred-thousand-dollars.

Glancing back at the TV, it shocked her to see so many super fans in the parking lot. Emily thought they would have scurried across Florida looking for the winning destination in the treasure hunt. There was big money at stake.

"Finally," Emily said out loud when Anthony called. "Did you see it?"

"Marc and I watched it a few times until Tiki overheard us. He started making the same dolphin sounds, flapping his wings and bobbing up and down. He seemed upset after hearing Marilyn's voice. It was pretty traumatic. We turned the TV to a show about beavers and gave him a couple of his favorite snacks to distract him."

"I'm sorry. That must have been horrible. Do you have any theories about these clues?"

"We were just talking about that. I looked online and there are a ton of places in Florida that offer dolphin encounters and an endless number of businesses or locations that use the word *dolphin* in their name or logo. Someone will figure it out."

"How will they crown a winner if Marilyn's still missing?"

"That's a good question. I don't know. Anything yet from Marathon?" Anthony asked. "There was nothing on the news about an investigation in the Keys."

"No. Nothing. Duncan was so mad yesterday. He avoided even looking at me when he got to Marilyn's house. Mike said he needs time to cool off, but I'm not so sure."

"You do have a habit of ending up in the middle of his murder investigations. He's worried you'll get hurt. That's all. I agree with Mike—give him time. It'll be okay."

"Thanks, Anthony. I'm leaving early for the hospital. See you soon."

• • •

The early morning drive along Gulf Beach Road offered a peaceful start to the workweek. She watched as residents walked along the ocean before filing into nearby coffee shops. Tourists stayed away during the intense summer heat, giving the locals a needed break from the crowds. Traffic was light, another reason Emily loved summer.

The news broadcast helped prepare her for the chaotic scene in her hospital parking lot. The crowd had grown since Saturday, spilling over into the barricaded area reserved for Emily's clients. Merchandising tents were larger and four food trucks lined the perimeter. After parking at the back door, Emily dropped her bags at her desk before joining Anthony.

"Did you see the cars parked in our customer area?" Emily asked.

"Franklin's working on it. I spoke with him a few minutes ago, and he's going to make sure that area is clear before we open. He seems to be a nice guy."

Emily nodded her agreement. "I'm afraid to look at the schedule. Have there been more cancelations?"

"A few. Kizmet is coming in this afternoon to recheck her eye. Otherwise, there are a couple of routine appointments, but no surgeries."

"If this keeps up, we may have to adjust the staff schedule. I don't want to cut anyone's hours."

"I'm working on payroll right now. Let's hope we get some good news from Mike and Duncan. If they find Marilyn, the paparazzi will go home and things can get back to normal. It's amazing how a simple avian nail trim appointment turned into a three-ring circus."

• • •

Emily took advantage of some quiet time during her morning appointment block to research the purchase of an ultrasound machine. Investing in this important diagnostic tool excited her because she currently had to refer her patients to a nearby specialty hospital when they needed an ultrasound. The company included basic training with the purchase of the machine, and Emily had her eye on an advanced continuing education course. But if business continued to be this slow, she would have to delay any sizeable investments.

Anthony came into her office and sat down. "I'm going to grab lunch from the new Greek food truck before I head home. Plus, I want to check in with Archie. Do you want anything?"

"Ooh, yes. If they have falafel, I'll take a pita sandwich; otherwise, you can pick for me. You know what I like. And thanks." Emily avoided the front parking lot since it often caused a stir amongst the super fans who peppered her with questions about Tiki.

"Anything new from Mike?" he asked.

"I'm checking my phone every ten minutes. It's so aggravating. It's because of me they have this lead to follow. You think that might warrant a return call."

"I'm sure if there's anything to share, he'll let you know."

"Can I ask you a question?"

Anthony raised his eyebrows and nodded slowly. Emily rarely asked for permission first.

"Are you and Marc considering adopting Tiki? You were adamant last week you were going to call the wild bird centers about re-homing him, and yet you haven't mentioned it all day."

"We've talked about it. Marc is even more attached to Tiki than I am, and I love him. What we want differs from what's best for him. That's the hard part."

"You've both given Tiki a wonderful home and should be proud of that. We can wait a few more days before deciding. I feel it in my bones that we're getting closer to finding Marilyn."

"I try to avoid thinking about it. I hope she's alive, but we have to be realistic. It's been over ten days."

Emily agreed. Every day that passed increased the chances of a horrible outcome. Time was the enemy in a case like this.

When Anthony returned with lunch, he handed Emily her sandwich, then grabbed a chair from the staff lounge and returned to the parking lot. It confused her until he shared an update about Archie.

"He's doing well and has a new group of friends standing with him. I bought him a Gatorade and told him to sit down and take a rest. Can you make sure someone brings the chair back inside before we close? I'm going home unless you need anything."

"I'm good. Tell Marc, thank you."

• • •

Mrs. Hedden arrived with Kizmet to recheck her corneal ulcer. Kizmet's eye had stayed open since her last appointment, and despite a few early bumps in the road, Mrs. Hedden mastered administering drops into the eye of a kitten.

The kitten purred throughout her exam and didn't object when Emily placed a drop of topical stain in her eye. Turning the lights off in the exam room helped focus the ophthalmoscope's blue light used to detect an injury.

"Great news!" Emily smiled. "The cornea isn't picking up any stain at all. The ulcer is fully healed."

Mrs. Hedden let out a celebratory cry. "Woo-hoo. Kizmet started hiding from me every time I reached for her eye drops. She's smart."

"Well, you did a great job," Emily said. Mrs. Hedden smiled broadly at the compliment.

• • •

Kizmet ended up being the last appointment—everyone else had rescheduled. Emily didn't want to close the hospital early, but it seemed pointless to stay open. She assured the staff they would be paid for the full day. None of this was their fault.

Emily locked up the hospital, her mind foggy and unfocused. Not wanting to waste her unexpected free time, she conserved what little energy she had for a walk up the beach to survey the future location of the sea turtle center, formerly Mrs. Klein's cottage. The drama surrounding Tiki and Marilyn had overshadowed their upcoming groundbreaking ceremony. Sarah's latest emails included the final architect's drawing, as well as some suggestions for the invitation list. Emily thought walking through the property would help her visualize the project.

To stay cool, she kept her feet in the water along the edge where the waves reverse course and retreat to the ocean depths—just deep enough to reach her ankles. The sun began its descent as families out for an afternoon swim packed up for the day. As she approached Mrs. Klein's cottage, the stress left her body. The ocean healed all. She pulled out her phone to download the architectural drawings to guide her as she walked the property when it vibrated, signaling a call from Mike.

"Em, we found him!"

CHAPTER TWENTY-SEVEN

"Yes!" Emily raised her fist, then pulled her bent elbow tight to her side in dramatic fashion. "Did he admit to kidnapping Marilyn?"

"Well, we don't actually have him in custody yet. We tracked his boat to a marina on Stock Island, which is a few miles east of Key West. He hired a local company to provision the boat, and they confirmed he was on board this morning. We have a team staking out both the boat and the entrance to the marina."

"But how do you know he's coming back? What if he's headed for the airport?"

"Don't think so, but we alerted airport security and local car rental businesses, just in case. Sheriff Wheeler had an undercover officer following him on foot in Old Town Key West. We held off on his arrest, hoping he would lead us to Marilyn. He went into a local bank, but unfortunately, the officer lost him in the crowd along Duval Street. Chad's best bet for a getaway is by boat. He'll be back."

Mike's confidence reassured her, but Chad had slipped through the cracks a few too many times. He didn't strike Emily as a criminal mastermind—maybe it was dumb luck. But someone desperate and cornered could become dangerous.

"Is Duncan with you?"

"Yes, he's with the team at the marina gate. I'm on a boat within eyesight of Chad's boat. If he's smart, he'll wait until dark before coming back. We'll know in a few hours."

"Did you see Marilyn and Tiki's video post from this morning?"

"We all did. The special agent on the case is dealing with the social media angle and the treasure hunt. That amount of money increases the risk of fraud. That's why they placed an undercover officer in the crowd at your hospital."

"What." Emily said, shocked to learn she had a secret agent mingling with the super fans in her parking lot. But it made sense. Of course, the authorities would send an undercover officer to monitor fringe elements in the crowd—people who might resort to criminal or violent acts to get their hands on the treasure.

"Listen, Em, I have to get back to the team. I don't know what to expect tonight, but I'll keep you updated as best as I can."

"Thanks, Mike. Be careful and tell Duncan the same—from me. I know he doesn't want to talk right now, but no matter what, he's my brother, and I love him."

"I'll tell him. Night, Em."

• • •

After Mike's call, she sat down in the sand, staring out at the ocean. *What was Chad up to?* None of the puzzle pieces fit together. During Mrs. Klein's murder investigation, Emily and Anthony would get together and work through the details of the case, just like they did on TV detective shows. It always came down to means, motive, and opportunity, and the list of suspects would slowly dwindle. She wished Anthony was here to work through it together.

Given Mike's update, Emily abandoned plans to walk through the future turtle center and called Anthony to share the news.

"I wish we were in Key West to see Chad in handcuffs," Anthony said. "He needs to be behind bars. The moment we met him, I knew he was no good."

"My timing is terrible, but I hoped we could meet tonight and dissect the investigation. We're pretty good when we put our heads together. I can get some takeout and bring it over to your place."

"Marc's home working on a big project. He'll be okay here alone with Tiki, so I can bring dinner to you. What are you craving?"

"Hmm. How about *Agave Sol*, the Mexican restaurant. Just thinking about their enchiladas and churros makes my mouth water."

"Done. I'll be there within the hour. Why don't you mix us up a batch of your famous margaritas. See you soon," he said before hanging up.

Her gloomy mood that had lingered ever since her confrontation with Duncan evaporated in a flash. Anthony always lifted her spirits. His undying optimism and big heart made it impossible not to get swept up by his enthusiasm. Emily picked up the pace to get back home to prepare for her crime-solving get-together with her best friend.

• • •

Anthony let himself in the front door. "Em, food's here."

"That smells so good. I set the table on the deck. Looks like we're in store for a fantastic sunset."

Emily rimmed her margarita glasses with salt and poured them each a cocktail before joining Anthony outside. They savored their meal and when their bellies were full, they each leaned back in their chair, taking a sip of their drink.

"So, on at least three separate occasions, Chad attempted to get his hands on Tiki Lulu. Once at the hospital and twice at your townhouse. Why does he want to abduct a parrot? To win the contest? To hold him for ransom?" Emily said.

"Yeah, he seemed pretty determined. And we know Chad's DNA was on the dead body, and we also know he was likely living with Colt at his grandmother's house. It doesn't mean he killed him."

Emily raised one eyebrow, signaling her doubt at Anthony's presumption of Chad's innocence. "What do the TV detectives call it? Oh yeah—circumstantial evidence. There's a boatload of that piling up around Chad."

"You're right. Who else could have kidnapped Marilyn or had access to her house in the Keys?" Anthony asked.

"Do you think she's still alive? I know we haven't wanted to talk about it, but it's getting hard to stay positive."

"My gut tells me she is. Plus, you said there had been no signs of violence at the grandmother's house, or the Keys mansion."

"Let's take the beach chairs down to the water for sunset. All this hypothesizing is hurting my brain." Emily cleared the food and their plates. "I'll make a to-go container for Marc."

"Sounds good. We haven't even worked through Marilyn and Tiki's treasure hunt. It can wait until after sunset. There might even be an update on the ten o'clock news."

Their plan was to have no plan, at least for the next hour. Sipping their margaritas, they watched the red fireball drop toward the horizon. Wisps of low-lying clouds framed their view.

Emily and Anthony had been staring at sunsets their entire lives. Legend has it that at the last moment before the sun disappears below the ocean, a streak of green light will flash across the sky. Anthony still talks about the time he saw the green flash during their senior class beach bonfire. Emily continued her unwavering stare, hoping her turn would be next. But no such luck. The blinding sun caused them to see sparkles, making her wonder if the likely source of the green flash might be retinal damage from direct sun exposure. Once the sun tucked itself in for the night, they gathered their chairs and moved back inside Emily's cottage.

"Anything?" Anthony asked as she scrolled through her messages.

"No. I hate waiting around for something to happen."

Anthony smiled. "I know you do. Patience, young Sherlock. Patience."

"What's the plan for tomorrow?" Emily said, changing the subject.

"Same as today. Marc will work from home in the morning, and I'll come into the hospital early, but I'll have to leave after lunch."

Emily nodded. "Wait, I forgot to tell you. There's a special agent working undercover in the paparazzi crowd at the hospital. They're worried the treasure hunt is attracting criminals and fraudsters."

"Fraudsters. Is that a word?" Anthony asked.

"I think so. I wonder who it is. I guess if they're doing their job right, we would never know."

Anthony sighed. "Well, Em. I'm think I'm going to head home and watch the news from bed. I'm tired. I know we've been distracted, but Sarah needs us to weigh in on the invite list for the groundbreaking ceremony. She knows about everything we're dealing with, but we have to make some time to look at it."

"You're right. It's not fair to leave it all to Sarah, Marlon, and Sharon. Let's make that a priority tomorrow over lunch. My treat this time." Emily plopped down on the couch and turned on the TV.

"This was fun. Just like old times. We can repurpose the whiteboard in my office for our crime board if Mike and Duncan don't sort things out soon." He grabbed his keys, Marc's leftovers, and waved goodbye on his way out the door.

"Bella." Emily called to her feline roommate as she patted the seat beside her. Bella's ears perked up before she slowly descended from her tree. The local TV station did a good job of covering Marilyn's missing person case and Tiki Lulu's treasure hunt. The reporter confirmed the police hotline received over two thousand tips, even though most of them were dead ends. Callers reported seeing Marilyn attending a hot yoga class and buying papayas at a farmers' market. Unfortunately, all that attention contributed to the growing crowd gathering daily in the hospital parking lot.

The news report included earlier footage of the paparazzi. As the camera scanned the crowd, Emily played a game of *guess which person is the undercover agent*. It was an impossible task.

Opening her laptop, she researched places in southwest Florida with *dolphin* in their name. She came up empty-handed when there were no street addresses to match the numbers in the hidden clues. When the search expanded to include the entire state of Florida, the long list became overwhelming. There were too many Dolphin Landscaping, Dolphin Donuts, or Dolphin Motels to count. The paparazzi had savvy social media skills and were likely only hours away from solving the puzzle.

Before calling it a night, Emily checked her phone one last time—still nothing from Key West. Mike thought it could be late before Chad returned to the boat, so she decided against calling him in case they were in the middle of a Chad take-down right now.

"Time for bed, Bella," she said before Bella stood up, stretched, then made her way to the bedroom, settling on her personal pillow. Emily followed behind, but found sleep to be elusive. She had too much on her mind, making it difficult to unwind as she waited for news from Key West. She turned off the *do not disturb* settings so any call during the night would ring through. After watching two episodes of an old BBC mystery show, she finally dozed off.

• • •

Emily woke feeling uneasy. Still no updates about Chad, and a local reporter broadcasting live from outside her hospital highlighted the challenges she would face once she got to work. It looked like the designated parking for hospital clients was already full of paparazzi. Anthony would have to enlist Franklin's help once again to clear the zone. What she wouldn't give to have a regular day at work.

She didn't linger over coffee but filled her travel thermos and headed out the door. She let Anthony know she would be there soon after stopping to pick up breakfast for the staff—a show of appreciation for their hard work.

After turning inland away from the beach, Emily prepared to merge onto the causeway when Duncan called. Seeing his name on the screen caused her heart rate to soar. She pulled into a parking lot at the base of the bridge to answer the phone.

"Hi, Duncan." She had so much she wanted to say but waited to follow his lead.

"Em, we got him. We arrested Chad on his boat last night when he tried to make an open water getaway. The Coast Guard had to get involved to help capture him."

Emily gasped in relief. Chad was finally in custody, and the tone in Duncan's voice made her wonder if had forgiven her despite their recent friction.

"That's the best news. Anthony, Marc, and I have been on pins and needles waiting for your call. Where is he now?"

"Behind bars in Marathon. Sheriff Wheeler's holding him on a resisting arrest charge while we sort the rest out. Chad will be moved back to Coral Shores to face charges for Dylan Colt's murder."

"Has he said anything about Marilyn? He has to know what's going on."

"He's waiting for his lawyer to show up, but we have another big lead we're following. I've got to go, but I wanted to tell you the news myself. Love you, Em." He hung up before she replied.

He didn't mention her pivotal role in the entire investigation, but talking with him reassured her that their bond was strong—unbreakable. It had been difficult to keep her emotions in check, considering their growing tension. If given the chance to do it over again, she might handle things differently. There was always room to work on her communication skills. It wasn't a lack of trust that kept her from confiding in Duncan. He was duty-bound to follow the law, but the slow pace of justice frustrated her, prompting her to act on her own. Whenever the time was right, Emily would apologize for pushing him away and let him know she loved him, too.

Chad's arrest was a big deal. She was eager to get to work and tell Anthony in person. They both needed to hear some good news.

CHAPTER TWENTY-EIGHT

Emily quickly dropped her purse on her desk and carried the bag of bagels and cream cheese into Anthony's office. He turned away from the computer to greet her.

"Morning. I didn't eat breakfast—your bagel timing is perfect," he said, helping himself to his favorite cinnamon raisin.

"I'm glad you're already sitting down because I have monumental news." Emily paused for effect. Unable to contain herself, she began dancing on the spot.

Anthony gave her a look to let her know he wasn't interested in playing a guessing game. "Out with it."

"They arrested Chad late last night."

"Yes!" Anthony jumped out of his chair and punched his fist over his head in celebration before joining her in a dance. When they caught their breath, he asked, "Where did they get him?"

"He tried to escape by boat out of a marina near Key West, but the Coast Guard caught him. He's in custody in Marathon. Mike and Duncan are there."

"I need to tell Marc. When I left this morning, he was online shopping for high-tech security systems. Since we can't work from home forever, he wanted increased protection for Tiki. Now, we don't have to worry anymore."

Emily knew they both loved having Tiki Lulu in their home, but nobody wanted to live in a fortress.

"Wait," Anthony said. "Did Chad say anything about Marilyn?"

"No. He refused to talk until his lawyer gets there."

"They need to get him to confess. Everything is riding on it."

"I agree. I'll keep my phone in my pocket. Until then, we need to clear space in the client parking lot. Are you up to enlisting Franklin's help?"

"Sure. I'll go outside after I finish my bagel. The schedule is light again. Our numbers aren't looking so good this month, but I don't think there's anything we can do about it."

Emily cringed, but she avoided worrying about things outside her control. It was a waste of energy and only stressed her out. Maybe the daily paparazzi circus would end soon, and things would get back to normal.

"Don't forget to call Marc," she said before returning to her office. With only two appointments scheduled for the morning, Emily resumed her research on ultrasound machine features but found it difficult to focus. What she wouldn't give for a new puppy exam.

• • •

Kensington Martinez, a twelve-year-old Bichon Frise, did not enjoy coming to the vet hospital but managing his kidney disease made it essential. After being hospitalized earlier this year when he stopped eating, his sky-high kidney enzymes returned to the normal range with intensive IV fluid therapy and medical support to treat an infection. Kensington became grumpy with any disruption to his daily routine, but Mrs. Martinez wanted to keep a close eye on his condition by rechecking his blood work every three months.

"I don't want to take any chances. The last time, he seemed okay one day and then super sick the next. There was no warning." Mrs. Martinez updated Emily on his daily activities. "I only feed him the special kidney diet you recommended. I'll do whatever it takes to keep him out of the hospital."

Emily agreed. To describe Kensington as feisty would be an understatement. During his last hospital stay, he tried to bite both Anthony and Catrinna. He did it out of fear, but as long as he felt safe, he was a wonderful patient. With Mrs. Martinez holding him, Emily did his exam and drew his blood sample in the room. Taking him away to the main treatment area would cause undue stress. It was important to be flexible and adapt to the needs of her patients. Plus, she had lots of time on her hands and was happy to make it work for both Kensington and Mrs. Martinez.

"I'll call you when his lab tests are final. His weight continues to be stable, which is a positive sign with kidney disease. Overall, great news."

"Thank you, Dr. Benton. Let's go, Kensington. I saw a food truck advertising crepes and thought I'd try it for lunch. Bye."

Emily followed them into the lobby to survey the activity outside. Franklin, the de facto leader of Tiki's paparazzi, cleared the client parking zone closest to their front doors. Emily considered him an ally at keeping the peace.

She stood staring out the window when Anthony joined her. "Just business as usual." He nudged her with his shoulder and smiled. "The upside is we have a variety of lunch choices thanks to the rotating food trucks. I saw a Korean BBQ truck pull in when I was outside checking on Archie."

Archie sat in the shade, sipping from a large water jug she recognized as the same one Anthony carried during marching band practice in high school. "Is that Big Beluga?" Emily asked, referencing the nickname Anthony gave his blue water thermos. He had often complained about carrying that jug to practices and band competitions.

Anthony grinned. "It's amazing that I've hung on to it all these years. Archie's eyes lit up when he saw its size."

"That's sweet."

"Sarah sent another email about the groundbreaking ceremony. It's scheduled for late Friday afternoon. She knows the hospital is still open, but it's the only time the mayor is available. Plus, the National Oceanic and Atmospheric Administration and the Fisheries representative can't make it on the weekend." He pointed to the crowd in the parking lot. "If things keep up outside, it won't be a big deal to close a few hours early. I think we should invite the entire staff to the ceremony," Anthony said.

"I agree. There will be lots of crossover between our roles as directors at the sea turtle center and our jobs here at the hospital. We should include them. Let's sit down and look at it together."

They returned to Anthony's office to read Sarah's email. Marlon and Sharon had rented a large tent and were coordinating with a local caterer to provide refreshments for the event. The invited guests included a *Who's Who* from Coral Shores and the Florida Association of Zoos and Aquariums, essential stakeholders in the new project. Emily and Anthony would adapt the hospital schedule to make it work.

"Sarah is sending out a press release in the morning and arranged for the local TV and print news organizations to be there. It's shaping up to be quite the bash," Anthony said. "She took care of all the important details, and I feel bad we weren't able to help."

"Me too, but we'll make it up to them in the weeks and months ahead. Once the center is open, we'll be hands on," Emily said.

When they completed their list of things to do between now and Friday afternoon, Anthony said, "I'm going to grab lunch for Marc, then head home. Do you need anything before I leave?"

"Thanks. I'm good, but I'll be better when I hear about Chad."

• • •

After Anthony packed up for the day, he conferred with Abigail about some hospital business, then waved goodbye to Emily on his way out. Just then, her phone rang.

"She's safe, Em. Marilyn is okay." Duncan shouted into the phone.

Overwhelmed with relief, Emily broke down crying. "Where was she?"

"We found documents inside the Marathon house for another nearby property on Grassy Key. It didn't turn up in our earlier searches because she assigned the deed to a separate trust. It's a two-story apartment complex on the bay, less than a mile from the Dolphin Research Center. The entire property was under renovation to create short-term studio apartments for wildlife and marine science students and researchers working in the Keys. That's where Chad held her—locked in an upstairs room."

"Is she hurt?"

"They took her to Fishermen's Community Hospital, but I think she'll be okay. Without power to the A/C unit, the temp inside was stifling. She's weak and dehydrated but able to walk out of the building on her own."

Emily realized she had to tell Anthony before he drove away and began running with the phone in hand.

"Em, I have to go, but I want you to know she'll be calling you soon about Tiki. He's been her only concern since her rescue. I told her about Anthony and Marc and their aviary, and she seemed grateful and relieved."

"I can't wait to hear her voice." Emily burst through the back door and began chasing after Anthony's car. "Can I call you back in a few minutes? I have so many people to tell, including the paparazzi in my parking lot."

"Chad's going to be charged with murder and kidnapping, and we'll be escorting him to Coral Shores this afternoon. We can talk more when I get back to town."

Emily waved her arms frantically to catch Anthony's attention. He saw her in the rearview mirror and slammed on the brakes before jumping out of the car. "What? What? Is an emergency coming in?"

"No." Emily laughed when she finally caught up to him. Anthony's face looked panicked, unsure of what was happening. "Marilyn's alive!" she shouted. "They found her."

Anthony grabbed her arms, before they alternated between hugging and jumping up and down. "Really, she's really, okay?"

Emily nodded emphatically. "Pull your van off the road and come with me. I'll fill you in on the way."

Delivering good news was fun, but finding Marilyn was more than just good news. The crowd of people in the parking lot shared a personal connection centered on their concern for Marilyn and Tiki's safety. Yes, there was a treasure hunt on the line, but that never seemed to be the primary motivation behind their gathering.

After first updating the staff, they headed straight for the parking lot. She waved at Archie, who stood when he saw Emily and Anthony walking with haste toward the team leader.

"Franklin, we need your help. I have to make an announcement and need to get everyone's attention." Emily's smile eased the concern on Franklin's face.

"I can do better than that," he said, and ran to a nearby tent to confer with a fellow super fan. He returned with a megaphone in hand. Franklin cleared his t-shirt display off a table and used a chair to step on top. Everyone in the crowd recognized him, and when he spoke, they listened. Once the music stopped, he said, "Dr. Benton has something important to tell us. Please be respectful and listen up." The crowd drew closer as he jumped down and handed her the bullhorn. "Here," he said, holding the chair for her.

"Thanks." She turned to Anthony who gave her a thumbs up.

Emily climbed up and turned to face the attentive crowd. "Thank you, Franklin, and thanks to all of you for the support you've shown Marilyn Peña and Tiki Lulu." Emily noticed Archie had moved to the front row. Anthony walked around the table to greet him and directed him to stand with Franklin, away from the crowd.

"We have amazing news. The police have found Marilyn. She's safe." Before Emily elaborated, the crowd erupted with cheers and applause. She had to wait a minute before the noise died down. "She's being evaluated by medical professionals but is in good spirits." The crowd once again drowned her out. Their joy was infectious, and Emily started laughing.

Someone shouted, "What about Tiki Lulu?"

"Tiki Lulu is happy, and healthy." Her voice carried across the parking lot.

Again, more shouts and cheers from the crowd asking, "Where is Tiki Lulu?"

"Tiki will be reunited with Marilyn, but those details are private. The police will be releasing more information soon. We appreciate your support. You've been wonderful, but I think it's time you all went home."

The music played as the crowd began dancing to the beat. They had no plans to vacate the parking lot until the celebration wound down organically. Emily stepped off the table and handed the megaphone to Franklin. Groups of super fans approached to thank them for caring for Tiki Lulu. Archie hugged them both before joining the revelers. He looked like a man who had a tremendous weight lifted off his shoulders. His eyes were bright, and he had a pop to his step.

As they turned to walk back toward the front of the hospital, Franklin approached them and asked, "Dr. Benton. Anthony. Can I speak with you inside, in private?" His formal tone carried a weight of authority. They nodded and led him to Anthony's office and closed the door. He reached for his back pocket and pulled out an ID badge. "My name is Special Agent Franklin Bonaventura, with the FBI."

Emily and Anthony turned to look at each other, eyebrows raised, but said nothing.

"It was my job to embed myself with the crowd outside. We needed to know if Marilyn's social media followers had anything to do with her kidnapping. Plus, it was the best way to monitor the treasure hunt and report any fraudulent or criminal activity."

"Thank you, Agent Bonaventura. Detective Mike Lane informed me there was an undercover agent in the crowd. We appreciate everything you did to keep them peaceful and the hospital open for our clients and their pets."

"You're welcome. I'll stay until they clear out for the night. I expect things will get back to normal by morning. There will be a press conference to announce the end of the case."

"What about the treasure hunt?" Anthony asked.

"That's all in Marilyn Peña's control. She enlisted an outside law firm as an unbiased third party to oversee the last step of the contest. That way, she stays neutral and avoids any claims of impropriety." Agent Bonaventura handed them each a business card, inviting them to call anytime if they had questions, then shook their hands before returning to the parking lot.

"Well, that makes sense now," Anthony said. "I knew he was a good guy. I need to call Marc. He's going to be so relieved."

Just then, Emily's phone rang. An unknown caller, but she recognized the 305-area code to be from the Miami and Florida Keys region and turned to show the phone to Anthony.

"Well, answer it," he said. "Maybe it's Marilyn."

Emily accepted the call. "Hello."

CHAPTER TWENTY-NINE

"Is this Dr. Emily Benton?" asked the caller.

"Yes. Who am I speaking with?" Her eyes opened wide, uncertain about the voice on the other end of the phone.

"My name is Susie Fairchild. Marilyn Peña is my best friend. I'm here with her at the hospital, and she would like to speak with you."

After a brief pause when the phone changed hands, a quiet voice said, "Dr. Benton. How is Tiki doing?"

Emily put the phone on speaker to include Anthony in the conversation. "Tiki's wonderful. Here, I'll let Anthony tell you all about him."

Anthony shared a detailed update about Tiki's diet and behaviors. He described Marc's obsession with mimicking all the components in the aviary at her Coral Shores home. He even told her about Tiki's favorite TV shows and his new friendship with Elvis.

At first, Marilyn said nothing, but when she spoke, it was obvious she was crying. "Anthony. Dr. Benton. Thank you from the bottom of my heart for everything you've done. As soon as I'm released from the hospital, Susie will bring me home. I can't wait to see him. I've been so worried and missed him so much."

"I know he missed you terribly. Whenever you're ready, Marc and I will bring Tiki to you. When do you think you'll be out of the hospital?" Anthony asked.

Susie came back on the phone. "Marilyn is a little overwhelmed right now. The doctor wants to keep her overnight for observation. They're treating her dehydration and will recheck her blood work in the morning before deciding whether to discharge her. We should be back in Coral Shores within a day or two. I'll call you when I have more specific details, but can I ask you a favor?"

"Sure. Anything," Emily replied.

"Can we arrange a FaceTime call with Tiki Lulu? It would boost her spirits to see him with her own eyes."

"I'm on my way home right now, and I can call you back within the hour to video chat with Tiki. He'll love that."

"Thank you, Anthony. Until Marilyn is feeling stronger, please call my number any time. I'll be by her side." They learned Susie had flown to the Keys from her home in Dallas on the first flight after Marilyn's rescue. She and Anthony exchanged contact information before ending the call.

"Em, I've got to go. I can't wait to tell Marc the good news," Anthony said.

"Please record their FaceTime call so I can see it, too. Now, go."

Anthony raced out the back door, leaving Emily standing alone in his office. She had so many questions about Chad, Dylan Colt's murder, and Marilyn's kidnapping, but the only thing that mattered was Marilyn's safe return and her imminent reunion with Tiki Lulu.

• • •

The hospital remained quiet through closing time as the crowd dwindled to include a few stragglers enjoying a last meal at the remaining food truck. Agent Bonaventura sat in his chair, on guard duty. Emily crossed her fingers hoping things would be normal by morning.

Anthony texted a recording of Tiki and Marilyn's video chat, which she watched too many times to count. Tiki talked and danced, clearly ecstatic to see his forever person. Marilyn got him to speak a handful of words they hadn't heard before. Marc and Anthony appeared happy to see them reunited, but Emily imagined they were feeling conflicted. If things turned out differently for Marilyn, they had planned to adopt Tiki. Now they would have to say goodbye to this plucky parrot.

• • •

Back at home, Emily ate leftovers at the kitchen island before bringing Bella onto the beach deck to take in the late-day sun. Her mother's chaise lounge was the perfect place to recap the events of the past week since she had nothing else to do except relax.

The ten o'clock news aired a report from an earlier press conference announcing the arrest of Chad Peña for the murder of Dylan Colt and the kidnapping and attempted extortion of Marilyn Peña. Multiple law enforcement agencies were present, and Mike fielded a few reporters' questions. He looked so handsome. Emily blushed watching him on TV.

A knock at the door startled her until a quick glance out the front window confirmed both Duncan and Mike's cars were in the driveway.

"Hi, Em," Duncan said. He gave her a quick hug, then walked into the kitchen, opened the fridge and grabbed a beer for himself and Mike. "Do you want anything?"

"I'm good," she said. "What are you both doing here? Has something happened?"

Mike leaned down and kissed her on the lips. "Everything's good. We wanted to update you in person. I told Duncan it was too late, but he insisted."

Duncan alternated looking at the two of them and shook his head. "That's not quite how the conversation went down, but we did both want to see you. Em, I'm sorry for the way I spoke to you in Marathon. I let my emotions get the better of me."

Emily sidled up to brother, who lifted his arm to wrap around her shoulder in a sibling embrace. "I'm sorry too. I often act before I think, and I know you were looking out for me."

"And don't let this go to your head, but thanks to your pursuit, we located Chad, and that led us to Marilyn. I told her so when we rescued her. Mike and I transferred Chad back to Coral Shores tonight, and he's behind bars awaiting a bail hearing," Duncan said.

Emily resisted gloating and accepted his compliment with a smile.

"That's better," Mike said, chiming in from the periphery. "I hate it when the two of you are fighting. It stresses me out."

Emily walked over to hug Mike, allowing him to pull her close. "Let's sit outside and you can tell me everything that wasn't included in the press conference," she said.

And it was a lot. Chad refused to talk with the authorities, but they no longer needed his confession, since Marilyn planned to testify about everything that happened. Mike elaborated on the missing details.

"Marilyn became suspicious of Chad when she caught him rifling through her desk and attempting to log in to her computer. He also asked a lot of questions about the treasure. That's why she brought Tiki to you that first day. She planned to confront him about cutting off his monthly allowance but became concerned he might lash out. He thought Marilyn hid the two hundred-thousand-dollar treasure in a physical location, like an old-fashioned pirate's chest. She prerecorded the video clues with

Tiki Lulu, but he hadn't seen them. When he wasn't able to log into her Flix account or access her laptop files, he attempted to kidnap Tiki Lulu, thinking he could get the clues directly from the source. He desperately wanted to find the money before a treasure hunter got to it."

"How does Dylan Colt play into all of this?"

Duncan shared the rest of the story. "According to Marilyn, Chad got drunk in a bar one night and bragged to Colt about his inside connection to the treasure. Colt pressured him into kidnapping Marilyn so she would tell them the location of the money. At first, they wore ski masks to hide their identity, but she could tell it was Chad and called him out. Marilyn refused to cooperate, and when Colt threatened her with a gun, Chad flipped out. She thinks he got scared things were spiraling out of control and hit Colt over the head with one of her metal sculptures, killing him. That's when he dragged Colt's dead body to the swamp and moved Marilyn to Colt's grandmother's house. He only kept her there for a couple of days before moving her to Marathon." Duncan sat back and took a sip of beer, allowing Mike to finish the story.

"The news coverage made him nervous, so he wanted to get out of town. She refused to give up any information about the treasure. That's why he kept trying to kidnap Tiki. He thought he would have better luck at interrogating a parrot."

"That's risky. She's so wealthy. Why didn't she just pay him off?" Emily asked.

"Marilyn said he didn't have it in him to do her physical harm. I think her words were, *He's lazy and incompetent, but he's not a killer*," Mike said.

"But he is a killer," Emily corrected. "He killed Colt."

"I'm only guessing, but I think she meant he wasn't a cold-blooded killer. He killed Colt in a moment of panic when Colt wanted to escalate his violence toward Marilyn to get her to talk. In a weird way, he did it to protect her, or to protect himself, or both."

"She called this afternoon from the hospital. Her friend Susie is planning to bring her home, and then Anthony and Marc will take Tiki to her. And they all lived happily ever after." Emily smiled. "Oh, I meant to tell you. I met Franklin Bonaventura, the undercover FBI agent. At first, we thought he was the ringleader of the whole mob, but he worked covertly to keep order and protect the hospital."

Duncan and Mike disclosed they had been in communication with him daily.

Duncan finished his beer and stood to leave. "We've been gone for two days, and I'm running on an hour of sleep. Night, Em. I'll talk to you tomorrow." He was halfway to his car when Emily charged out of the house after him. Startled, he turned to face her, but before he said anything, she hugged him tight.

"I'm sorry. I know I can be a handful, and you were just doing your job."

When she finally let go, Duncan said, "Handful?" then smiled.

"Okay, but I'm working on it." Emily laughed. "Can we agree—I can take care of myself, and you need to learn to trust me."

"You've got some great detective skills," he said before his expression turned serious. "I'll always have your back, Em. I hope you know that."

"I do. I love you, big brother." A weight lifted as soon as she said the words. They hugged one more time and as Duncan drove away, Emily turned to see Mike standing in the doorway with a smile.

"I saw you on the news earlier," she said as they walked back inside. She turned to whisper in his ear, "Impressive."

Mike laughed. "I hate those press conferences. So much posturing."

"Well, you and Duncan should be proud. You cracked the case."

Mike pushed the hair away from her eyes, then cradled her face with his hands. "I think you mean we cracked the case." He kissed her gently at first, but Emily demanded more. When they came up for air, Mike asked, "Let's make plans for the weekend. How about Friday night?"

"Oh, I can't. Remember, our groundbreaking ceremony for the sea turtle center is Friday at four. Duncan and Jane will be there with the kids and Elvis. Sarah is flying in tomorrow and would love to see everyone. Can you come?"

"I'll be there, and I can help with anything you need." Mike left after one more quick kiss.

Despite the late hour, she knew Anthony would be eager to hear the latest details. The parts of the case that had baffled them now came into focus. With the guilty party behind bars and Marilyn safely at home, the only thing left up in the air was the treasure hunt—unless a lucky winner had already been crowned.

CHAPTER THIRTY

It was strange to see an empty hospital parking lot. No paparazzi, no food trucks, and no Archie. Anthony would not be in until mid-morning, since he had to shop and prepare Tiki's food for the next week. He didn't want Marilyn to worry about getting parrot provisions before she returned home.

Susie texted an update. The doctor had discharged Marilyn from the hospital, and they were on their way to her Marathon house. Marilyn wanted to make sure Chad hadn't trashed the place and looked forward to a long, hot shower and sleeping in her own bed. There was no love lost between Marilyn and Chad. She told Susie she would be fine if she never saw his face again. She had no desire to confront him. He was dead to her the moment he betrayed her.

A yacht service based in Key West drove her boat back from Stock Island and would arrive that afternoon. Marilyn and Susie planned to stay in Marathon overnight until a professional crime scene cleanup service erased all evidence of Dylan Colt's murder at her Coral Shores house. Marilyn wanted to hire someone to *sage* the house, ridding it of all the evil spirits. Emily recommended her mom's friend, Otter, for the task. She had followed Marilyn and Tiki's story, and Emily thought she would love to help.

• • •

Emily and Abigail sat at the reception desk, reorganizing the schedule for Friday afternoon. "Dr. Benton. So far, everyone can make it to the ceremony. Do you still want me to arrange a car service to drive the staff from here to the turtle center?"

"Yes, right now, there's limited parking at the site, but I had an idea." Emily pulled up a website for a local limo service.

"Wow. That would be so much fun. I've never ridden in a limo before."

"I want it to be a surprise. It's been a tough couple of weeks, and we all deserve a little treat. Anthony and I will be busy schmoozing with the guests, so I made a dinner reservation at Bravo Italiano after the official event wraps up."

"What a wonderful plan," Abigail said. "I'll tell everyone the event ends in the early evening so they clear their schedules. I can't wait. Will you be joining us for dinner?"

"Unfortunately, I don't think so. Sarah Klein scheduled an interview with the local newspaper after the ceremony, but I called ahead to the restaurant and gave them my credit card number. They usually add the gratuity for large groups, but can you make sure the waitstaff gets a generous tip?"

"Sure. Thanks, Dr. Benton."

• • •

Life slowly returned to normal. Wary clients who'd been nervous about navigating the mob called to reschedule, and the appointment calendar quickly filled up.

When Anthony arrived at work, he had news to report.

"Marilyn posted a new video to her Flix account. She must have recorded it this morning from inside the aviary at her Marathon house. She thanked all her supporters for their love and confirmed Tiki Lulu was thriving and staying with a friend. Tomorrow at two p.m., she's live-streaming a reunion party and will make a special announcement."

As Emily watched the video, Susie texted another update. She and Marilyn would be back in Coral Shores first thing tomorrow. Otter had completed her spiritual cleansing of the home and reassured them only good energy remained. Given all that the women were handling, they were delighted to learn Anthony and Marc had taken care of Tiki's meal prep and were on standby, waiting for their call.

"Em, do you want to come over for dinner? This is our last night with Tiki, and I thought the kids and Elvis would like to say goodbye to him. I called Jane, and she's good with the plan."

"That sounds perfect. I'm in."

• • •

Still balancing work and Tiki's care, Anthony left early to give Marc a hand, missing the chance to meet their newest patient—Janou Link, a six-month-old Keeshond. Her owners, Nora and Bruce Link, brought her in for a wellness checkup and to schedule her spay surgery. They were new to the area and learned about the hospital from the TV news coverage.

"It's so great to meet you, Dr. Benton. We saw you on TV announcing Marilyn and Tiki's safe return to the crowd, and we said to each other, *That's where we want to bring Janou.*"

Janou, a twenty-pound ball of fluff, had the thickest, most luxurious fur Emily had ever seen. Nora expressed an interest in training Janou to be a therapy dog, and part of the visit included a consultation with the vet about how to pursue that goal. Emily had two other clients whose therapy dogs visited the area children's hospital and senior centers, and thought they would be great resources. With Janou's puppy vaccine series completed before their move, Emily put her spay on the schedule for the following week. After showing off her training and tricks for a few cookies, Janou pranced into the lobby as if auditioning for her future role as a therapy dog. What a great way to end the workday.

• • •

Tasked with bringing dessert to Tiki's farewell party, Emily picked up a box of guava pastries from a local Cuban bakery. After a quick trip home to feed Bella, she drove over to Marc and Anthony's place. The moment she let herself in the front door, she heard Mac and Ava giggling. Elvis and Tiki were up to their usual antics, entertaining the crowd.

"Hi Em," Jane said, meeting her at the door. She took the box from Emily and set it on the counter, then turned to hug her, squeezing so tight Emily struggled to exhale. "I was so worried about you. Duncan told me everything you did leading to Marilyn's rescue."

"I'm okay. We're all okay," she said. "I'm sorry I haven't got back to you. It's been a beast of a week."

"Don't worry about that for a minute. We can catch up once the dust settles. Are you excited about Friday?"

"I am. Now that Marilyn is coming home, Anthony and I can turn our attention to the turtle center."

"Speaking of the turtle center," Anthony said as he joined them in the kitchen. "Sarah will be here soon. She arrived this afternoon, and after seeing all the news coverage about Marilyn and Tiki, she wanted to meet him." A knock at the door prompted him to add, "And there she is."

Dinner turned into an official party. They were only missing Duncan and Mike, who were working on the murder and abduction case against Chad. After brainstorming with Sarah about Friday's event, Emily noticed Marc sitting quietly in the chair next to Tiki's aviary. He had forged a strong bond with the parrot, and she imagined he had conflicted emotions about saying goodbye. She walked up behind him and put her hand on his shoulder. "Are you all right?"

Marc smiled up at her. "I am. I'm happy he's going home, but I'll miss him. More than I ever imagined."

"Of course, you will. I'm sure Marilyn would welcome you anytime you want to see him."

"I spoke with her today, and that's exactly what she said. An open-door policy for Tiki."

After dinner, Tiki cycled through his nightly routine. He perched on one leg with his head nestled in his feathers. Everyone else followed his cue.

• • •

Emily arrived early to work, eager for Anthony to get there and share the details about the long-awaited reunion. After spending the morning at Marilyn's house, any mixed emotions he and Marc had about saying goodbye to Tiki disappeared the moment they saw him in his extravagant aviary. He flew from tree to tree, exploring every perch and food station. Occasionally, he would land on Marilyn's shoulder and after a few *Hellos* and *Whatcha doings*, he would nuzzle her neck and coo. Anthony also told Marilyn all about Archie and his loss of Bonkers.

That same day, Marilyn called Emily to thank her for everything she had done, since Emily had to work during the reunion. She put the call on speakerphone for Anthony to hear.

"Emily, we missed you this morning, but we'll see you soon," Marilyn said, her voice sounding strong. "The worse thing about being held captive was not knowing if Tiki was safe. I didn't care about myself, and I understand how Archie let his own health take a back seat. Thank you for telling me about him. I'd like to invite Archie over to spend time with Tiki. Do you think that's a good idea?"

"That sounds like a brilliant idea. I'll forward his contact information," Anthony said. "Archie will be thrilled."

• • •

With a busy hospital schedule, Emily and Anthony struggled to steal a moment away from their patients to work on plans for the groundbreaking ceremony. Anthony set an alarm for two p.m. to watch Marilyn's Flix livestream. She had arranged for the local news channel to be present for the recording.

"Everyone, come quick." Anthony ran through the hospital to gather the staff in his office. Marilyn and Tiki Lulu were on his computer screen, and the corner graphic showed half a million followers were online right now.

"We want to thank all our fans and supporters for the outpouring of love we received during a very dark and difficult time," Marilyn said. "As you can see, Tiki and I are doing great. Say hello, Tiki."

"Hello. Hola." Tiki bounced his head up and down, spreading his wings in a grand gesture.

"Now, on to more exciting news. We have a winner! Babs and Burton Ollivander were the first to figure out that the number anagram is the address for the Dolphin Research Center on Grassy Key, in the Florida Keys—58901 Overseas Highway." A picture of the retired couple standing in front of the two-story dolphin statue at the nonprofit research center giving a thumbs up filled the screen. Marilyn continued, "I grew up in the Keys and volunteered at the center during my younger days. That's where my love affair with parrots began. Even though it's a dolphin center, they also provide permanent homes to many parrots rescued for a variety of reasons. Sometimes, parrots outlive their family members and have no place to go." Marilyn turned the camera to zoom in on Tiki. Archie stood next to him, feeding him a piece of mango. The number of Flix viewers soared past one million.

"Yes," Anthony exclaimed. "Look at Archie's face. He looks ten years younger." Marilyn had wasted no time arranging their introduction. "I bet we're witnessing the start of a lifelong friendship."

The camera panned back to Marilyn. "The Ollivanders have won the two hundred-thousand-dollar prize, and they've chosen the Marathon Wild Bird Center to receive the matching donation. Congratulations Marathon Wild Bird Center—you're a very deserving charity." Marilyn clapped while Tiki bobbed up and down.

"Each of the wild bird centers taking part in my treasure hunt will also receive one hundred-thousand-dollars to help with their operational costs. They are: Everglades Wonder Gardens in Bonita Springs, Save our Seabirds in Sarasota, Florida Exotic Bird Sanctuary in Hudson, Pelican Harbor Seabird Station in Miami, and Flamingo Gardens in Davie. I'm also making a similar donation to my beloved Dolphin Research Center to thank them for hosting my scavenger hunt finale. Tiki and I want to encourage all of you to support your local wildlife nonprofit centers. They need your help." Marilyn took a deep breath before continuing. She struggled to get the words out and wiped a tear from her eyes.

"Now, to the most important news. Our friends at the Coral Shores Veterinary Hospital are real-life guardian angels. Anthony, Marc, and Dr. Emily Benton's courage and love are the reason Tiki and I are safe at home. I'll never be able to repay them, but I'm going to try. I'm making a one-million-dollar donation to the Eliza Klein Sea Turtle Education Center. Anthony and Emily are directors of the center, and we can't wait for the doors to open at this special facility."

Emily missed what Marilyn said next because Anthony and the staff started screaming with joy. She turned to Anthony and asked, "Did you know about this?"

Anthony grabbed her hands. "I had no idea. She tried to pay Marc and me this morning, for caring for Tiki, but we refused." Anthony's phone started ringing. He alternated between calls from Marc and Sarah. Marilyn's generosity overwhelmed them all.

By the time Marilyn wrapped up her Flix announcement, she had over two million viewers.

• • •

When Sarah, Anthony, Marlon, and Sharon met for dinner at Emily's on the eve of the groundbreaking ceremony, they had lots to talk about. Marilyn's big announcement set off a frenzy of media attention. Local and national news outlets clamored for interviews. Concerned they were unprepared for a large crowd, Sarah and Emily consulted with Duncan. He recommended a local company that employed off-duty police officers to manage traffic, parking, security, and whatever else popped up.

When there were no details left to scrutinize, they said good night. Sarah teased she had a few surprises for the group to be revealed at the event.

Emily needed some time to wind down and joined Bella on the couch to watch the late-night news. The judge denied Chad's bail request, so he would wait behind bars for his trial on murder and kidnapping charges. Marilyn and Tiki's Flix announcement surpassed five million views and kept climbing. Local wildlife centers reported record attendance and unprecedented small-dollar donations. So much good had come from such an evil act.

As Emily got ready for bed, Mike called. "You sure had a big day. I can't wait for tomorrow's ceremony."

"It's almost too much, and I never thought I'd say that about a charity."

"In case you want some extra help, we can ride over together. I can set up chairs or manage the crowd. Whatever you need."

"I'll have to be there early. Can you get away from work?"

"I cleared the afternoon for you, Em. Just let me know what time to pick you up, and I'd love to celebrate your success over dinner on Saturday."

She didn't have to see Mike in person to end up with a stomach full of butterflies. His enthusiastic support of her career and respect for her contribution in solving the case made him more attractive to her—if that was even possible. Emily's success did not threaten him as he embraced his role as her biggest cheerleader.

When she lay her head down to sleep, images of flying parrots and baby sea turtles filled her slumbering mind.

CHAPTER THIRTY-ONE

Emily and Anthony came to work early. They had lots to do since the hospital would close at two p.m. Emily hoped to get away before then, but she struggled to stay focused.

Jane sent a picture of Elvis after his morning grooming visit. A bright, blue bandana imprinted with images of little turtle hatchlings stood out against his snowy white fur. He looked adorable. Sarah contracted with a famous designer friend of hers to create a logo and product line for the new center. Elvis's bandana would be for sale once the gift shop opened, alongside T-shirts, reusable shopping bags, reusable straws, and water bottles made from recycled plastic pulled from the ocean. Sarah sourced everything from materials in keeping with their environmentally responsible mandate. They wanted to set an example to prove it was possible to be financially successful and help the environment at the same time.

A local artist commissioned to create a drawing of Elvis planned to reveal his work at the ceremony. Elvis's image posted on signs throughout the center would guide guests to the adjacent dog-friendly area of the beach, far away from the fragile turtle nests. Since the turtle center had been named after his original forever person, Eliza Klein, it made sense to use Elvis's likeness.

He had become a local celebrity in his own right and loved the attention.

Marlon and Sharon were in constant contact with the team. The tents were up, chairs in place, speaker system tested, and banners hung. They were a dynamic duo, and their commitment ensured the center would be a tremendous success. Even the weather cooperated. Late afternoon pop-up storms were common during Florida summers, but the forecast looked clear, without a cloud in the sky.

After the last appointment checked out, Emily walked into Anthony's office. "Do you need me for anything else? Mike is picking me up in an hour."

"I'm good. I'm leaving soon, too. Abigail has everything covered here." He reached for her hand to stop her from walking out of his office. When she turned to face him, he said, "Today's the day, Em. This will forever change our lives. I've been so busy checking things off my list, I haven't stopped to think about the significance. Becoming directors of the sea turtle center is a dream come true. Your mom would be proud of us."

Emily smiled and took a breath before hugging him tight. He was right, as usual. Anthony had an uncanny ability to focus on the important things, forcing all the clutter to the periphery. He helped keep her centered.

• • •

Arriving home early on a work day threw Bella for a loop, upsetting her daily routine. She appeared extra groggy and took longer than normal before demanding a pre-dinner appetizer. Emily freshened up and spent a minute on her hair and make-up. Multiple media outlets would be present for the ceremony, including a professional photographer Sarah hired to capture the event.

When Mike arrived, Emily planned to get more details about the case, since it would be difficult to talk with a crowd around.

• • •

"You look beautiful, Emily," Mike said.

"Thanks. Come on in. We have a few minutes until we need to leave."

He helped himself to a glass of iced tea, and they both sat down outside on her deck.

"So, what's the latest?" she asked. "I have so many questions about Chad's case."

"Like what?"

"Has he confessed to any of his crimes?"

"No, he's refusing to cooperate. He's working with a court-appointed lawyer, but there's a mountain of evidence against him. Marilyn, as an eyewitness, made it crystal clear she's looking forward to her day in court so she can tell her story. According to Marilyn, Chad has caused trouble ever since he was a toddler. Marilyn was his closest family after his parents died, and she's now disowned him for good."

"She's been sending me daily updates about Tiki Lulu." Emily showed Mike the latest pictures. "He now has his own publicist, and Marilyn is working to trademark Tiki's name and image. The wild bird centers were interested in branded items to sell in their gift shops, and she's going to donate all the profits to wildlife charities. A real win-win."

"I watched their interviews on the big cable TV shows. They're a remarkable team." Emily agreed. Marilyn and Tiki's contribution to wildlife conservation was priceless.

• • •

When Emily and Mike arrived at the groundbreaking ceremony, they were grateful Sarah had roped off parking spots for the guests of honor since media vans lined the street.

"I'm sure glad we hired extra support for today," Sarah said when they joined her in the main tent. Mike excused himself to check in with the off-duty officers. He wanted to ensure they had a solid plan for handling the crowd.

They all had specific roles for the day. Emily and Anthony would escort the various marine industry representatives, as Sharon and Marlon welcomed local community and business leaders. Sarah's responsibilities included guiding the mayor through his official duties. Experienced volunteers from the Coral Shores Turtle Project engaged the kids at an activity booth, complete with coloring books about sea turtles and washable turtle tattoos.

When the limo carrying the hospital staff arrived, the smiles on their faces as they exited the vehicle confirmed Emily's transportation arrangements were a hit. They were having a blast.

Jane, Duncan, Mac, Ava, and Elvis's arrival added to the festive atmosphere. Elvis had a peppy step to his gait, happy to accept pets and belly rubs from his adoring fans. The kids asked to have their picture taken with their famous dog, standing next to the oversized painted image of Elvis.

After Emily's honored guests were seated, she noticed a second limo parked on the road. Confused about who it could be, she saw Sarah approaching the vehicle with a wide smile on her face. The limo driver opened the door, and Marilyn emerged in full parrot regalia. The vibrant, red streak in her hair complemented her flowing sun dress adorned with an imprint of Tiki's image. After Marilyn, Archie followed, almost unrecognizable in a dapper linen suit, crisp white shirt, and a tropical colored bow tie covered with images of little parrots. A straw hat completed the outfit. They walked arm in arm, greeting their friends and fans along the way.

Emily and Anthony joined Sarah as she introduced the newcomers to the remaining guests of honor, all of whom were excited to meet the local celebrity.

Marilyn apologized for leaving Tiki Lulu at home. "He's been through so much," she said. "But don't worry. We'll be posting about today's event on our next Flix livestream."

Emily stood next to Sarah and leaned in to whisper, "Is this your surprise?"

"One of them." She grabbed Emily's hand, pulling her toward the speaker's podium. Hidden behind the table was a brass-plated shovel with a polished wood handle, engraved with today's date. Listed on the back of the shovel were the names of the Board of Directors. "After the first shovelful of dirt, I'm going to frame this and mount it on the wall inside our welcome center—below this photo." Sarah then pulled out a framed picture of her mom. Taken years ago, it showed Eliza, with Elvis at her side, teaching a young group of turtle volunteers on the beach.

"Oh, Sarah. It's beautiful. It captures her perfectly."

Sarah smiled but wiped away a tear. "I wish she was here today. I like to believe she's watching over us as we take this next big step.

At their last meeting, the board unanimously decided Sarah should be the person to perform the ceremonial task with the shovel. The Eliza Klein Sea Turtle Education Center honored the memory of her mother, and because of Mrs. Klein's vision and generosity, the Coral Shores community now had their very own state-of-the-art facility.

Sarah and Emily's presence at the front of the tent prompted the guests to take their seats for the main event. Emily smiled at her niece and nephew in the first row, with Elvis at their feet. Marilyn, Archie, and Marc were in the next row, chatting like old friends. Mike stood beside Jane and Duncan and locked eyes with Emily from across the yard. Their intense gaze acknowledged that their relationship had grown deeper and more intimate after all they had endured in recent days. Emily put her hand on her heart as if it were possible to physically tame the flutter.

Standing at the back of the tent, Anthony waved his arms to get Emily and Sarah's attention, then pointed at his watch.

"It's time," Emily said. "Are you ready?"

"Absolutely." Sarah squeezed Emily's hand, then stepped up to the microphone. "Welcome, everyone, to the future Eliza Klein Sea Turtle Conservation Center…"

ABOUT THE AUTHOR

DL Mitchell is the author of the Coral Shores Veterinary Mystery series and a 2024 Nominee for Georgia Author of the Year. She brings her unique perspective as a practicing small animal veterinarian to the world of mystery fiction. With experience in bustling, big-city hospitals, her transition to a house call concierge veterinary practice has enriched her storytelling with firsthand encounters and insights into the human-animal bond.

She loves spending time with her husband, daughter, and their menagerie of pets, planning the next travel adventure, and running nearby trails. She's a scuba diver but gets seasick, and when she's on the road, she travels with her espresso machine and her blow-up, stand up paddle board.

OTHER TITLES BY DL MITCHELL

NOTE FROM DL MITCHELL

Word-of-mouth is crucial for any author to succeed. If you enjoyed *Parrot Prose*, please leave a review online—anywhere you are able. Even if it's just a sentence or two. It would make all the difference and would be very much appreciated.

Visit my website at DLMitchellMystery.com for information about book signings, new releases, and more.

Thanks!
DL Mitchell

We hope you enjoyed reading this title from:

BLACK ROSE writing

www.blackrosewriting.com

Subscribe to our mailing list – *The Rosevine* – and receive **FREE** books, daily deals, and stay current with news about upcoming releases and our hottest authors.
Scan the QR code below to sign up.

Already a subscriber? Please accept a sincere thank you for being a fan of Black Rose Writing authors.

View other Black Rose Writing titles at www.blackrosewriting.com/books and use promo code **PRINT** to receive a **20% discount** when purchasing.